MEMORY ROAD

DICK SCHMIDT

LANDSLIDE
PUBLISHING

Landslide Publishing, Inc.
201 Plaza Real, Suite 140
Boca Raton, Florida 33432

Copyedited by
Carol Killman Rosenberg • www.carolkillmanrosenberg.com

Cover and interior design by
Gary A. Rosenberg • www.thebookcouple.com

Printed in the United States of America

To Barbara

AUTHOR'S NOTE

In an open letter to the American public, former president Ronald Reagan disclosed that he had learned of his prognosis with Alzheimer's disease. With this novel, it is my hope to emphasize the need for each of us to recognize the relevance that those stricken with this terrible life-stealing affliction still have to their families as well as to the rest of society.

November 5, 1994

My Fellow Americans,

I have recently been told that I am one of the millions of Americans who will be afflicted with Alzheimer's disease.

Upon learning this news, Nancy and I had to decide whether as private citizens we would keep this a private matter or whether we would make this news known in a public way.

In the past, Nancy suffered from breast cancer and I had my cancer surgeries. We found through our open disclosures we were able to raise public awareness. We were happy that as a result many more people underwent testing. They were treated in early stages and able to return to normal, healthy lives.

So now we feel it is important to share it with you. In opening our hearts, we hope this might promote greater awareness of this condition. Perhaps it will encourage a clearer understanding of the individuals and families who are affected by it.

At the moment I feel just fine. I intend to live the remainder of the years God gives me on this Earth doing the things I have always done. I will continue to share life's journey with my beloved Nancy and my family. I plan to enjoy the great outdoors and stay in touch with my friends and supporters.

Unfortunately, as Alzheimer's disease progresses, the family often bears a heavy burden. I only wish there was some way I could spare Nancy from this painful experience. When the time comes, I am confident that with your help she will face it with faith and courage.

In closing, let me thank you, the American people, for giving me the great honor of allowing me to serve as your president. When the Lord calls me home, whenever that day may be, I will leave with the greatest love for this country of ours and eternal optimism for its future.

I now begin the journey that will lead me into the sunset of my life. I know that for America there will always be a bright dawn ahead.

Thank you, my friends. May God always bless you.

Sincerely,

Ronald Reagan

PROLOGUE

There was no view from the secure interior conference room on the sixth floor of the National Security Agency, a modern glass structure located on Route 32, just south of the Baltimore Washington Parkway in Fort Meade, Maryland. The fluorescent lights cast an eerie brightness over the three suits assembled for the unusual meeting, representatives of three government agencies not known for interagency cooperation. The light served to exaggerate thinning hair and worry lines on the faces of the participants, which included Hank Brogan, Deputy Director of National Clandestine Services of the Central Intelligence Agency; Hollis Cavner, Chief of Staff for the Director of the National Security Agency; and John Hallanger, Executive Assistant Director of the National Security Branch of the Federal Bureau of Investigation.

Hank Brogan, who had initiated the meeting, looked at the other two with nervous apprehension as he outlined his situation for the representatives of the other two agencies. The meeting had been going on for over half an hour, and already he could sense their unease. Absent was his usual toothy smile, as he pled his case for cooperation among competing organizations to manage the complications that had led to the assembly.

Hallanger could contain himself no longer. "So, let me get this straight, Hank," he interrupted, turning to Brogan. "You have a problem with a retired senior agent who may be in a position to expose dangerous information, through no fault of his own, as result of his advancing dementia, so severe that you feel he needs to be supervised. Since the Central Intelligence Agency has no jurisdiction over domestic affairs, you have requested the authority of the National Security Agency through the Director, hence Hollis's attendance, to direct the Bureau, *me,* to assign resources to oversee what is essentially an involuntary incarceration of an American citizen for the rest of his life. Does that about sum it up?"

Brogan's face reddened as anger welled within him. "That's an unfair characterization of the situation. This is hardly an incarceration, and you know it. Masterson was station chief in Brussels and, in that capacity, ran networks throughout the Mideast and Russia. He retired only three years ago, and his knowledge is still relevant. He has advancing dementia. He is probably not even aware that he may pose a threat. We don't know who he may be talking to, and he is not capable of the judgment necessary to prevent divulging what he knows to the wrong people. We are not alone in our concern." Referring to the Israeli intelligence agency, he continued, "Mossad already knows about his condition, and if they know, so may the Iranians and Russians. I don't have to explain to you what the Israelis will do to contain this situation, but it will not be as compassionate as our proposal, that's for sure!" He pounded his fist on the table for effect. "I just need some help here." He turned to Hollis for support.

Cavner squirmed in his chair as he looked back at John Hallanger, knowing he already had his marching orders. "Jack, I know this situation makes you feel uncomfortable, but this has already been cleared by my boss. I have been directed to authorize you to proceed with Hank's request. You are to coordinate and oversee an operation to obtain a court-approved guardianship for Stewart Masterson, which will place him in an assisted living facility under your control until such time as his condition has deteriorated to the point where he no longer represents a threat to national security. At that time, we can revisit the matter to determine what options will serve Masterson's best interest going forward. Hank has a point; as much as this may seem distasteful to you and the Bureau, you represent the better among crummy options for a guy who has served his country with distinction, and I suggest you do the best you can for him and his family."

Resigned to a decision that had already been made, Hallanger turned to face Brogan. "What have you got for me to work with?"

Brogan slid a thick dossier across the table.

"The file contains all the pertinent personal information we have on Masterson. He is currently living in Boca Raton, Florida. His wife, Helen, died a year ago from breast cancer, and he has a daughter, Karen Kenny, who lives locally in Silver Spring and a son, Robert, who lives in Seattle. Before her passing, his wife had already expressed concern over Masterson's behavior and judgment, and his daughter is in the process of trying to get a guardianship appointment in the state of Florida as we speak, so you will have to move swiftly to countermand that action if you are going to have your man in place. She is a single mom, schoolteacher, but there is some information in the file about her that may help you discredit and disqualify her as an appropriate guardian appointment. We'll leave the mechanics to you how best to orchestrate that. We suggest you arrange to place Masterson in an assisted living facility somewhere where you have people on the inside that can monitor his routines, and report back to us if contact is made by foreigners."

Feelings of disgust welled up inside Hallanger, ordinarily known for his politically correct demeanor. "For an agency that isn't supposed to dabble in domestic affairs," he said sarcastically, "you guys certainly have put a lot of preparation and thought into this. You really are a bunch of schmucks!" He opened the file and looked through its contents. "I will have to run this out of the Miami office. Fulton McBride is the Special Agent in Charge; you can rely on his discretion. God help us if this gets out. I will go see him in person."

With little else to say, the meeting ended on that somber note, as the three packed up their papers and headed for the door. Hallanger couldn't resist one last barb. "Hank, you ever think how the agency will deal with you when you retire in a few years?"

In fact, this situation had loosed those very thoughts in Hank Brogan's mind, usually in the middle of the night when he couldn't sleep.

CHAPTER ONE

"Hi, Daddy. It's Karen. How are you doing?" Karen asked quietly, some concern in her voice because her father hadn't answered until after several rings.

"I'm fine, just a little lonely right now," Masterson replied. "Have you given any more thought to a visit? I know your mother would like it if you could spend more time with me."

Karen felt a little exasperated. "Daddy! I was just there last week; don't you remember? You spent all your time at the mausoleum. I came all the way down there to be with you, but you spent most of your time visiting Mom. Please, Dad, you need to find some other interests. Mom's been gone almost a year now. You need to rebuild your life. Have you given any thought to what we talked about?"

"I don't remember; what did we talk about?" Masterson sounded confused.

"We talked about you being around other people, friends, who can help you rebuild your life. You can't spend all your waking hours visiting Mom's ashes in a cemetery. We all miss her. I'm worried about you; things are piling up. Don't you remember I had to pay all your bills for you? FPL was getting ready to cut off your electricity."

"I know; I'm getting behind. I'll try to catch up, I promise. I just miss her so much; it seems even more lately. The only time I feel I know what I'm doing is when I visit her. I'm more comfortable there. She's always there for me, and the mausoleum is open twenty-four hours, so I can go when I feel the need."

"Daddy, this is more serious than you want to admit. I want to talk to you again about moving back up to Maryland to live with me and the kids. I can help you out if you are nearby, and the kids would love it if Grandpa was always around." It occurred to Karen that the last thing her father would like is to feel irrelevant, so she added, "And you would be a big help looking after them. It would be nice to have a man around the house again."

Masterson sighed, followed by a long pause.

"Daddy, are you there?"

He sighed again. "Yes, I'm still here. You know, that would be nice, but I don't think I can be that far away from Helen for so long, you know?"

Frustrated, Karen reflected for a moment. "You know, you could bring her with you. There are lots of nice chapels and memorial parks around here where she could be nearby, and you could still visit whenever you wanted." She knew it was useless to argue with him about something he did not want to do. It only made him more combative. She had to create an appeal, or he would never go for it. "We miss you too, Dad."

Karen debated reminding him that he was about to lose his driving privileges in Florida because his mandatory in-person license renewal was due before his birthday this year, and she doubted he could pass an exam in person if he had to. Not wanting to upset him further, she decided against bringing the subject up. He didn't feel it was going to be a problem, which was really the issue anyway, wasn't it? The realization set in that she was going to need another visit to nudge him along.

"Well, just think about it for now, Dad. I'll call you later in the week. Why don't you call one of your friends and play golf, or something. It may do you good, and take your mind off of Mom for a few hours."

"Okay, Karen, whatever you say."

"Love you, Daddy. Goodnight."

"Love you too, sweetie."

Karen thought about their conversation for a few minutes. In fact, she had proceeded much further than her father knew. She had already talked to a local family lawyer about a guardianship for her father. The lawyer had explained to her that she would have to get the guardianship approved by a circuit court judge in Palm Beach County, and then if she wanted to relocate him to Maryland, the judge would have to authorize that, as well. A lawyer in Florida, awaiting her approval to go ahead, had already drawn up the petition. Under Maryland law, with her father's acquiescence and a little evidence as to his condition, she would be granted legal authority over his affairs, assuming it was uncontested. And who would object? She was advised it would be essentially the same in Florida. Her brother, Robert, would support her, as long as he did not have to be responsible for their father's care, and he lived in the Pacific Northwest, anyway, with a family of his own to look after. Although he was quite successful in his own right, his financial resources were fully encumbered by his own needs.

Karen reflected on her own limited circumstances. She was a forty-four-year-old, single mother raising two boys—Bart, fourteen, and Tim, eleven. She had a good job in the Montgomery County School System with good benefits. The boys went to nearby Barrie School, which made carpooling easy for her, but financially she was stretched. Good fortune had allowed her to live in her childhood home after she and her ex-husband split up five years ago, just a couple of years before her dad retired from his government job in Brussels with the Central Intelligence Agency and moved to Florida. The addition of her father to the household would provide some relief in her circumstances, as some of his retirement income could be applied to the family needs, and of course, she could invest the proceeds from the sale of the Boca Raton home for their benefits. She knew that this money would be required for her dad's maintenance in the not too distant future when he would more than likely not be able to care for himself.

It tore her up to witness the progression of Alzheimer's on her father. He most likely would not even remember the early stage diagnosis he received just before her mom died. She had hoped it would be a blessing for him, not to remember, but the reverse proved true. Initially he handled her dying well, but as time passed and he felt more and more alone, he became dependent on those memories of his life with her, eventually to the exclusion of everything else. Just the week before, she had visited him to evaluate what steps she must take, and he had made little time for her, spending most of his days at the mausoleum with her mother's ashes. Several times during her visit when he left the house on an errand, he returned to the driveway after a few minutes having lost his focus on what he had set out to do.

Karen resolved to take action the following day, starting with a visit to the lawyer, followed by another visit to her father to work her magic and convince him it was his idea to relocate to Silver Spring. It was three hours earlier on the West Coast, so Karen took advantage of the hour to call her brother to advise him of her plan.

While Karen Kenny was busy visiting her father the week before, John Hallanger was spending a few days not too far away in Miami at the Bureau field office in Miramar. The beautiful new glass building was located on Southwest 145th Avenue. He met privately with Special Agent in Charge Fulton McBride to develop a strategy for taking control of Stewart Masterson.

After a review of the files and lists of available resources, they came up with a plan. A search of Karen Kenny's background had not revealed much, but her ex-husband had pled a felony arrest for possession of cocaine with intent (to sell) to a misdemeanor and had served six months in county lockup in Fairfax County in the late nineties. Karen herself had been arrested at the same time, but no charges were ever filed after the prosecutor determined that she was an innocent passenger in the car that was stopped. Her husband's arrest and subsequent scrapes with the law had ultimately led to the dissolution of the marriage early in the new millennium.

McBride's plan was to associate Karen Kenny's involvement in her husband's drug business with some creative record keeping and use this "evidence" to discredit her as a viable person to be responsible for her father. This intervention in her petition would be presented on short notice after learning she had made her request of the court, wherever that might be, not leaving her enough time to prepare a defense. The seriousness of Stewart Masterson's advancing incapacity would be emphasized, requiring the judge to make a quick ruling on the alternative arrangement proposed by the Bureau, who, after all, is just looking out for one of its own, so to speak. Confidential witnesses would all be available to promote the fabrication, as it were. In no time, Stewart Masterson would be a ward of the Bureau, living out his final years in Tropical Isles Senior Assisted Living Facility in Pompano Beach, for the good of the nation's security.

Hallanger looked at the outline and nodded thoughtfully. "Good plan, Fultie. You have pulled a lot of stuff together on short notice. Let me know what kind of backup you need from my office for any action that needs to be taken in Maryland. Again, great plan."

"Just for the record, Jack, I think this sucks. I've never felt so bad about anything I've ever done since I've been with the Bureau. Having said that, I will see that the plan is implemented as efficiently as possible. I understand the pressure you are under in Washington.

The only help I will need is credible people to put in a courtroom in Maryland if that's the direction the daughter goes. You're assuming she will try for a guardianship here in Florida, right?"

"Yes, that's our assumption. He's a Florida resident now, and moving the jurisdiction will be difficult for his daughter, I suspect. We have learned, however, that she has sought counsel in Maryland, so we need to be prepared for that eventuality."

The meeting concluded. Hallanger rose and headed for the conference room door. McBride stepped in front of him and suggested, "I can get us on the Trump course at Doral this afternoon, if you want to get in eighteen."

Hallanger frowned, not rising to the bait. "Didn't bring my sticks with me, but thanks for asking."

ಲಂಛ

Masterson answered on the second ring. "Hello."

At the sound of his voice, his daughter burst into uncontrollable sobs. "Daddy, I didn't get it."

"Didn't get what, dear?"

"The guardianship for you, Daddy. It was awful!" Karen's voice quivered with sobs. "You're not going to be able to move home, back to Maryland, I mean."

"Oh, I forgot. You are going to arrange it so that Mom and I can come back to Silver Spring and live with you and the boys. What do you mean, we can't?"

Karen could barely understand him through her grief. "Daddy, it was terrible. People came from your office where you used to work, well not where you used to work, exactly, but from another government agency."

Masterson listened intently, but the meaning was not really clear to him. He remembered he worked in Brussels at the embassy, but he didn't understand why they would want to make his daughter cry. He felt sad for her and a little angry that the embassy would want to make his daughter so unhappy. He did not have good feelings about Brussels. He felt some people there were a threat to him, and he was a little concerned, but he didn't know why.

Karen tried to control herself. She took deep breaths in an attempt to calm herself down. She explained further, "They told the judge that I was not fit to be your guardian, that I had a criminal association with known drug dealers. They implied that I just wanted to get your money. They convinced the judge that your care was best left to the government, and that they would arrange for your safekeeping. They were so mean, and they told such lies to the judge. They had all these people to help them convince the judge to allow their representative to put you in an assisted living facility in Florida. They even asked the judge to prohibit me from visiting you without their approval, but my lawyer wouldn't let them get away with that."

Masterson listened patiently, not understanding much of the content beyond the fact that he and Helen would not be moving to Maryland to be with their grandchildren. He remembered he liked it there. He felt comfortable there. When Karen had explained on her last visit what her plan was, he had resisted at first. Finally it occurred to him that he was happy around his daughter, almost as happy as when he went to visit Helen, and so he felt good about the prospect of being with Karen and having Helen nearby. Helen's beautiful face flashed before him and comforted him. He felt the need to go to the mausoleum and be with her, to explain. He told Karen so.

"Dad, please wait. I don't know how much of this you can understand, but I need you to listen to me for a minute. Can you do that?"

"Sure, kitten, anything you say." Masterson's thoughts were already formulating a plan to drive the few blocks to Helen. He held the phone to his ear anyway.

"They, your old bosses, are going to send someone down to talk to you and make the arrangements. My lawyer got the judge to instruct them that they are not to meet with you until I am there, so we are going to coordinate a meeting the first part of the week, in a few days, to come see you and explain things. Do you understand?"

"Yes, you're coming to see me on Monday. You be sure to let me know what time, so I can be here to let you in. I don't want to be on one of my visits with your mother."

"You got it, Dad. Good job. That's all you need to know for now. I'll be at the house on Monday in the late morning. Have a good weekend, and say hi to Mom for me, will ya?"

"Will do."

There was nothing more Karen could offer at the moment, so she hung up and started crying again. When she was more settled, she called her lawyer and asked if he could accompany her to Florida to help keep her from being bullied. He said he would, and Karen was appreciative that the lawyer seemed to be taking a personal interest in her situation.

క౦౧

Masterson spent the majority of the weekend piddling around the house pulling out boxes of memorabilia he and Helen had amassed over a lifetime together, imagining how he would pack them up to move back to Maryland, not yet fully aware of what Karen had been trying to explain to him. He made several visits to Helen's niche at the mausoleum where he spoke to her in the quiet of the serene gardens surrounding the columbarium.

He also spent some time walking the quiet neighborhood of the Coconut Palm subdivision just east of Federal Highway at the south end of Boca Raton and reflected on the few years he had spent with Helen in this place since his retirement. They enjoyed remodeling the small home located on an interior lot, as they marveled at the amount of new construction, home after home of the original

Bermuda-style residences being knocked down to be replaced by huge, lot line to lot line, Mediterranean stucco monsters that were in vogue. His own home would have been one of the victims of tear down had he and Helen not seen it as perfect for their retirement needs, needing only a little refurbishment to make it livable. They were fortunate that prices in the heart of the recession allowed them to purchase it for the value of the dirt, the structure having no value in a replacement market.

On Monday, Masterson remembered to stay home to receive Karen. He was a little surprised when she arrived with a nice young man whom she introduced as her attorney. They sat in the family room and talked about the events of the past week. Karen's lawyer, Masterson couldn't remember his name, spoke quietly and slowly as he prepared Karen and her father for the most likely series of events they faced. Masterson didn't really get the particulars, but in general, he understood that some people from the government were going to look after him. He was becoming increasingly uncomfortable with this. He offered coffee several times, always declined. Karen's young friend was impressive, wearing a suit and tie and all. He seemed friendly and kind to Karen, so Masterson trusted him. They all directed their attention to the front of the house when a black Ford sedan pulled in the driveway.

Masterson asserted himself and greeted two well-dressed, clean-cut gentlemen at the door when the bell rang. Standing behind him, Karen sized up the FBI agents as they proffered introductions. The older of the two looked uncomfortable, dressed in an unremarkable charcoal suit, white button-down shirt, and a rep tie. His associate was young, probably barely out of the Academy. He looked studious in tortoiseshell horn-rimmed glasses.

"Mr. Masterson, I am Fulton McBride, Special Agent in Charge of the Miami office of the Federal Bureau, and with me this morning is Agent Lyle Ornstein, also of the Miami office."

They extended their hands and shook all around. McBride was

tall, about fifty years old, with hair graying around the temples. He had a confident look about him. His partner was younger, shorter, and very fit looking, but relaxed in his manner.

Introductions made, McBride suggested, "Ms. Kenny, is there someplace comfortable where we can sit and discuss our plans. I can appreciate how difficult this situation is for you and your family, and I want you to know that I and the Bureau will do everything in our power to make this a positive experience."

Karen could not resist the opening. "You mean, you're from the government, and you're here to help us?" The sarcasm hung in the air like a fart, McBride and his partner looking at each other nervously.

Masterson directed them back to the family room, where the two agents sat on the sofa facing the sliding-glass patio doors. Separated by a coffee table, Masterson, his daughter, and her attorney sat facing them in comfortable armchairs. McBride became aware immediately that he and Ornstein were disadvantaged by the glare off the patio, unable to see clearly the faces of the family whose lives they had come to disrupt.

Masterson had been a person in charge his whole life, and although he was not entirely sure what this meeting was all about, they were in his home visiting his family. In character, he took the lead: "Mr. McBride, you may be aware that I have been in government service my adult life. I find it curious to receive members of the FBI in my home. Perhaps you can shed some light on why you are here, so that my daughter and her friend can be helpful to me."

McBride was a fast study. He already figured that he had to play to Masterson's sense of relevance, while trying to persuade his daughter that he was not an enemy. The attorney he felt he could handle because McBride had all the legal cards in his briefcase. This was going to be a lot easier if he had willing participants, and he was aware of the number his cohorts had done on Karen Kenny in court the previous week.

"Ms. Kenny," he began, "I can only imagine how betrayed you feel after the judge's ruling last week in West Palm Beach. The methods notwithstanding, we are where we are, and I would like to put the best face on this we can, for the benefit of all concerned." Trying to distance himself from the tactics the Bureau used to discredit her, McBride reviewed the circumstances before everybody, making sure to direct his conversation to Masterson as well as the others. He noticed that Masterson acted his part well, but he didn't really follow everything that was being said. Emboldened that he could be direct in front of Masterson without risking alienating him, he did his best to make his case. He spun the circumstances on the fact that Karen's father's Alzheimer's disease was irretrievably progressing, the end result of which would require him to be in a facility, which could provide more intense supervised care than she could offer. Furthermore, the cost would now be borne by the government, so that her father's assets could be preserved. He offered additional consolation that Karen would have no restrictions on her ability to visit her father, irrespective of what the judge had provided for in his order.

Karen fumed. "No matter how you try to spin this, I will never forgive you for what you did to me in public last week. I am a grammar school teacher. I don't have the resources to bring my family to Florida so that we can enjoy what time we have with my dad. What you did is unforgivable, and there is no way you can convince me that he will be better off here than with his loving family in the years ahead."

"Notwithstanding your feelings, Karen, may I call you Karen?" McBride began.

"No you may not! We are not friends, Mr. McBride; don't bother trying to treat me as one."

McBride blanched but continued, "Ultimately, it is no longer your call." He went on to outline that the Bureau had made arrangements to place Karen's father at Tropic Isle Senior Assisted Living Facility, located just south of Boca Raton in Pompano Beach. The accommodation package was the highest level of care they offered. He would have his own apartment where he could reside as long as he was able to care for himself, after which time he would be relocated to an area within the facility with the appropriate level of care. Tropic Isle had all manner of activities where her father could participate with supervision. He would not be allowed to bring his automobile, however. "It's my understanding he will not have the use of his car much longer, anyway."

Masterson picked up on this. "What do you mean, *not use my car?* How will I get to the mausoleum to see Helen?"

"The home has transportation available on demand for reasonable supervised visits off the premises," McBride offered. "They have to be supervised because Tropic Isle is responsible for your safety, Mr. Masterson."

Masterson wasn't too sure about all this, but he felt sure Karen could explain it in more detail after the agents left.

The remainder of the afternoon was spent going over logistics. Karen made arrangements for a sub to cover her classes for the next few days, so that she could stay in Florida and help pack up the accumulations of her dad's lifetime and prepare him for the move south. Her attorney hadn't been of much tactical help, other than comfort, but he was able to assure her that McBride's documents and court orders were in order. McBride explained the reason for Lyle Ornstein's presence. Lyle was the person designated by the judge in West Palm Beach to be Masterson's legal guardian. His plan was to visit Mr. Masterson weekly to assure his needs were being met.

Lyle lived in North Miami, so he would be available on short notice to deal with any personal issues that might come up regarding Masterson's legal requirements. His background was in accounting. As a CPA, he would be able to help sort out Masterson's final accounting and make sure that his funds would be looked after. With the court's authority, he could execute documents on Masterson's behalf, such as the sale of his late-model, midsize Mercedes, and payments for storage of anything Masterson couldn't take with him.

With most things settled, the agents agreed to drop Karen's attorney at the airport in Fort Lauderdale for his evening flight back to Baltimore, while Karen and her dad began the process of boxing up what was in the house.

With tears in their eyes, they pored over photo albums created during a lifetime. Progress was slow, as each picture brought back a memory to be shared, prompting further discussion. Years of living in Europe when Masterson was responsible for critical espionage networks in the Mideast and Russia took hours to relive. They ordered Domino's for dinner and worked late into the night.

Tuesday morning they began afresh, stopping only for a quick visit to see Helen and enjoy the beautiful gardens surrounding her final resting place. Karen couldn't help but notice how at peace her dad was poring over his past, and she could see firsthand what a calming effect the place had on him. It was, in fact, her idea to visit Mom; her dad hadn't brought the subject up once.

Later, Karen separated the photos into groups, one for her and one for her brother. A special few of her mother she put into a single album for her dad to take with him. Clothing was categorized, some to be given away to charity or Goodwill, newer stuff to move with her dad. Some of the furniture could be used, and Karen made arrangements for it to be trucked to the assisted living facility. She rented a storage unit in Deerfield Beach to place those items that couldn't be decided upon until some future date.

Each evening she called her boys to see how they were doing. Her close friend and fourth-grade teacher at her grammar school was staying in her home while she was away, looking after the kids. It was good experience for her, as she was engaged to be married and contemplated starting a family of her own soon—that is, assuming the experience with Bart and Timmy didn't put her off. Lauren, her friend, was good for staying through Friday, and putting the kids on a plane Friday afternoon, so that they would have a chance to spend the weekend with their grandfather before everyone had to report back to school on Monday.

For his part, Masterson understood that his daughter's wishes had been overruled by a higher authority and that he was going to be living somewhere else with other people, but still nearby where Helen rested. That gave him some comfort, but he was unsettled about the prospect of moving out of his small home where he knew where everything was. On Friday evening, his grandkids came to visit him. Amid great hugs, Masterson was embarrassed at how sparse his home looked with all the personal items boxed up and sitting by the front door. They all went out for pizza and a movie, and while Masterson couldn't really concentrate enough to follow the plot, he enjoyed being with his family. He was in a comfortable place again, and near-term memories were more available to him.

Karen, her dad, and the boys had a great weekend together. On Saturday they paid a visit to Tropic Isle to look at her dad's new apartment and to set it up with some personal items, so he would feel somewhat at home when he arrived Monday morning. She and Masterson marveled at the attention to detail they witnessed in the lobby and reception area. It had more the appearance of a luxury five-star hotel than the retirement home they anticipated. The staff was very cordial, and excepting the occasional orderlies dressed in fresh white uniforms, the main building did resemble a quality apartment building. Behind the reception area were several living room–style seating arrangements with sofas and armchairs. The whole ground floor was very inviting for guests to visit, without feeling out of place in the living wings, which extended diagonally left and right behind an active group of dining rooms, each designed to have a different feel from casual to formal. Small shops were fit in space available between other functions, and the administrative offices off to the south side looked like those of class-A commercial office buildings. Décor made heavy use of marble and richly stained woods, with quality fabrics everywhere to absorb noise.

The director, a balding, nervous-looking gentleman who introduced himself as Mr. Reinhardt, took the time to show the family the apartment on the third floor where Masterson would be living. The residence hallways were wide and the one-bedroom apartment spacious. The doors to all the apartments were spaced irregularly to eliminate the regimented look found in most multifamily residences, and they were very wide and substantial, undoubtedly to accommodate wheelchairs when necessary. The effect was to make the interior of the living areas look more like townhomes with heavy outdoor-style entrances. In fact, Karen noticed that each entrance was somewhat distinctive, making each apartment feel unique. The furnishings were sparse, as her dad's furniture had not arrived yet, but she felt much better understanding that he would be living in comfortable, familiar surroundings. With the personal effects, pictures, and stuff, it would make him feel right at home, she hoped.

Karen looked in the bedroom, finding it spacious as well with a modern bath and shower off to the side, incorporating assist features to reduce exposure to falls and an emergency call cord. The kitchen was small, but it had everything her father would need. Mr. Reinhardt explained that the stove had automatic shutoff software installed, so that residents wouldn't have to worry about things burning up.

"We encourage our guests to use the rather extensive public dining options downstairs, but the small kitchens are suitable for a quick snack or breakfast, so people don't have to get dressed to find a bite to eat, any time of day or night," he added.

Karen was impressed by the views. The third floor gave an

elevated sight line to the surrounding neighborhood to the east, which was mostly residential. She was amazed at how much green she saw from this slight elevation; there was much more vegetation than she would have imagined from what she remembered seeing at street level, yet the apartment was not so high that it felt separated from the surrounding terrain.

Karen had left the boys on the first floor to explore, and she was even more surprised to see how excited they were at all the interesting things they had found, including a really *dope* fitness center and game room. "They even have video games played on seventy-inch televisions!" Bart exclaimed. "Can we visit Grandpa when he moves here, Mom?" Tim asked, expressing his excitement.

Masterson smiled. "Sure you can," he said, tousling Tim's mop of unruly hair.

Karen smiled too, knowing that they wouldn't be spending much time with their grandpa on these visits with all the distractions.

On the way out of the building, Reinhardt showed them the expansive pool deck and surrounding gardens, which were substantial enough to contain walkways and paths through the foliage. The pool deck was nicely appointed with outdoor patio furniture situated in clusters. There was plenty of covered space by the building where more casual wicker furniture with comfortable cushions provided seating for small groups who wanted to enjoy the outdoors without the intense Florida sun to make things uncomfortable during the day or in the balmy evenings.

Feeling much better about things, Karen made arrangements to make the handoff to Lyle Ornstein after the weekend. She and the boys said their goodbyes Sunday late afternoon and caught an evening flight back to Baltimore, and her dad went to bed prepared to meet Lyle Ornstein in the morning to move to his new quarters.

CHAPTER TWO

When he came out of his modest Florida home in the morning to go to work, Dick Smith was somewhat surprised to find his Mercedes S550 running in his carport in Fort Lauderdale. It was one of those perfect, clear blue days, not a cloud in the sky. Warm for March, the day was starting out in the low seventies with little humidity.

Dick was looking forward to some *me* time. His wife had left on an early flight to visit her mother in New York, and he had some time for himself. Today he was scheduled for his Wednesday afternoon golf game at Coral Ridge Country Club with the usual suspects. He and his friends played a regular low-stakes game midweek, risking at the most twenty bucks or winning a hundred or thereabouts, plus bragging rights.

At first he noticed the telltale puddle of water running out from under the car, a sign the air conditioning had been operating, then the dew that covered windows, a related condition. *God damn it!* he thought. He checked the inside to make sure there was still gas in the car (there was) and the key was in the cup holder where he'd left it when he was home (it was).

This was not the first time the car's automatic gas-saving feature had bit him in the ass. In their arrogance, Mercedes engineers had developed software for their cars to "assist" an ignorant customer base in the management of their automobile needs. When the brake was applied firmly, such as at a stoplight or when the driver had reached his destination, the brake hold feature initiated an engine shutdown to save gas. When the gas pedal was pressured to go or when the air-conditioning coils warmed to the point of being ineffective, the car started back up. Sometimes when he was in a hurry, Smith exited the car when the feature was engaged, only to have the car start up again after he was out of earshot of the running auto, usually not far from the quiet German car. In fact, not something Smith shared with just anybody, when he first bought the vehicle, he returned to the parking garage at Fort Lauderdale–Hollywood International Airport from a weekend trip to find his car was out of gas.

I hate this car, he thought, although in his heart he was proud to drive a top-of-the-line Mercedes in his midthirties, not an accomplishment many of his golf buddies could match. What he really objected to was the arrogant way Mercedes engineered their cars, as though they knew better the needs of their customers. In his soul, however, he knew he would lease another when the current one came up for renewal.

He put his clubs and golf shoes in the trunk and headed to his office to get in a morning's work. Wednesdays he put in a half day before heading over to the club for the afternoon. His mind was speculating on what he was going to do with his free evening to take advantage of his wife's absence. He might visit a few local hotspots and try to get lucky, or just go to a titty bar and enjoy the entertainment. The Pure Gold was just up the road in Pompano Beach, a quality club he had frequented, so he wouldn't have to drive far to get home in an impaired condition. That was probably a better alternative, less complication and drama. Maybe someone in his golf group would like to join, although that was unlikely considering how pussy whipped his friends were. The irony that the only reason he could go was because his wife was out of town escaped his mental process.

ↄⲟⲥ

During his first weeks at Tropic Isle, Masterson was dominated by feelings of isolation and emptiness. He missed Helen terribly, and his loneliness only deepened as time progressed. In his mind, she was just up the road a ways. He thought about her incessantly, filling his days with memories of her, poring over the photo album Karen had put together for him. Opportunities to visit her memorial at Eternal Gardens were passed over by the administration at Tropic Isles, and it had been so long since he had made the trip; the awareness of Helen's passing had dimmed since his relocation. His preoccupation with memories of her had replaced the agony of her death, and he now thought of her as a force out there somewhere. That feeling accessed a part of his brain that conceived that he could still be with her in some abstract way. Emotion ruled his consciousness, giving him false hope that he could still find her and fill the void in his heart.

On a balmy March evening, Masterson sat among other seniors at a group table in the main dining room. He didn't particularly enjoy dining with others, but it was better than having a meal served in his room sitting in front of his fifty-inch Samsung trying to remember how to find the CNN channel. Most of the others liked to talk about the "good old days" before the United States became an embarrassment among nations. Masterson could tell a story or two that would stand their hair on end, but he knew he had to be careful talking about his past. He would tell them that the nation was not always as weak as it appeared. He knew America had plenty of influence in world affairs; leaders just couldn't talk about it publicly.

His closest friend at the table was Bevy Martin. Bevy knew something about living on the edge. He had been a fighter pilot in Vietnam when he was shot down on his one hundred ninety-ninth mission. Although based in Ubon, Thailand, he'd spent most of the war in Hanoi, courtesy of Ho Chi Minh, where he was one of only a handful of prisoners to actually make an escape during his incarceration. Unfortunately for him, he sought asylum at the French Embassy in Hanoi, which turned out to be a poor choice, as they promptly turned him back over to the North Vietnamese after giving him a shower and fresh clothes. Bevy was finally released in 1973 after the negotiated peace, where he returned to the States and flew for a major flag carrier. Now he spent his days in the relative calm of Tropic Isle, weakened by the aging process. His family, scattered around the country, was not sufficiently motivated to care for him, so he opted to use his limited resources to buy a life estate in the retirement community, his wife having predeceased him.

Bevy was pleased to have Stewart Masterson around, someone with whom he had found common interest, living and reminiscing in an older world where they shared common memories. Bevy recognized that Stewart was impaired, but they enjoyed sharing a bond in lives of former relevance. He was able to help his friend with daily activities that Stewart found taxing. Stewart shared what history he still had at his command, often speaking about his wife, Helen, as if she were still around, somewhere just up the road, but Bevy had long ago connected the dots that the love of Stewart's life was deceased. Out of compassion, he did not share this with his friend. He had met with Stewart's daughter, a lovely girl named Karen, on her visit the previous week, during which he learned more detail about Stewart's background. He promised her that he would look after her father, and he sensed her relief that Stewart had someone on the premises who cared. The only other visitor Bevy was aware of was some official-looking young man who checked on him each week. Bevy thought his name was Oranburg or something like that, and his interest was more clinical in nature than compassionate. He was pleasant enough, in any event.

For Masterson, life was not so pleasant. His feelings of loneliness dominated his days, and he missed Helen terribly, no longer associating her with trips to a mausoleum; he missed the *real* her. He had only been at Tropic Isles six weeks, but he did not feel that he was in a place where he belonged. In his mind, he was reminded of time he spent on the road staying at Courtyard Inns or European hotels. All his needs had been attended to, but he was not in a place that felt like home.

Tropic Isle had varied activities, several dining rooms to choose from, a first-class physical fitness center, swimming pool and sun decks, and spacious gardens for an evening stroll. But when he tried to get past the grand reception area, he was always stopped by the front desk and turned back. Once he tried to assert himself to go for a walk outside, but hospital-garbed attendants were called to intercede, and he was escorted to his apartment. Masterson just wanted to be home where he was among those he loved and who in return loved him. Barring a few friends, he was not finding that feeling here, and compulsion to find that place of comfort was swelling within his core. But it was just a feeling, without a specific identification of place. He just knew it was not here at Tropic Isle.

He finally gave up trying to get out, as he realized he had no destination in mind. He had the suspicion that he was being watched, and this made him more uncomfortable. Lately, when he even ventured toward the front of the building, he sensed that people were moving to positions to intercept him before he could get to the front door. As his loneliness deepened, he began focusing on things he could control. Grooming had always been important to him. He showered regularly and took time selecting what he was going to wear. Always a preppie dresser, he took care in the selection of his wardrobe, usually wearing khakis and a polo shirt, light socks, and tasseled loafers. He kept his hair relatively short, but still long enough to comb, parting it on the left side. He was one of the fortunate ones who had good genes for hair with little evidence of thinning. The blond color had lapsed into silver, however. But still he didn't look his age, so in Florida particularly, he could blend in anywhere.

On this particular chilly Florida evening, the family table conversation was all over the place. Usually the conversation turned to the upcoming presidential primaries, where none of the candidates met with anyone's approval. Bevy said the world had gone mad, as some businessman named Trump seemed to be marching toward the Republican nomination. Most of this was lost on Masterson, whose only image of the potential nominee was a guy who looked like he had a squirrel on his head. The caliber of discussion was a little subdued, as several of the widows were in attendance.

"What are you planning for the holiday next month, boys?" one of the ladies asked.

"We're going to hide our own Easter eggs" was Masterson's stock reply, the irony of his own humor not lost on him. He had learned to rely on a few cute, canned responses to help conceal his failing memory from others; he felt as though it put those around him more at ease.

Each of the men was putting forth an effort to make a good impression on the ladies, companionship being a sought-after commodity at Tropic Isle. The woman to Masterson's right volunteered that her children and grandchildren were coming in for a visit after dinner.

"Would any of you like to meet them?" she asked hopefully. The group was unresponsive for the most part, suddenly becoming preoccupied with their desserts. Masterson felt sorry for her at her obvious disappointment and volunteered to participate. He sort of liked Gracie, anyway. Bevy gave him a smirk and a wink, rolling his eyes, which made Masterson smile.

"I thought we could sit out on the patio by the pool; it's such a nice evening. That will give the grandchildren a place to run around. You know how children are, with all the nervous energy. They probably aren't much interested in what we old people have to say anyway."

"I'll be in my apartment, number three-oh-six. Just buzz my room when they get here, and I'll come right down." Masterson smiled at her.

The meal concluded, the diners slid their chairs back and, at varying speeds and mobility, made their ways to their next destinations. Most went to the card room where they would play bridge and listen to the background television noise, usually from *FOX News,* although those who made it to eight o'clock would probably switch to CNN and the democratic debates scheduled for the night. Masterson made his way to the elevators and back to his room to wait for Gracie's call. He lay across the foot of his bed for a moment and fell asleep. At seven o'clock, his bedside phone startled him from his sleep, and he fumbled for it, pulling it to him by the spiral cord.

"Hello," he answered, wondering who would be calling him in the evening. *Maybe it's Karen,* he thought.

"Hi, Stewart; it's Gracie from dinner," the woman reminded him, knowing he may need a little help. "Do you still want to come down to meet my family? They're all here."

Masterson worked through the fog and remembered the dinner conversation. "I'll be right down."

"It's chilly outside; you may want to put on a sweater or jacket," she suggested.

Masterson grabbed a yellow sweater out of his drawer and put it on, giving himself a sideways glance in the living room mirror; he approved of his appearance. He hesitated a moment and decided to add a belt to his suspenders, sliding a beige windbreaker off a hanger from his hall closet. He didn't give the door a thought as it swung closed behind him unlocked as he entered the hallway and walked to the elevators.

In the great hall area behind the reception desk, he was introduced to Gracie's family. They went out the glass patio doors to the pool deck, and Masterson felt the chill of the early spring Florida air and put on his windbreaker. As they sat around a large round coffee table, it occurred to him that these "kids" would not be running around outside. Gracie's children were in their late forties, and the kids were of college age. He couldn't remember anyone's name except for Gracie's, but he had become experienced at hiding his shortcoming. He sat back on the cushioned patio sofa and tried to follow the conversation. He tried to answer the few questions that were directed his way, but mostly just enjoyed the comfort of being among people who were pleasant and weren't trying to get him to do something he didn't want to do. The teenagers, two girls and a boy, sat together at the next table and chatted among themselves.

After what seemed to Masterson to be a long time, Gracie and the others began standing and saying their goodbyes. Masterson stood likewise and shook hands and smiled politely. He moved to Gracie to give her a hug goodnight, when she suggested, "I'm going to see them out; why don't you come with us?"

Dressed in his khakis and yellow sweater, overlaid by his beige cotton windbreaker, Masterson fit right in as they paraded by the reception desk to the entry circle in front of the building, chatting away as any family assembly might. The orderlies didn't even look up from their iPhones as Masterson passed by.

Gracie's son retrieved the family van from the parking lot and pulled under the portico, as Gracie hugged her daughter and grandchildren for a final time, and the group piled into the van. Gracie stood in the overhead lighting and waved goodbye to her family, and turned to thank her "gentleman friend" for joining her on such a lovely evening.

Now, where did he go? she wondered as she turned around, finding no one in the vicinity. Assuming Masterson had just gone upstairs to his apartment, she didn't give him another thought as she hugged herself to ward off the cool night air and walked indoors.

✺

Smith met his buddies at Coral Ridge Country Club around noon, where they got in eighteen holes before the late-winter sun reached the horizon. He had a passable round, shooting in the mideighties, good enough to win a few bucks. Following the round, they gathered in the men's locker room to divide up some cash and have a few drinks before heading their separate ways. Their conversation covered the usual rehash of hole-by-hole play, complaining about the bad breaks they got, not focusing much on the lucky putts they drained. As they were breaking up to leave for their respective homes, Smith tossed out what had been on his mind.

"I'm batching it tonight. Does anybody have any interest in catching some action at the Pure Gold? I've got some good use for the twenties you guys gave up to me this afternoon. I'm thinking they might look nice sticking out of some girl's garter." He had everyone's attention, but to a man they declined, offering up one domestic excuse after another. It was as Smith had forecast. All pussy whipped. With three scotches under his belt, he made for the door where the valet pointed to his car in the lot adjacent the entrance.

"The car is where we parked it, Mr. Smith," the valet told him, as he grabbed Smith's clubs off the bag drop and put them diagonally in the trunk. "We couldn't bring it up to the door because you forgot to give us the keys. You must have taken them with you."

31

Smith remembered he had taken his personal items out of his pockets when he played golf, which included his cell phone and car key, and put them in a side pocket of his golf bag. *Not the first time I've done that,* he thought.

Smith tossed his golf shoes in on top and pushed the auto trunk closer, tipped the valet five bucks, and headed off on Federal Highway to make his way north to the Pure Gold. The sun was already below the horizon, but not so far that the western sky could hide the blazing gold and red sunset. Smith drove with the windows up to ward off the evening chill. He was in excellent spirits from within and without; an excitement was stirring as he made his way north. By the time he got to the shopping mall where his destination was located, he was downright stoked about his planned *me* time. He pulled into an empty parking space some distance from the nightclub entrance, not wanting to risk that someone might associate his car with his planned activities.

It was completely dark as he pulled into a space near the curb. In his exuberance, he approached the parking bumper a little fast and applied his brake firmly. As designed, the brake hold feature integrated into his Mercedes software activated, and the car's gas-saving feature shut down the engine. Without giving it a second thought, Smith exited the car and headed for the neon-accented entrance of the Pure Gold Gentleman's Club. So quiet was the Mercedes that he didn't even notice when the car started back up again. He was halfway to the front door by then. The car purred quietly in its space somewhat apart from the spaces filled by busy shoppers in the mall. The key fob was still in his golf bag in the trunk.

❧

Masterson moved out to the curb on the edge of the busy boulevard. After a few fits and starts, he sprinted across four lanes of traffic to the median in the middle of Federal Highway and surveyed his situation. Already he felt a sense of freedom being out from under the portico lights of Tropic Isle where he could just see Gracie entering the automatic glass doors at the entrance.

Across the remaining few lanes of traffic was a shopping mall where stores were lit up in attention-getting light displays. The buildings towered over the one-story strip retail stores along the rest of the highway, and Masterson felt he would enjoy some anonymity among the larger buildings of the mall. He could see cars pulling in the parking areas, circling about looking for free spaces. The light at the nearby intersection turned red, and the flow of traffic slowed significantly, allowing Masterson an opportunity to risk walking across the second half of the roadway. He stepped over the curb at the other side and slipped in between the cars that were parked near the parking lot apron. He knew he would be less visible in a crowd, although he needn't have worried. Absolutely no one had any idea that he was anywhere other than in his room. The mall entrance doors were just ahead, and he made his way toward the inside of the shopping center, checking his "six" every few paces to see if anyone was paying him any mind.

To his left above an outside business entrance was a flashy neon sign, just down from the grand entrance to the shopping center. From his angle he could make out Pure Gold Gentlemen's Club in a purplish neon hue, with golden arrow strobes flashing downward to large black doors. There was a large fellow standing outside the door checking out customers as they arrived. He was wearing a dark suit, and that made Masterson nervous. He was not comfortable around dark-suited people who hung out around doorways, so he turned and walked in the other direction toward the parked cars. He was unsure of what to do next, so he continued to walk the perimeter of the parking lot.

That's peculiar! Masterson thought as he ran his hand along the sides of the parked cars. The windows on the car next to him were fogged over. He drew a smiley face in the foggy surface of the side window. Looking down, he noticed a puddle of water forming under the front of the car, which was a new-looking silver Mercedes, the big fancy model. Masterson remembered he had a mid-size version a few years older that had been taken away from him when he moved to the assisted living facility. The man from the government told him he was not allowed to drive anymore when he collected Masterson's wallet, credit cards, and other identification, told him he wouldn't be needing that stuff anymore, that he and the staff at Tropic Isle would take care of all his transportation requirements.

Masterson moved forward and put his hand on the hood and felt its warmth, comforting in the chilly air, but he could also feel the car vibrating. *It's running,* he thought. *Who leaves his car running in a shopping center parking lot, especially a hundred thousand dollar car?*

Masterson looked around and didn't see anybody near him. The car wasn't parked near any of the mall entrances. There were still open spaces near the mall entrance, where someone wanting to just dash in for a quick purchase might leave a vehicle running, but not here, a hundred yards away. He took a chance. Opening the driver's door, he slid in behind the wheel. Sure enough, the instrument screen was all lit up from behind. Whoever's car it was had the seat set about right, so he must have been about Masterson's size. The little gas tank icon on the dash showed twenty-five percent.

Masterson thought about his situation for a moment and made a decision. He knew Federal Highway, traveled it hundreds of times over the years he had been in Florida. He remembered Helen, and how much he missed her drilled deep in his chest. She was just up the road, he knew. His need to be with her consumed him. Tears of joy flowed down his cheeks as he stepped on the brake and slipped the car into reverse out of habit, instinct guiding his progress now as he backed out of the parking space and followed the aisle to the entrance of the mall parking lot.

It was dark now, and the fast-moving lights confused him as he edged cautiously out into traffic. Finding a hole in the southbound lanes, he gunned it and merged with the northbound traffic on the other side of the median, cutting off a Ford Mustang in the fast lane. He was rewarded with a lengthy blast on the horn and a hand gesture from the driver's window, as the angry driver swerved to the inside lane to avoid a collision. The noise got Masterson's heart rate up a little, but in no time, he settled down, feeling more comfortable in the steady flow of the traffic. He marveled at the smooth handling of the larger Mercedes, which was bigger than the one he had owned. As he adapted to the automobile and its responses, he speeded up, racing against some kind of internal timetable, which seemed to be directing his progress toward Helen. As he proceeded north, his impatience grew at the thought of seeing his beloved wife again. He began weaving in and out of traffic in the left lanes of northbound Federal Highway.

Sergeant Randy Ruback was nearing the end of his patrol shift with the Broward County Sherriff's Office. He was part of a deployment that handled traffic monitoring in Deerfield Beach, a small town at the north end of Broward County whose budget could not handle the cost of a full-blown police department; hence that responsibility had been farmed out. It was a political win for both city and county, as the revenue, while considerably less than the cost of full traffic monitoring for the city, was far greater than the few vehicles and staff required for the county, overhead having already been covered.

Ruback was engaged in routine traffic observation along US 1, known locally as Federal Highway. The work was slow, even for a Wednesday evening, and there wasn't much for him to do. He positioned his patrol unit in a service drive between a restaurant and strip center near Tenth Street, watching for unusual activity among the passersby on the road.

Ruback wasn't particularly liked by his fellow officers, partly attributable to his gruff manner and appearance. He was large and intimidating with the 'roided-out appearance of someone who spent all his free time in a gym. His hair was military short, and he enjoyed wearing his uniform too much. Ruback was one of a few who came to work dressed in his work outfit, complete with leather Sam Browne belt and gear, which he also often wore at home where he lived alone and during errands around town. Officially, this was frowned upon by his superiors, but he felt it commanded respect from those who came in contact with him, a characteristic that he placed a high value on. He often mistook trepidation of those he encountered for appreciation of the authority he represented, and correspondingly he did not react well to those who showed disrespect. Often inviting confrontation, Ruback did not observe common civilities when addressing people in new situations, as he felt it was not necessary given his position. Why should he go out of his way to be nice to people, when they should respond to him based solely on his countenance? He did, however, follow verbal protocol whenever dealing with a situation for which he had been trained. Warmth was not an industry standard when asking, "Your driver's license, registration, and proof of insurance, please."

On this particular evening, traffic was flowing evenly past him toward the light at Tenth Street, just up the road. As he scanned the oncoming traffic, he noticed a pair of headlights swerving to the inside lane, passing a slower car and returning to the outside lane again, obviously speeding. Ruback wasn't interested in a protracted arrest and detention that would increase his shift, but he still had a half hour to go, and this looked like a routine traffic matter, anyway.

Too late for radar, Ruback eased out into traffic and followed the erratic path of the silver Mercedes, while he called dispatch and passed on a description and license of the vehicle. The light turned yellow as the pair approached the intersection at Tenth. Ruback looked up to the top of his windshield just in time to notice the light switch red as the Mercedes passed under. Clear of the intersection, Ruback pulled up behind the unaware Benz. He put on his patrol lights and hit the button on his dash for a pulse of his siren to get the driver's attention. There was no immediate reaction from the Mercedes, so he hit the siren pulse again, and a third time. Finally the car's turn signal came on as the Mercedes worked its way to the right lane curb and turned onto the access lane to the shopping center at the southeast corner of Hillsboro and Federal.

Ruback tapped in the license plate numbers for the Mercedes on his patrol unit's computer and brought up the registration for a new S550 leased to Richard Smith, whose address was in Fort Lauderdale. No warrants or arrests showed up on the computer screen. He grabbed his flashlight and got out of the car, cautiously approaching the driver's side of the Mercedes.

Things were progressing swimmingly for Masterson until the blue, white, and red lights started flashing in his rearview mirror. He continued for a block or two hoping they would go away, but the urgency of the siren beeps convinced him otherwise. He knew this was authority behind him and that he must pull over, so he started checking his mirrors for opportunities to get to the right-hand lane. A wall of fear overtook him as he maneuvered to the entrance of a large shopping center at Hillsboro Boulevard, almost to Boca Raton. He slouched in his seat and watched his rearview mirror for the activity in the patrol car that pulled up behind him. His heart rate rose to over one hundred as the colored strobe lights continued their blinding flashes. He saw his face reflect alternating shades of ghostly blue, warm rose, and revealing white in rapid succession in the mirror. For the moment he had no concern or even awareness that he was driving a car that was not his. His primary thought was that this was an inconvenience keeping him away from Helen and that the authority behind the patrol car was no friend of his.

After several moments, the police car door opened and a huge uniformed officer got out. As he approached the car, Masterson saw him light up a flashlight and shine it around the interior of his car. Coupled with the staccato flashes from the patrol lights, the intrusion of the flashlight beam really felt like an invasion of his space, and Masterson's alert level amped up a couple of notches.

The officer looked in the driver's window and said something to Masterson that he could not hear. The officer made a circular motion with his finger. Masterson fumbled around the unfamiliar door ledge trying to find a power window control button. Finding none, and somewhat frustrated to hear what the officer was saying, he pulled on the door handle and started to open the door. The officer aggressively pushed the door shut with his knee and signaled more vigorously for Masterson to roll the window down. The tenseness of the situation made Masterson all the more anxious, as he twisted about in his seat trying to find the window actuator, finally locating it on the door arm rest. It took three tries to get the right button, but finally, the driver's door window slid silently down, and Masterson found himself looking into a powerful Maglite. He could no longer see anything beyond the car window, but he heard the officer's voice from behind the light's brilliance.

"What's the matter with you, buddy? You look trapped in there. Let me see your license and registration, please," Ruback instructed in a monotone.

Masterson stared back blankly in the direction of the light. Ruback asked again, getting more impatient, "Driver's license and registration, sir!"

Masterson fumbled around, feeling his pockets, which were empty, except for a comb. Failing to find anything, he looked up and shrugged his shoulders, holding his palms up, suggesting he was out of options to comply.

"What's your name, sir?" Ruback asked, sensing there was something wrong here. *Is this guy drunk?* He didn't smell alcohol. Masterson just continued gazing upward toward the light and the voice coming from behind it. He asked again, a little louder, "What is your name? Identify yourself!"

"I'm Stewart Masterson," he replied, blinking into the bright light. He tried to put his hand in front of the flashlight to protect his eyes.

"Mr. Masterson, I think you'd better step out of the car." Ruback stepped back and motioned with his flashlight for Masterson to get out of the car, waving circular motions on the pavement below the door. Masterson complied. Standing face to face, Ruback asked him why he didn't have any identification.

He replied, "I don't carry any since I moved to my new home. I have no need of any."

Ruback became more impatient. "You do if you are going to drive on public roads. Where is your new home? Where did you get this car? Is this your car?" he barked in Masterson's face.

Masterson backed up a step, leaning his rear on the door, trying to get away from the annoying policemen. "I live just down the road a little, and I just got this car," he offered as an answer.

Ruback had had enough of this guy's bullshit. Placing his right hand on Masterson's left shoulder, he tried to rotate him roughly toward the doorframe. "Okay, buddy. That's enough from you. Turn and face the car; put your hands on the door and spread your legs." Ruback tried to sweep one of Masterson's feet to the side.

Feeling fearful, Masterson resisted the force from the officer, and he tried to turn the other way to face him. He didn't like being pushed around by anybody, particularly this hulk of uniformed authority. His stare became more intense.

Ruback was incensed. He misinterpreted Masterson's fear and confusion for disrespect, and he would have no part of it. Now he was pissed, and he was not about to put up with the old man's attitude change. As Masterson turned toward him, Ruback gave him a big shove with his hand in the middle of his chest, intending to pin him up against the car.

Masterson may not have been able to process new thought and communication as well as he used to, but his training and instinct were as current as ever. Signals that had been going to the lower cortex of his brain where they could not always connect with history stored there, now were redirected to the part of his brain that short-circuited the processing part, and reflex actions that had been learned over countless years of training in response and execution were excited directly from the spinal cord. His fight-or-flight response was fully engaged, and physical threat met with Masterson's trained responses, not requiring any deductive brain processes.

As Ruback pushed against his chest, Masterson rotated, so as not to be disadvantaged by being pinned up against the car. In the first instant, he resisted the pressure on his chest, then backed away a half pace, causing Ruback to extend his arm to continue pushing. Masterson rose up on his toes to give himself a height advantage and clasped both his hands over the top of Ruback's hand on his chest, pressing as hard as he could to add to Ruback's thrust. When he had maximum leverage, Masterson rotated forward from his hips in a snapping motion, holding the officer's hand firmly against his chest and squatted, taking all his weight off his feet momentarily.

The effect was rather dramatic. One moment a rather normal-sized man was standing before him, and the next, Ruback found himself strangely overpowered. The force of Masterson's rotation, coupled with the inflexible position of Ruback's hand on his chest caused the palmar radiocarpal and ulnocarpal ligaments to snap, as they were stretched to their limits. As the ligaments parted, Ruback's wrist joints dislocated at both the radial and ulna, and the hinge to his hand became useless. There was immediate pain as the ligaments stretched to the snapping point, but surprisingly, there was relief thereafter when they severed. Instinctively, Ruback leaned forward to ameliorate the pressure on his wrist, which was when Masterson used his accelerated momentum to continue his thrust forward and head butt Ruback ferociously on the bridge of his nose. The excruciating pain did not abate until the big man lost consciousness, his nose spread across his cheeks and blood pouring from his nostrils.

Masterson looked down at the unconscious police officer and felt relief that he had removed an impediment to being with his beloved Helen. He engaged no emotion other than having removed a threat to his objective. He could tell from the flow of blood he had not killed the police officer, and he was aware that he would be best served to get out of the area, lest someone else interfere. He rubbed his forehead where he had made contact, not noticing any damage as the force of the blow had landed squarely on soft cartilage of Ruback's nose. Masterson's forehead would just be a little bruised.

Lying on his back with his arms out to the side and one knee elevated, Ruback looked much like a discarded marionette. Masterson deftly stepped over the officer's body and slid behind the wheel of the Mercedes and closed the door. On instinct, he depressed the brake and put the car in gear. As he stepped on the gas, he felt the stilled engine come to life, and he moved carefully from the curb, so as not to disturb the sleeping police officer. When he was clear of the scene, he moved into northbound traffic on Federal Highway, caught a green light at Hillsboro, and proceeded north toward Boca Raton where he felt familiarity with his surroundings. He did not even notice the police cruiser's flashing lights in his rearview mirror as he pulled away.

A half mile ahead, the density along the road lessened, and US 1 became a manicured boulevard, with a wide grassy parkway dividing the north and southbound traffic. As the landscape became more and more familiar to Masterson, the excitement within him grew. He knew he was getting close to his Helen, his heart rate quickened, and his face flushed in anticipation. He was progressing solely on instinct at this point, his gut guiding the operation of the Mercedes. He didn't even notice when he passed the traffic signal at the entrance to the gated community where he and Helen used to live, the retirement home they shared until that government official told him he had to move. He raced to the next signal where the highway narrowed at a busy intersection. New construction eleven stories high filled one of the four corners, and Masterson knew now where he was from months of driving this route daily. He must turn left here to find Helen. He waited what seemed like an eternity at the light, as traffic followed the dictated lights and arrows, but Masterson was focused on only one arrow, the left turn arrow. *Finally!*

The car in front of him didn't move into the intersection fast enough for Masterson, so he gave him a blast from the horn. As the car moved slowly ahead, Masterson floored the Mercedes and passed the SUV on the outside of the turn and accelerated to the next light where he was at the head of the line to cross the intersection at the railroad tracks and Dixie Highway. Heart pounding and adrenaline flowing, he crossed the tracks when the light turned, then made the sweep around the bend of the road. He knew he was so close! *Just one more light,* his gut told him.

Again his patience was tested as the light turned red when he approached. *Almost there!* Through the light! *There, on the right:* Eternal Gardens, a huge marble façade archway, beautiful plantings surrounding, and vines growing on the columns and connecting on the archway overhead. Masterson pulled through the entrance to the dimly lit parking lot behind. He was here! Helen was here! No cars in the lot, so he parked in the first space alongside the walkway to the spacious gardens beyond. He stepped on the brake, stopping the car, and threw open the door. He didn't bother shutting the car off; it did that by itself. He didn't notice when it started back up again as he walked up the path through the archway.

He bolted up the walkway, so excited, knowing that his emptiness was about to be fulfilled. Helen was here. As he entered the gardens, he passed a reception hut occupied by a uniformed guard who was sitting at his desk watching a small television in the corner. Masterson felt comfort in this place, and he slowed for a moment to survey his surroundings. As he paused by the office, the guard looked up and smiled in recognition.

"Hi, Mr. Masterson. It's so good to see you again; you've been away awhile, haven't you? I haven't seen you in over a month. You have always been one of my regulars in the evening." Masterson looked at the guard, vaguely remembering the friendly face. The guard continued, "No need to stop, Mr. Masterson, I'll sign you in. Have a nice visit." The guard returned to the election debate on the screen.

Instinct had brought Masterson to this place, but now as he looked around the gardens, he felt some confusion. Before him were a series of serpentine stone edifices, all very formal. Beautiful gardens of rosebushes, gardenias, and bougainvillea were planted everywhere. The stone fixtures were faced in light marble with engraving. As he absorbed what he saw in front of him, his excitement at the prospect of seeing his beloved Helen began to crumble. He was engulfed by an overwhelming sense of dread. Synapses were firing, and distant memories were slowing being recovered, as his inner compass guided him to the third arc of stone monuments, top row, second from the left.

A wall of unbearable weight fell upon him as he looked at the marble engraved faceplate on the niche before him:

HELEN CROSS MASTERSON
JUNE 6TH, 1944 – JANUARY 2ND, 2015

The synapses connected and the full burden of the loss of his wife took him to his knees. His heart twisted in agony, as he realized he was not to going to be with his beloved Helen. His awareness finally penetrated the lower reaches of the limbic system of his brain, freeing his recall of Helen's passing, the months of rapid decline as the cancer took her beautiful life from him. Slumped in a round-shouldered collapse, his body shook with heaving sobs as he hugged himself, as if to hold himself together against the horrible burden he felt pressing down upon him.

It took him several minutes to compose himself and stand to look at the niche again. Finally when he did, he absorbed the significance of the engraving on the marble face. Still shaking as occasional waves of grief overcame him, lips trembling, he traced the outline of her name on the engraving with his finger. Older memories swept through his mind as images from his younger years flashed before him. His sadness slowly shifted to serenity, and his need to be with her changed form. He wanted to see her urn, the repository for her ashes and the last tangible evidence of her existence. As he surveyed the marble face, he noticed the bronze metal fasteners at each of the four corners of the marble faceplate. He reached for the one on the lower right and tried to grip the palm relief of the metal between his index finger and thumb, so as to unscrew it. His fingers slipped. He tried again, squeezing harder and pushing to gain more traction. Slowly the polished fitting began to yield. First a quarter turn, then a half, finally it rotated smoothly. The threads were very fine, so it took a dozen turns before the metal fastener fell into his hand.

The lower left released easily, but the upper right was fit very tightly. He tried multiple times, but he could not get enough traction with his fingers on the tiny bronze fitting. His hands were moist, sweating a little in spite of the cool, dry evening. He pulled his shirttail out of his trousers and lifted it up his torso. After a few tries using the cloth for friction, he was able to loosen the fitting. The last, upper left did not prove to be a problem. The marble plate was fit snugly in the niche frame. Masterson put his hands on the flat surface and tried to work it loose. After some massaging, the marble slab shifted a little. Using the thick-tined end of his comb, he was able to get some leverage under the marble at a corner, where the bronze fitting had been removed, and pry the edge of the stone out enough to where he could remove it. He laid it gently on the ground in front of the wall and stood, looking directly into the niche where the amphora-shaped urn contained his beloved wife's ashes.

The urn was made of brushed pewter, lightly polished, and inscribed with Helen's birth and death dates under the caption *Dearly Missed* beautifully engraved in script. Masterson stood a moment taking in the setting, his heart aching anew, as though he had lost his love for a second time. Gently he reached for the urn and lifted it out of the enclosure, holding it tightly to his breast. Slowly he rotated his back to the wall and slid down on his haunches, quietly sobbing as he placed his face against the cold metal.

He felt Helen's spirit penetrate his chest, as he held her close, and a renewed sense of calm overtook him. *Now, now there, my love,* he said. Memories from long ago worked through his mind as he let himself go, giving in to them. His son, Bobby, the Little League star, hit a home run to win his series championship. Karen, the apple of his eye, won an essay contest in high school just before the family moved to Europe to begin his foreign rotation with the Central Intelligence Agency. Helen, when she accepted his proposal of marriage on the mall in the heart of Washington. Early memories came at him nonstop. He couldn't quite bring his son into focus in recent memory, and he felt as though he was a long way away. Karen, his daughter, was still available to him in his mind.

Overcome with loneliness, only made worse by the fleeting memories and the awareness that he was holding what was left of his wife in an urn, Masterson stood and faced the hole in the stone wall before him. As he reluctantly placed Helen's urn in the open space, his attention was diverted to the small canvas bag tucked in the corner. It was about the size of a Dopp kit used for toiletries when traveling, canvas of a greenish-gray color, with a heavy-duty zipper across the top. It had been pushed into the corner of the niche alongside where the urn was placed. Masterson gave the corner a tug and felt the weight of the bag, probably a few pounds, as he pulled it out of its hiding place. Masterson had no earthly idea why the bag was in Helen's final resting place, and yet, its presence didn't seem entirely unfamiliar to him. He couldn't describe the feeling. In fact, he had placed the bag there himself, not wanting to dispose of the only remaining connection to his clandestine past, his go bag, containing essentials he might have needed when he was in active service if he had to make a quick run for it. He moved it around the side of the stone wall where he had more light from the overhead lamps and studied it for a moment, unsure if he should examine the contents here or in privacy somewhere else. His curiosity got the better of him in time, as he thought, *Who is going to see me here, of all places?*

Slowly he unzipped the bag. The zipper caught once on the corner of some bound papers, which jutted out from inside. He pushed them down with his thumb on the other hand, and the zip moved more freely. When it was fully open, Masterson pushed on the ends of the bag, bowing the middle so he could see inside better. He didn't really know what to make of what he had discovered. Stacked neatly across the bottom and at one end were bound bundles of currency. Fanning the corners, Masterson quickly determined they were one hundred dollar bills. He pulled them out and counted five stacks, all appearing to be one hundred dollar denominations, each bound with a paper band indicating $10,000. Next he removed a baggie, which contained several credit cards in names he didn't recognize and matching identification, mostly driver's licenses and a couple passports. The photos all resembled him. The last item he removed from the bag was a stainless steel nine-millimeter pistol and two full spare magazines.

Masterson looked nervously over his shoulder to make sure no one else was around. Satisfied, he packed his booty back in the canvas bag and turned his attention to the niche. He knew instinctively his newfound assets made him vulnerable. He needed to keep this recent development to himself. He leaned in to the niche and gave his beloved a gentle kiss goodbye, and then thinking better of it, pulled her back out and set her on the ground, and carefully placed the marble piece over the front. Finding the bronze fasteners in the grass at his feet, he screwed them in one by one. When the job was completed, he felt comfortable that things looked undisturbed. Tucking his polo shirt back in his pants and pulling his sweater back into place, he surveyed the surrounding area for signs of something amiss. Finding none, he zipped his windbreaker up halfway, tucked the urn under his left arm inside the jacket, and picked up the bag by the loop at one end and made his way out of the garden. He tried to walk normally, holding the urn in place with his elbow, so as not to draw attention to himself.

"Good night, Mr. Masterson" came unexpectedly from the guardhouse, but Masterson managed a smile and nod to the guard.

"See you next visit," the guard added before returning to the presidential debates on his small flat screen TV.

Masterson walked the short way down the flowered path, passed under the arch with all its vines, and angled to his car, the only one in the lot. He found it peculiar that the car was covered in dew and the headlights were on, just the same as he found it originally in the shopping center parking lot. That seemed like a long time ago. When he opened the driver's door, he felt the rush of chilled air, colder even than the chilly evening air about him. Then he noticed the instrument lights on the dash were lit. As he sat, he became aware that the car was running. *Strange!* he thought. *I'm sure it wasn't running when I got out.*

Placing Helen's urn on the seat next to him, he sat there in the quiet of the space and thought about what to do next. He felt Helen's presence would be of help to him now; just having her near gave him the strength to sort out what he should do next. He knew somebody was probably looking for him with the intent to take him back to that place. *Ugh!* He needed to find a refuge where he was needed, where he would be around people who cared about him. He needed to find home! The closest thing to home he could think of was his daughter, Karen. He did remember she lived in his old house, the same house he grew up in, because it had been his parents' house, as well.

It shouldn't be hard, he thought. He remembered his house from childhood, so etched in his brain it was. As a youngster he had vacationed in Florida with his parents, and they had always driven down US 1. He had a car, money, and even a driver's license, should he need one. He had no idea what he would need with a pistol, but it couldn't hurt having it around. He felt better about things already. He had a plan. He was going home to Karen, and she would know what to do. Comforted that he had a way forward, he put the Mercedes in reverse and backed out of the space.

At the Federal Highway intersection, Masterson turned left off of Camino Real on to US 1 and started his long trek northward, with his beloved Helen belted safely by his side on the front passenger seat of the shiny new Mercedes. He knew she was not really there, but the pewter metaphor served to keep him company, to give him someone with whom he could share his thoughts. "Helen, if my memory serves me correctly, if we just stay on this road, we will find our way back home and to Karen."

CHAPTER THREE

While Stewart Masterson was continuing his adventure northward, the Broward Sheriff's Office was trying to determine the whereabouts of Officer Randy Ruback. He had last reported in to the dispatcher that he was pulling over a silver Mercedes Benz on Federal Highway in Deerfield Beach, but he hadn't reported back in for the last thirty minutes. The watch commander ordered a nearby unit to surveil the last known location for Ruback. It didn't take long for the officers to find Ruback's flashing lights in the turnoff to the shopping center at the southeast corner of Hillsboro Boulevard and US 1. They reported the location to dispatch and were instructed to use caution while investigating the scene.

While the other officer remained in the car, the driver got out and approached the cruiser slowly, one hand on his sidearm, the other holding his Maglite. He saw nothing unusual until he worked his way to the front of the police car where he discovered a large uniformed man, presumably Sergeant Ruback, lying motionless, his back on the pavement, arms out to the side, one leg extended and one bent upward at the knee. His face was covered in blood, which looked like it radiated from his nose, and he was snoring peacefully in repose. The officer quickly motioned to his partner to join him, as he knelt to feel Ruback's carotid for a pulse. The officer was alive, but out cold.

They tried to resuscitate Ruback with gentle slaps, but were unable to get any response beyond a soft moan from the unconscious policeman who seemed peacefully asleep, snoring softly due to clogged sinuses, a result of his condition. The officers noted that Ruback's eyes were dilated and barely responsive to the flashlight beam. "This looks serious," the first officer said to his partner. "I'll stay with him while you report this in and request an EMS crew. We can probably do more harm than good if we try to wake him up." The second officer agreed and returned to his police unit to call in.

Having decided his condition was serious enough to wait for the EMS crew before venturing farther, they waited a few moments until they heard the approaching sirens and moved to the edge of the roadway to help identify their location to the incoming ambulance.

The EMS crew scrambled from the back of their vehicle with a backboard and other equipment and were directed to the injured officer by the policemen.

"Do either of you know what went down here?" the EMS driver asked of the responding patrolmen.

"No. He is just as we found him. We were unable to get any response, and we didn't want to risk making the situation worse by trying to rouse him," one of the officers replied.

The paramedics went about their business, checking vitals, and so on. When they were satisfied the downed sergeant was stable, they moved him to the stretcher, secured his neck in a flexible brace, and transferred him to the ambulance. They made their way south to North Broward Medical Center emergency room, lights blazing and sirens blaring.

The Broward Sherriff's Office sent Charlie McCutcheon, an investigator, to the hospital to see if he could learn anything from the downed officer. One of the uniformed police officers drove Ruback's patrol unit back to headquarters, after he had copied the information off the car's open computer screen page. He radioed in that the most recent inquiry involved a 2016 silver Mercedes Benz S550 sedan and the searched vanity plate number. The sheriff's office forwarded the information to McCutcheon, who called the registered operator of the car, a Richard Smith, who resided at 2750 NE 45th Street in Fort Lauderdale. There was no answer. He did not leave a message.

After a few minutes with the attendings in the emergency room, Sergeant Ruback began to respond with groaning noises but was still incapable of saying anything coherent. The CT scan revealed that he had a concussion, a crushed nasal bone, and severely bruised cartilage of the middle nose. There were no other signs of trauma, and the doctors were waiting for their patient to regain consciousness naturally. After a few more minutes of IV fluids, Ruback began to evidence that he could see, and his eyes started to react to light stimulus. His breathing was difficult, as he could not make an airway through his nose.

As Ruback regained his consciousness, he was most bothered by the bright lights in the emergency room, followed by the pounding in his head and the dryness in his mouth. He noticed people bustling around him, and his head felt like it was about to burst. When he moved his arm, it caught the attention of his doctor, who said, "Welcome back to the world of the living, Sergeant. You have been away for a while. Can you hear me and understand?"

Ruback blinked and tried to nod.

"Do you know where you are? If it's difficult to talk, just nod."

Ruback moved his head sideways, indicating no, he did not.

"You are in the emergency room at North Broward General Hospital. You were attacked, we suspect, and you have a concussion and a badly broken nose. I would like to do some tests on you to check your responses."

The young doctor made tests of the police officer's responses to stimuli, light, and so on. Satisfied, he asked his patient if he could speak.

"My head is killing me," Ruback managed to scratch out.

"I have no doubt; I can only give you some Tylenol right now. Anything stronger may aggravate your condition. Would you like some?"

Ruback nodded and weakly said yes.

The doctor motioned to the nurse to get the Tylenol and continued, "It will be best if you can sit up. When you feel up to it, you may try to blow your nose to clear out the blood and fluids. It will help you breathe better, but it won't be pleasant. There's nothing we can do to repair the damage. It will have to heal on its own. Nothing in your nose has been displaced, so it doesn't have to be reset—lucky for you. We will move you to an outpatient room while you get orientated. There is an officer here from your department who would like to speak with you when you are able. We recommend you stay here for a couple of hours to make sure nothing unexpected sneaks up, then we will give you a protective face plate, and if your balance is good enough, you can be discharged. Follow-up care will be provided in the instructions we give you."

"What about my wrist?" Ruback said, wincing as he tried to lift his right arm off the gurney. The swelling was only now becoming noticeable.

"We don't know anything about your wrist," said the doctor as he probed cautiously around the swelling and discolored joint. "Wow, that's in pretty bad shape. We're going to need another X-ray. Nurse?" he called over his shoulder. He gave the nurse quiet instructions, as though sharing a secret, the way hospital doctors often did.

While Ruback was being wheeled off for another X-ray, McCutcheon, who was waiting in the reception area, tried the Smith number again; still no answer. He checked his watch and noted it was just after nine o'clock. He sat in the waiting room thumbing through a dated *People* magazine while he waited for Ruback to return. The attendant at the reception desk notified him shortly before ten, and he was escorted to the outpatient examining room. He was shocked to see his fellow officer in such bad shape. His face was swollen so grotesquely that his eyes were barely visible as though at the back of tunnels, his skin discolored by the trauma to a purplish hue that faded to yellow across his cheeks. A nurse was fitting his nose for a plastic protective shield, which he gently taped in place. His right arm was bandaged over a splint that ran halfway up his forearm from the palm of his hand.

Ruback acknowledged McCutcheon with a wave of his other hand, as he was asked, "Can you talk?" He nodded unperceptively. "What can you tell me? We know you were engaged in a routine traffic stop. We have the ID on the car and the owner."

Ruback began his reply, sounding awful, his voice gravelly and nasal, just as the doctor came back in the room with the results of the X-ray. He was informed that his wrist had been dislocated and the ligaments controlling movement severed, which is why he did not feel pain when the joint was exercised. Furthermore, nothing could be done now, because of the swelling, but that surgery would be required for the repair to reattach the ligaments before he would regain use of his hand, followed by weeks of physical therapy, after which he would most likely have full use of the affected limb.

A half hour later McCutcheon reported in what he had learned, which wasn't much beyond a vague description of the assailant and the fact that the sergeant had deducted the suspect was not the owner of the car. The description was sketchy as to the perpetrator's age and size due to Ruback's embarrassment that he had been so severely subdued by a senior citizen.

McCutcheon summarized his report and emailed it to his

precinct to put an alert out on the notices wire to be on the lookout for a 2016 Mercedes Benz, silver, license number a vanity plate: HEDGER, and driver suspected of assault on a policeman. The BOLO (be on the lookout) was forwarded to Palm Beach County law-enforcement agencies as well as those in Broward County, due to the proximity of the assault and the northbound direction of the traffic at the scene. McCutcheon tried Smith's home phone again. Still, no answer.

∽∾∾

Back at the Pure Gold Gentlemen's Club, Dick Smith had a grand old time shoving first twenties, and then later as his cash supplies dwindled, tens, fives, and occasionally a few ones in young ladies' garter belts, as they twisted and gyrated on his table. With vacant stares, they slowly shed what few articles of clothing they had, until finally, Smith could see it all. He was amazed at the wholesomeness of these women; in high school, he could have taken any of them home to his parents, who would have welcomed them with open arms.

Early in the evening, while he was still dispensing twenties, the occasional young woman made eye contact with him, suggesting a trip to a back room for a lap dance or such, but it didn't take long for the pros to determine that he had already had way too much to drink, and they moved on to better prospects. The girls were all young and gorgeous, and they did their best to look sad and vulnerable, as though hoping for a white knight to spirit them away to some other world of safety. The act was effective to keep the money coming, but the fact of the matter was that these girls were seasoned con artists, and the successful ones brought in better than thirty thousand dollars a month, outearning most of their customers.

As the evening wore on, Dick got sloppier and sloppier, until finally one of the strippers did him the favor of suggesting he had had too much to drink and that he ought to go home. She and her friends were beginning to find him annoying. That hurt Dick's feelings more than anything else; he settled his bar bill with a credit card, stiffing the dancer and not hearing her "Fuck you!" above the noise and music as he headed to the door. It never occurred to him that the charge would be there for him to explain to his wife in about a month when the VISA bill arrived.

The chilled evening air brought some clarity to his vision, as he stepped outside. He knew he wasn't doing very well when he stumbled to his knees as he stepped off the curb heading for the parking lot. Smith remembered about where he had left his car, away from the gentlemen's club entrance, so he wobbled off in that direction. Due to the lateness of the hour, there weren't very many cars in that part of the lot, so he was a little surprised that he didn't see it right off. He checked his watch, noting it was almost midnight, and realized the shopping center had been closed for almost two hours. He paced along the edge of the parking lot, becoming frustrated that he could not locate his car. He was sure it was in this area, and there were few cars around to conceal his Mercedes.

Smith reversed his direction and ended up at the club where he started. *Okay, let's do this logically,* he said to himself. He circumnavigated the entire shopping center parking lot, remembering that he had parked near an outside curb. No car! He began at the west side and walked the length of the parking lot one space in from the side. No car! He repeated the process row by row until he got to the outside curb on the east side, and still no car! Most of the lot was vacant, and he still could not identify his Mercedes. Slowly the idea that it was missing worked its way through the fog in his mind, and he considered his options. He knew he was in no condition to drive, and he really didn't want to try to explain to anyone why he was in the area at this hour, particularly the police. He now suspected his car had been stolen, and he was surer of it when he realized he did not have his key in his pocket. After careful consideration, Smith decided his best option was to call a cab and go home to deal with the situation in the morning when he would be more presentable and able. If the car had been stolen, it was going to be an insurance matter, anyway.

A quick search of his pockets brought to Smith's attention that he didn't have a phone, either, so he wouldn't be calling Uber. Slowly the common denominators worked out in his brain, as he remembered the incident at the country club with the valet. His car fob and cell phone were in his golf bag in the trunk of his car. His shoulders slumped as he slowly turned and headed for the only open place he knew, the Pure Gold Gentlemen's Club, purple neon accented with yellow arrows above, where he could source a cab at this hour. Feeling like a complete ass, he made his way to the door, explained his need to use a phone to the doorman, and went inside to the hostess. He was not greeted with enthusiasm, but he was able to slur out his need for a taxi and was accommodated by a hostess who was just a little impressed that the man in front of her had enough presence of mind to know he was in no condition to drive and not too proud to admit it.

Smith rode in silence in the back of a local taxi trying to put together a scenario for the morning when he called the police to report his car stolen. He thought first he would drive his wife's car up to the shopping center to take one last look around before embarrassing himself, just in case. Failing in that option, he would just have to call the police and make some excuse for why he had waited until the following day to report a missing hundred thousand dollar vehicle. All this was becoming too much for Smith, as he started to nod off on the way home. He appreciated the taxi's broken air conditioning because the open windows helped freshen the locker room smell he'd noticed when he got in. The driver awakened him for directions as they neared the turn onto Bayview Drive, near his house.

ഓൻ

Masterson settled in for a long trip up US 1 in the Mercedes, his focus firmly centered on finding his way to his daughter in Silver Spring. He was fully aware that the trip was going to be a challenge, as he was also aware that there were alternative routes he could take. But he recognized his capacity was limited somewhat, concluding that it would be best for him to stick with a plan that had some familiarity. As a preteen, he had vacationed several times with his family in South Florida. Airlines were expensive for a family of four, so he and his older brother had spent the better part of two days playing games in the backseat of the family Buick, annoying their parents in the front with questions of *When do we get there?* and bargaining for rest stops and Dr Peppers at ten, two, and four. Masterson smiled to himself as he remembered the plain roadside motels the family stopped at in the evening after a long day's drive. He joked about it with Helen, belted in the passenger's seat beside him.

"Honey, we're going to have fun on this trip. You remember we didn't travel much by car with the kids, except to the shore in the summers," he reminded her, knowing full well she was not really present. It gave him comfort to think about her as being with him, so he didn't feel as alone while the streetlights passed him by. "You need to help me keep my full attention on these road signs to make sure we don't miss a turn. US 1 can be tricky in some of the towns we will go through." He reached over and gave the urn a pat on the top.

Masterson's body was in a perpetual state of doping, as the freshness of his situation kept a steady flow of adrenaline to his central nervous system from his adrenal glands. Ironically, the chemical result was to stimulate the same neural connectors that his prescription for Aricept was designed to, which was fortunate for him, since he didn't think to include it in his unplanned departure from Tropic

Isle. At the end of the day, Masterson was performing at his peak for the moment.

It was after nine thirty and the traffic was light on a weekday in March, so Masterson made good time through Boca Raton. He kept a vigilant eye out for anyone expressing special interest in him, but for the most part, he felt he was somewhat familiar with his surroundings, for the time being. As the miles wore on, though, he sensed more and more that he was not totally aware of where he was. He was not yet tired thanks to his brief nap earlier in the evening, though that nap seemed like it had happened a week ago. He focused on the moment, dealing only with keeping to his planned route, knowing that if he was diligent, US 1 would take him to Washington, D.C., where he felt sure he would know his way around.

The traffic thinned even more as he worked through the urban roadway south of West Palm Beach. The number of lanes varied between four and six, and the traffic lights spaced closer or farther apart, depending on whether he was near the center of one of the towns, or not. Masterson continued to be annoyed by the car at stoplights, when for no apparent reason, the motor shut off while the car was stopped. He quit being concerned after realizing that it always started again when he stepped on the gas. He remarked on the oddity to Helen, but got no response.

Things continued smoothly until Masterson got to West Palm Beach, where street signs were more oriented to local names than highway designation. Going through the north side of downtown West Palm, he missed the left turn sign off Quadrille, and he continued north into a different sort of neighborhood. There was no other traffic around to speak of, so there was no flow to indicate the direction change, but Masterson had developed a keen sense of instinct in his years of clandestine service. His gut told him reliably when something was amiss, and over the years, he had learned to rely on this valuable intuition. It had saved his life on many occasions.

"Helen, this doesn't feel right. The street was lined with small businesses back there, and now all I see are vacant lots, and fenced in open areas, and we were on a one way street, which is now two way."

Satisfied that his wife was in agreement, Masterson turned the car around and headed slowly back to where he saw oncoming headlights veering off to the west at the traffic light a few blocks ahead. When the light turned green, he ventured slowly into the intersection, ignoring the *WRONG WAY* warning, possible because there was no oncoming traffic. Craning his neck around to the right, he could see the US 1 left turn sign at the front of the intersection, so he made a quick U-turn and a left to get back on the proper route north.

"Helen, we were lucky. We have to watch out for that. If we get off this highway, I have no idea how we will find our way." His heart was racing a little, but he was greatly relieved to be back on track. The misstep and recovery also added a little confidence to the overwhelming task Masterson knew he had in front of him.

As he continued north through Riviera Beach, he could see the massive transformer grid opposite the Palm Beach Inlet. The tallest sailboat masts hauled out at the marinas that lined the western shore of the Intracoastal were visible over the tops of the buildings on US 1. In the heart of downtown Riviera Beach, he couldn't help but notice the prostitutes hanging out along the side of the road in small groups of two, three, and four, highlighted by streetlamps, but with brick and concrete exit strategies alongside the sidewalks they walked. None took so much as a passing interest in the silver Mercedes working its way north on the highway.

Moments later, the road ahead widened, and the landscape improved considerably. The speed limit picked up as well, and Masterson made good time in the lessening traffic but was careful not to speed excessively, lest he attract the attention of another policeman. He had had enough of those encounters for one evening.

After a final downtown in North Palm Beach, the roadway

became somewhat rural, as Masterson passed through one high-end development and gated community after another. The grass was manicured, and the communities were walled off, much like the one he lived in before he was shipped off to Tropic Isles. The shopping centers had high-end stores, and everything was clean and tidy. Masterson was delighted when he crossed over a waterway on a high bridge, and he could see an almost full moon reflecting on the calm water below him.

Past the bridge, he pulled over to the side of the road to look in awe at the beautiful, old-fashioned lighthouse that stood at the water's edge across the Intracoastal from him, aglow from the moon just overhead. He stopped at an opening in the planted landscape to share the view with Helen. "Look at that scene, dear. It should be on a postcard."

Reluctantly he eased back onto the road, lest he call attention to himself late at night in this isolated spot. The two rode together for the next hour in silence, passing more high-end residential areas, some of the names vaguely familiar to him. It was just after eleven o'clock. After going through Hobe Sound, which Masterson remembered as a very wealthy, old-money area, he noticed an Indian motorcycle dealership on his right. His memories shifted back to his college years when he raced motorcycles himself, quite successfully on TT and other dirt track circuits. Although his rides of choice were the popular English makes like Triumph and BSA, he had an appreciation for the American standard of yesteryear, the Indian, a big bore monster whose popularity preceded the Harley Davidson.

When he moved into a more urban area, Masterson noticed the sign proclaiming that he was entering Stuart, Florida. The irony was not lost on him that he shared a name with the pretty little town, spelling notwithstanding. As he climbed higher over another landmark bridge, offering him a view of the wide expanse of the Indian River, the extension of the Intracoastal, he noticed a neatly laid out community airport on the southern shore off to the right. "Look at that, Helen. How convenient that airport must be for the people who live around here. It's part of the community!"

As he came down the other side of the bridge, he was alarmed by a tone and a flashing light on the dashboard in front of him. LOW FUEL blinking in his face was certainly getting his attention. He scanned the panel, trying not to panic. On the lower left, he saw an icon of a gas pump, which, although showing over half full on the icon, was indicating a percentage of less than five percent. The flashing just made it seem all the more serious.

"Helen, I haven't even thought about gas."

The highway ahead was lined with gas stations, mostly empty at this hour of the night. He pulled into Hess, the first one on his side of the road and slid into a line of pumps on his right, selecting the middle one, out of habit. The only other car at the pumps was a pickup truck at the far end. As he braked, the car shut off again. He turned to face Helen's urn, looking for some support, as he was feeling a little confused. He knew how to put gas in his car, but he was unsure how to pay for it. Feeling his pockets, he remembered he had no wallet, identification, credit cards, or money. He was reminded of how helpless he felt earlier in the evening when he was stopped by that pushy policemen right after he found this car.

He looked down at Helen, as if expecting an answer, and he noticed the canvas bag next to her urn on the seat. He remembered it contained all sorts of things he would need on his journey, especially money. He opened it and fumbled through the contents, pulling out the plastic baggie that contained the credit cards. He didn't recognize any of the names, but he figured, *What the hell,* and selected the VISA card. Without thinking about it, he went to the side of the car and pressed the gas fill door, and it released open. Turning to the pump, again relying on instincts, he placed the card in the slot, aligning it with the magnetic strip as depicted on the instructions. He waited a moment while the screen said PROCESSING. Looking around the area for potential signs of danger, Masterson redirected his attention to the gas pump screen and read: EXPIRED CARD, TRY ANOTHER? So, he did, achieving the same result. All four credit cards were rejected. He held them up in the dim overhead light to try to read the expiration dates, but he didn't have his reading glasses with him, so he was unable to make anything out.

In good light, he had been able to read most things since his cataract surgery, but the engraving was not distinct enough, nor the light bright enough for him to make it out. Either way, he figured, the result was the same. He wouldn't be using those credit cards. Masterson sat back in the driver's seat and tried to work out a solution with Helen, when he thought of the money. He stuck his fingers in the small canvas bag and pulled out a sheath of bills wrapped in a band that said clearly: $10,000, replacing the credit cards in the baggie, why he didn't know. Masterson slid out about half a dozen or so hundred dollar bills and slipped them in his left front pants pocket. He zipped up the bag and shoved it under the driver's seat where it would be out of sight to a passerby.

"Well, wish me luck, honey." Masterson nodded to the urn, before he stepped out of the car and made his way to the convenience store at the center of the service station. Inside he was greeted by a peculiarly tattooed young man with beady eyes, the sides of his head shaved, which accentuated the mop of hair that graced the top, giving him a sort of weasel look. Masterson explained that he needed to buy a tank of gas, but that his credit card had expired, not wanting to give out any more information than was necessary.

"You'll have to pay cash, then" came the uninterested reply.

"All I have is a hundred," Masterson volunteered.

"Then you're out of luck, unless you don't want more than twenty in change." Pointing at the small sign below the register indicating that no change in excess of twenty dollars would be provided, he continued, "we safe all bills twenty and up after nine o'clock; I couldn't get to them if I wanted to. Sorry, buddy," he added, not looking particularly empathetic.

Masterson thought about this a minute. He knew the money wasn't an issue; he certainly had plenty of hundreds, but they did leave a trail, and people remembered stuff like that. He did not want to be remembered, at least until after he got to his daughter's house. After that, he didn't care; he knew the two of them could work things out. The last thing he wanted was to get stopped en route to Maryland and get sent back to that lonely place.

"Tell you what," he proposed, pointing at the colorful pictures of menu selections on the wall behind the tattooed man and handing him a hundred dollar bill, "take the hundred, and heat me up one of those beef burritos while I go pump a tank of gas for myself. Then I might pick out a few things to add to the bill, you can give me my twenty change and keep the rest. That work for you?"

"Whatever" was the noncommittal reply. The kid marked the bill with an authentication pen and held it up to the overhead fluorescent lights. Satisfied, he opened the fuel-selector valve on pump seven, where the Mercedes was parked, and returned to his Marvel comic book.

Relieved that his trip did not come to an inglorious end, Masterson stepped lively to his car. He removed the pump nozzle, and after considering the options, selected high-test, not for the performance, but to lessen his financial loss on the deal. *Hell, I may have the beginnings of dementia, but I'm not stupid!* he chuckled to himself.

The Mercedes took twenty-one point eight gallons of high-test at a cost of sixty-five dollars, seventy-three cents. He returned to the island convenience store and picked up his steaming burrito, added a sixteen-ounce root beer, a bottle of water, and a couple of candy bars for a total bill of seventy-three, eighty-five, and collected his twenty dollar bill in exchange. *Not bad,* he thought. *I'm out less than ten bucks!* He left his late-night dinner on the counter for a minute while he went to the men's room at the back of the store. Refreshed, he picked up the paper bag containing his burrito and snacks and headed back to the gas pumps.

Back in his car, he pulled to the side of the service station by the highway and devoured the burrito, cooling the overmicrowaved filling with sips of his beverage. In a few minutes, he concluded his meal with a belch, nodding to the passenger seat. "Please forgive me, Helen. That didn't represent my best behavior."

Renewed now that he had some food in his stomach, he continued north on US 1, comforted that he had a full tank of gas. He was not tired for the moment, but he did think about what he was going to do about finding a place to sleep. He looked over at Helen's urn and said, "What do you think about stopping for the night, dear? Why don't we just continue until I get weary and then look for a roadside motel to rest for the night? As I recall, there are many to choose from as we head in and out of the small towns on the highway."

Masterson's plan would have been a good one if this were 1956, the last time he made the trip with his parents on US 1, but the interstate highway system had changed all that over the years, as long-distance travel plans moved vacationers to the interchanges of the superhighways, and the rest accommodations with them. Masterson did notice the occasional fifties-style motels along the sides of the road as he entered and left small towns, so he felt comfortable he would be able to find a place to sleep when the time came that it was needed. He did not notice that most were unlit at this time of the night.

An hour later, the Mercedes slowed as the highway became more urban in nature when he reached the outskirts of Melbourne. As he moved into downtown, a light drizzle began, and his wipers, which were set on automatic, began to sweep intermittently, clearing up a blurring windshield. He was beginning to feel the effects of a long day, so he leaned toward Helen and asked, "What do you think, dear? Had enough for one day? I'm getting tired, and I could use some shuteye. Let's pick out one of these motels we're passing and get a room for the night."

Helen didn't respond, which Masterson took for her acquiescence. He had just passed the historic landmark "Ice House" on the west side of the road when he spotted an old-style, wood-frame motel, with a blinking neon arrow pointing down to an unlit sign that said: VACANCY. He wasn't very impressed with the building, but he turned into the lot anyway. There were no cars in the parking lot and no lights on in the corner office. The place didn't look too inviting, so Masterson pulled back out onto the highway and continued his search northward.

He found two other prospects in the next several blocks, but neither of them looked inviting either, if even open for business. Finally, ahead on the left was a familiar-looking structure that resembled a modern roadside motel, and he turned into the parking lot in anticipation that he had found something suitable. He pulled under the portico and looked inside to the lobby, but he didn't see anyone at the front desk. Then he noticed the sign over the glass doors in front: MELBOURNE ELDERCARE.

Oops! Not what I'm looking for, he thought, and then he noticed the tombstone signage at the driveway that announced he was at a senior living facility. How ironic! It sure looked like a motel from the outside. Again he moved back to the highway. Masterson was becoming a little concerned as he grew more tired and frustrated. He was already at the north side of the town of Melbourne, and the highway was opening up again. He pressed on.

The rain stopped, and he could see the Indian River glistening off to his right, as the moon moved higher in its transit. At the north end of Melbourne, he passed Masterson Street, and that gave him a chuckle. The road out of town continued to be lined with small businesses, although it was more rural in nature. He had passed a mile of new car dealerships in Melbourne, but now he saw construction-related warehouses. He passed Titusville and other small towns, but it was not until he reached Cocoa, Florida, that he saw something helpful. It was now nearly one o'clock in the morning, and Masterson could barely keep his eyes open. Ahead on the right was an Americas Best Value Inn, well lighted and apparently open for business. Encouraged, Masterson turned onto the angled street and headed up the berm separating the entrance to the office from the access road. On closer inspection, he could see the place was a mess inside. The office was filled with broken furniture and vending machines staggered around the lobby. If it was open, it certainly didn't look like a place where Masterson would like to sleep, possibly on dirty linen.

Wearily, he pulled through the covered entrance and retraced his path to the highway once again. "Helen," he said to his muse, "I don't think I can go much further. We'll go up the road a bit, but I'm afraid we will have to take the next place we see, regardless of its condition, or return back here."

A half hour later, he pulled into the small town of Mims, Florida. It was after one o'clock in the morning, and Masterson did not feel it would be safe for him to continue, even a little ways farther. The town was small, and the businesses that dotted the roadside were not orderly, often unkempt and littered with abandoned vehicles. Partway into town, he saw a bright storefront ahead and to the right. The area was neat and welcoming, somewhat lighted, and the building was new and inviting. He noticed the strange trapezoid-shaped sign above the front of the building: TRACTOR SUPPLY CO. At the corners of the parking lot were stacks of fencing at one end and motorized gardening vehicles at the other.

Masterson pulled up to the front of the store where the lighting was sufficient for safety, but not so bright that it would intrude on a few winks of sleep. He noted the residual stench of his burrito wrapper and paper napkin, so he took a moment and policed the inside of his car for debris from his late-night snack, stuffing it inside the paper bag it came in, and stepped out into the nippy, fresh air to deposit it in the nearby waste bin located next to the large glass front doors. He made a quick pit stop to relieve himself around the side of the building in the shadows. Walking back to the car, he could hear the humming of the big parking lot lamps as they guzzled electricity.

He surveyed the interior of the car, satisfied that Helen would approve of his attention to cleanup detail, and slid back into the driver's seat, exhausted. Getting a little annoyed that the car was again still running, he pushed the start/stop button to see if he could make the engine turn off. It did. Suddenly concerned, he gave it another push to make sure the car would restart, which it did, much to his relief. He shut it off again.

His mouth tasted funky, but there wasn't anything he could do about that. He rinsed it with a little of the water from the bottle he had purchased at the gas station, and set about figuring how best to position himself to get some sleep. He considered getting in the backseat but settled for a partial recline in the front, where he could wedge his head in the corner next to the door, using his wadded-up windbreaker as a makeshift pillow of sorts. He gave Helen's urn a gentle pat and bade her goodnight, wriggling himself into a comfortable position, a little on his left side. In less than a moment, he fell into a deep sleep, uninterrupted by dreams of any sort.

The sun began to brighten the morning sky around six a.m., and traffic increased ever so slowly on the highway in front of the store, but Masterson was totally oblivious to this, as his exhaustion forced his sleep well past his usual morning wakeup. His body position had not changed from the moment he closed his eyes, so in need of rest was he. The only ambient noise was of the occasional car passing by the store, the parking lot lights having shut off automatically earlier in the morning. The Mercedes was so quiet inside that Masterson did not hear the crunch of the tires on the gravel parking surface as the shiny new Chevy Silverado turned into the lot and parked over by the fencing shortly after eight o'clock.

A youngish man got out of the truck, dressed in black pants and a white short-sleeved shirt bearing a logo over his left breast pocket similar to the one on the store sign and a name tag on the right. He looked curiously at the Mercedes parked at the front door to his store and walked over to the driver's side and peered in. He saw an older man asleep in the front seat, curled up on his left side, with what appeared to be a metal bucket next to him in the passenger seat. *Most unusual,* he thought, *the store isn't scheduled to open for at least an hour; it's clearly marked on the front door.*

Most of his customers didn't drive S-Class Mercedes Benz's either. He became concerned that the gentleman may be in some kind of distress, so he tapped gently on the window, trying not to startle the older man. When he got no response, he tried more aggressively to get the man's attention by tapping the glass with his car keys. That produced instant results.

Masterson startled at the sharp tapping, as he fought his way out of a sound sleep. At first he could barely move, his old bones having fixed in place for over six hours, his ligaments resisting displacement. The building blocked the brightest of the rising sun, but the light was still sudden and unexpected, and it overcame him somewhat. At first he didn't really move, but as the tapping became more insistent, he lifted his head and looked upward at the kind young face of a man in his mid- to late thirties peering down at him. His face was so close to the window that his breath left fog traces on the glass from his nostrils as he exhaled.

Masterson slowly repositioned himself in his seat and he heard the man speaking to him, "Are you all right, sir?" The tapping stopped. Masterson could not really make out too clearly what the man was saying, and the windows wouldn't respond when he tried to put them down, same as when he was stopped by the policeman what seemed like so long ago. He fumbled for the door handle and cracked it open a few inches.

The young man stepped back a pace or two. "Are you all right, sir?" he repeated.

Masterson was still trying to make sense of the situation; he remembered he was on some kind of a mission. He put his hands on the seat bottom to straighten himself up in the seat, which was difficult because it was almost fully reclined. Fumbling with his hands, he looked down, and noticed the urn in the seat next to him. A mixture of emotions and memories welled up within him. He was both comforted by Helen's presence and concerned, as the series of events that brought him to this parking lot began to work their way up his brain stem, partly triggered by the rush of adrenaline at trying to figure out if he was in trouble for his encroachment on this property.

"Yes, everything is fine, young man," Masterson managed to get out. "Forgive me for stopping on your property for a while." He couldn't help noticing the matching logos on the man's shirt and the store sign overhead. "I had a long day's drive and felt I couldn't continue safely, so I borrowed your parking lot for a rest. It was well lit, and I felt safe here. I hope you don't mind."

"Certainly not!" the young man replied. "And welcome to Tractor Supply. My name is Jerry Milgram, and I am the manager here. I just now got in to open the store and get ready for the day's business. You look like you could use some freshening up. Would you like to come in and use our restroom to clean up?"

Masterson was relieved that he was not in trouble, and the idea of washing his face appealed to him. "Thank you very much, young man. I would like that. Give me a minute to figure out how to put this seat back upright, so I can get out, and I'll be right in."

Milgram smiled and watched curiously as the older man fiddled with knobs and controls inside the car, trying to sort out the seat. "Here, let me help you with that." He opened the door a little wider, identified the seat back adjuster, and raised it to a comfortable driving position. He thought it odd that the owner of the car wasn't very familiar with it.

As he leaned in he realized that the metal bucket belted in the passenger seat was in fact a memorial burial urn of some sort with engraving on it. Out of politeness he didn't say anything, but he began running different scenarios in his mind. The old man didn't seem quite right, but he made allowances on account of his age. His thoughts were confirmed somewhat when the older gentleman leaned over to the urn and patted it affectionately, quietly speaking to it. Then he slowly unfolded himself from his sleeping position and awkwardly positioned his feet on the gravel and stood cautiously, holding the doorframe for support.

When he had his balance, he stepped around the door and closed it behind him, taking in a big breath of fresh air, not as chilly as last night. Offering his extended hand, he introduced himself to Milgram. "Thank you so much for your courtesy. My name is Stewart Masterson."

"Pleased to meet you, Mr. Masterson. Where are you headed this morning?"

"I'm on my way to see my daughter in Maryland. I didn't leave South Florida until last night. This was as far as I got," Masterson volunteered.

Milgram was starting to connect the dots. The poor guy must have lost his wife, and he was taking her back home somewhere.

"Well, the least I can do is show you some Tractor Supply hospitality, Mr. Masterson. Come on inside, and I'll get some coffee started up while you use the facilities to freshen up."

The two walked to the front door, which Milgram opened with a set of keys on a retractable cord on his belt. Inside, he disarmed the beeping security system and hit the wall switches adjacent the door to light the place up.

Masterson stepped inside behind him and surveyed his surroundings. He sure didn't see what he expected. There were no tractors or other heavy farm machinery. The store was huge open space, much like the inside of a big store in a mall. The merchandise was lined on shelves that were arranged in a logical orderly fashion, much like a Walmart. One end offered heavier machinery, such as riding mowers and plumbing equipment, and the other side consisted mostly of soft goods, gardening supplies, and clothing.

"I guess from the name I was expecting heavy farm machinery," Masterson stated as if asking a question.

"The origins of the company come from that kind of retail. Its beginnings stem from meeting all the retail needs of farmers, primarily by mail order. The company was founded back in the Great Depression. As the farming industry consolidated over the years, the company shifted its emphasis to smaller boutique operations, gentleman farmers, so to speak. You can get most anything for your outdoor growing requirements here, including what you need for the household. We even sell clothing now."

Milgram led them through the stacks of merchandise, and Masterson could see what the man meant. At the back of the store was a comfortable employee lounge. Milgram paused at the doorway and pointed across the hall to the restrooms. "I think you'll find everything you'll need in there, Mr. Masterson. Take your time, and when you come out, I'll have fresh, hot coffee for you in the lounge."

Masterson stepped in the men's room, which he found clean and efficient. He took off his sweater and shirt and cleaned himself up as best he could. He noticed a day's stubble on his cheeks and chin, but there wasn't much he could do about that. About the only thing he had in his pocket was a comb, which he ran through his hair, wetting down a few cowlicks, remaining evidence of his night in the car. Afterward, he joined the store manager in the lounge for a few minutes while they drank their coffees.

Jerry Milgram kept the conversation light, not wanting to pry, but at the same time probing to see if there was anything amiss or if he could be of any help to the nice old guy. He learned what he could, concluding that Masterson was a kind older gentleman who was just taking his wife's remains back home to his daughter. He did seem somewhat confused, but he didn't seem to be having any difficulty, although Milgram did find it peculiar that Masterson was intent on driving to Maryland on US 1, when the obvious preferred route would have been on the interstate. When he inquired, Masterson just replied with, "I prefer it this way." Satisfied he had done all that could be expected of a Good Samaritan, he ushered the gentleman back to the storefront entrance and wished him well.

"Thank you ever so much for your kindness, sir." Masterson had already forgotten Milgram's name, but he would remember the unusual store logo and forever associate it with kindness and helpfulness. He knew he would be getting hungry soon, and the manager had advised him that he would have all manner of "in and out" restaurants to choose from going north on US 1.

Feeling good about the start to his day, Masterson got back in his Mercedes, smiled over at Helen, and hit the start button on the dash. Again, he was greatly relieved that the car started right up. He didn't question his good fortune, as he backed up and turned out of the gravel parking lot and pulled into morning rush hour traffic. Just north of the small town of Mims, the highway paralleled the waterway, and he had a clear view of the monstrous NASA building at

Cape Canaveral across the river, clouded somewhat in the early morning haze, the temperature being hotter than the previous day. The sheer size of the building made it difficult to determine how far away it was, the haze being the only indication that it was much farther than one would first imagine.

As he approached St. Augustine, his stomach began to rumble. It was mid-morning, and he began to search the roadside establishments more intently to find a good place to eat. Ahead on the left, he saw a strange sight. A full-sized, side-wheel riverboat was parked next to the roadway. As he passed, Masterson marveled at the building when he realized it was a carwash. "That's a first!" He grinned in Helen's direction. "I almost wish we needed a wash, just to check it out," he added.

He passed several possibilities for dining, but they were all fast food restaurants, and he wanted to sit down and order a meal like a civilized person. Besides, the queuing and bustle amid too many selections made for a confusing experience for Masterson inside the fast food joints like McDonald's. He much preferred to sit and contemplate his dining decisions where he wouldn't feel rushed.

Before he got to the downtown of the city, he spotted a pleasant-looking roadside diner to his liking. Leroy's Café looked like just the place to eat, and he turned into the uncrowded parking lot on the west side of the roadway. Inside he was given outdoor or indoor options, and he chose the air conditioning, as the morning was getting a little humid for his taste. He left Helen in the car, knowing that bringing her with him would only invite unwanted questions and explanations.

The service was friendly and efficient; the waitresses seemed like hardworking women trying to put a good face on a thankless job, where they spent their entire day on their feet, dependent on the goodwill of others for a living. He appreciated being treated well, as though he mattered. He left a hundred dollar bill on the table, secured by his empty coffee cup, after a satisfying country meal of eggs over easy, grits, and bacon.

He visited the restroom where he was greeted by an unusual sign thanking him for his patronage at the "Road Kill Café" where he was cautioned "never to assume it's a raisin," among other irreverent admonitions. It took a minute, but the humor was not lost on him. He chuckled to himself. On the way out the door, his waitress tried to hand him change, but he brushed her hand aside with a smile, to her utter and total astonishment.

CHAPTER FOUR

The call to McBride came on his direct line at the Bureau office in Miramar.

"Mr. McBride, this is Jerry Reinhardt. I'm the day manager of Tropic Isle Assisted Living Facility in Pompano Beach. You asked me to call you or Agent Ornstein directly with any matters that came up regarding our resident, Stewart Masterson."

"Yes, Mr. Reinhardt, I remember. What have you got for me?"

"Well, sir, we can't locate him."

"What do you mean, you can't locate him?" replied a confused McBride.

"I mean, sir, that we do not know where he is. This morning he did not come down for breakfast, which is not all that unusual. Many of our residents do not come down, preferring to have juice or make coffee in their apartments, but we have a protocol for that, as you can imagine. If a resident doesn't check in by ten o'clock, we call or check the room discreetly, to make sure everything is in order. As you know, Mr. Masterson is only one of our guests with diminished abilities, just the only one under the care of the FBI."

"Go on."

Reinhardt continued, "So, this morning, when Mr. Masterson didn't show up for breakfast, we rang his apartment at ten o'clock, as per the protocol. When he didn't answer, we sent an orderly to his room, who notified us that the unit was unoccupied, unlocked, and the bed had not been slept in. We checked with his known social acquaintances, and none had seen him since last evening, when he visited with another of our resident's family on the patio."

"How do you know the bed wasn't slept in? Maybe he just made it up this morning."

"We thought of that. The linen is changed every Wednesday. The sheets were still freshly pressed this morning."

An exasperated McBride exploded. "You've got to be kidding. We pay you plenty to keep track of a demented seventy-two-year-old man, and you can't do that? You expend every effort, use every resource to find Masterson and report back to me or Lyle Ornstein immediately. You got that?!"

A fearful Reinhardt tried to defend himself. Tropic Isle was indeed paid a premium to provide special attention to Mr. Masterson, and he personally received a special financial inducement to make sure the special attention was provided. "Mr. McBride, I assure you we take every precaution to prevent this from happening, but sometimes these people just get out. We usually find them nearby in very short order. I'm sure that will be the case here."

"It better be, but that's not very consistent with an unused bed," McBride said contrarily. "I'm sending Agent Ornstein down there right now. Please give him your full cooperation." He slammed down the phone.

McBride's first call was to Ornstein. "Lyle, get your ass up to Tropic Isle as soon as you can. Masterson is unaccounted for, and I don't think that those idiots have the sense of urgency we need right now. Assess the situation and get back to me by two o'clock. That's about all the time we have before I have to let Hallanger know about the slip. Hopefully we can have it all cleared up by then, and I won't have to call anybody."

"I'm on it!" was Ornstein's eager reply. He knew his boss didn't want him to waste words on unimportant chitchat.

⁀⁊⁊⁀

Karen Kenny wasn't having a very good day, either. It was just past midweek, and she had a note in her inbox to see the principal of the Barrie School at her earliest convenience. Her reaction was not dissimilar to what one would expect if a student had received such a summons. Notices of faculty summons to the administrative offices, when not in connection with a student matter, were not usually about something rewarding.

"You wanted to see me, Dr. Graham?" Karen asked demurely after knocking lightly on the principal's open door.

"Yes, Miss Kenny. Come in; close the door behind you and take a seat."

Graham was a typical bureaucratic-looking man, balding, wearing wire-rimmed glasses perched peculiarly on his forehead, because they were for distance, not reading, his myopia being a natural solution to the aging requirement for reading correction.

The principal's demeanor was judgmental in Karen's opinion, and she was concerned. "What can I do for you?" she asked, leaning forward in her seat.

"A matter of some concern regarding you has come to our attention," Graham replied.

Karen felt an icy stab in her midsection. *What now?!* she thought with agitation.

Graham continued, trying to sound official, "As you know, we here at the Barrie School have a very strict zero-tolerance policy regarding drugs, our business being children and all, and you were

77

required to inform us of any drug involvement in your background when you applied for your job. . . ." He let that drift off, hanging in the air for a moment to gauge her response.

"I don't know what you are talking about, Dr. Graham. I have no history of drug involvement or use!" As the words passed her lips, a feeling of doom fell over her, as she recalled her asshole of an ex-husband. *Would his past never be done with me?* she wondered.

"Unfortunately, Miss Kenny, we have received evidence to the contrary." Graham held up a blurry copy of a fax with his thumb and forefinger, as though it might have come in contact with anthrax or some such thing. "This came in this morning."

"What is that?" Karen asked nervously, leaning over Graham's desk to get a better look. All she could see was a letterhead that read ARREST REPORT, MONTGOMERY COUNTY and, below that, a filled-out form.

Graham handed her the paper, continuing as she studied it. "It is a copy of an arrest report involving you and your husband—"

"*Ex*-husband!" Karen emphasized.

"Ex-husband then, involving you and your *ex*-husband in 1999 for drug possession with intent to sell. Those are pretty serious charges, Miss Kenny."

"But those charges were dropped," Karen pleaded. "I had nothing whatsoever to do with the charges, which my ex-husband ultimately faced. Even the prosecutor admitted I was only a passenger in the car."

"Nevertheless, you were arrested, and we at Barrie have an obligation to the parents of all the students to insure the safety of the children and insulate them from undesirable elements. Where there's smoke, there's usually fire. You failed to inform us of your arrest when you applied, and so we were denied the chance to evaluate your situation when you were offered your teaching position. I have no choice but to place you on suspension, with pay, until such time as the school's board of trustees can make an official review and report back to us their recommendations."

Karen slumped in her chair. Nothing was going right in her life. First her father, and now this. The more she thought about the situation, the more irritated she became. A spark lit within her. "Just how did you come by this information, may I ask?"

"That is irrelevant, I'm afraid," Graham answered glibly. In fact, he couldn't answer because he didn't know; the fax had come in during the morning without a cover from a phone number bearing a Virginia area code. A check with the local police verified the validity after they reviewed Montgomery County records. He continued, "For what it's worth, this is difficult for us. Your work here has been exemplary, and your contribution will be missed. My hope for you is that this mess can be cleared up, and we can put it behind us. That will be all for now, Miss Kenny."

Karen left the building feeling crushed. She didn't pack up any of her personal effects, as she felt sure she would be exonerated in time, able to return to the teaching job she loved. *At least I have my salary for the time being,* she thought.

On the way home, she considered some of the positives that could come out of this. She would have a paid vacation, some time to invest in Tim and Bart, and maybe reach out for her dad. She hadn't talked to him in a while; she thought she might give him a call when she got home. Her plan to "change the reel" almost worked, but by the time Karen pulled into her driveway, all she could think about was finding out who the son of a bitch was who sent the fax to her boss. She felt sure it had something to do with the government people responsible for costing her the guardianship for her father. It was consistent with the way they behaved in court many weeks earlier.

Once inside, Karen turned her thoughts to her dad. She made herself a cup of flavored coffee, courtesy of Keurig, and reaching for the portable phone on the kitchen wall by the door, flopped on the easy chair in the corner of what passed for a family room in the small house. She knew the number of Tropic Isle by heart, dialed it, and waited for the human response at the other end.

"Tropic Isle, how may I direct your call?" said a pleasant male voice.

Karen pictured the young black man sitting behind the circular reception desk in the front lobby, surrounded by pleasantly decorated seating areas where visitors could gather without intruding on the intimacy of the residential hallways. "Apartment three-oh-six, please," Karen answered.

There was a click as the call was transferred; after four rings, her call was picked up by the automatic voice mail: "You have reached Stewart Masterson. I am not available to take your call right now, but you may leave a message."

It was a very formal recording. *Just like my father,* Karen thought, and then said aloud following the beep, "Hi, Dad. Sorry I missed you. You're probably out chasing terrorists. Call your daughter when you have a moment; it's the one number I know you'll never forget."

Karen's phone was the same number her father had grown up with when he was a little boy. Only the (301) area code had been added, and the exchange changed from Maryland 2, to 622. She figured he would remember the number long after he forgot the rest of his family, so long had it been in his consciousness. If she hadn't heard by dinner, she would try again.

She turned her thoughts to the motives and possibilities that could cause someone to send that incriminating and misleading fax to her employer. She couldn't shake the feeling that the people from the FBI had something to do with it. Who else would dig up that piece of trash at this time? It was too much of a coincidence. But why?

Karen knew she needed help, and she turned to Charlie Edgerton, the attorney who had helped her with the guardianship she had tried to arrange. After she related the details of the day's events, he suggested she give him a little time to consider what her options might be. She said she would wait to hear from him. He did volunteer that he thought she had a legal advantage with the school's board of trustees and that she would have no trouble getting her job back. Charlie suggested she take advantage of the free time afforded her in the meantime. He volunteered to meet with her in the evening for a quick bite, if she was comfortable with that, knowing that she did not have spare resources to pay for attorneys. Karen told him she was good for now, but that she would call him as things progressed.

She reflected for a moment on Charlie's offer to meet in the evening. The way he phrased it, the offer sounded a little like a business date, emphasis on date. Karen was forty-four, unmarried, and had no prospects, with two kids to raise on her own. She didn't have much time or opportunity for romance, so she gave each possibility that came her way serious consideration, short of feeling desperate. She could not put the consideration of any eligible male off the table, and at the risk of appearing mercenary in her approach to her situation, every candidate got an evaluation of sorts, whether he had expressed an interest, or not.

Charlie was a nice guy, seemed to take a genuine interest in her difficulties, and was always willing to go the extra mile, as evidenced by his willingness to make the trip to Florida a couple months ago to have her back when she met with the FBI agents at her dad's house. He was certainly presentable enough, a preppy dresser. She liked that; it reminded her of her dad. She couldn't tell his age, but it seemed about right, probably midforties. He didn't wear a wedding ring, but she had seen pictures of what looked like preteen children, a boy and a girl, on his credenza in his office, and there was no photographic evidence of a Mrs. Edgerton visible.

After a moment's hesitation, she called him back and suggested it might be a good idea if they could meet, perhaps tomorrow night?

Charlie paused for a moment, understanding the consequences of his response, and said, "It will work best for me if I can come right from work. Can you meet me at seven o'clock at the Olive Garden, the one in the Mall at Prince Georges, across from the Metro station? Does that work for you?"

He, too, tried not to leave any opportunities on the table. Karen was certainly attractive enough, as well as professional and smart. He felt sorry for the way she had been railroaded by the government, so he already had a kind of emotional attachment of sorts. He said his goodbyes and called his babysitter to lock her in for the evening, sat back in his desk chair, and smiled, feeling proud of himself.

~ ∽ ~

The first four bars of "Sweet Home Alabama" rocked from McBride's pocket while he was heading out for a bite to eat. "Yeah," he answered his cell phone gruffly, having already identified that Ornstein was the caller. "What have you got for me?"

"Not much and nothing good, Fultie," Ornstein ventured in the familiar.

"Let's hear it."

"Well, as near as I can determine, Mr. Masterson just went for a walk about eight o'clock last night. Do you want all the background?" the junior agent began.

"Yeah, let's have it all. Maybe I'll hear something you missed." McBride sighed.

"Everything here was normal through dinner. It doesn't look like anything was planned. At dinner with mixed company, Masterson accepted an invitation to visit after dinner with a lady and her family, which he did. He was dressed normally for the circumstances, that is sweater and a jacket, because they were assembling on the pool deck outside, and it was a little chilly. The woman, a Gracie somebody, is apparently a little taken with our man, although there doesn't seem to be any involvement beyond friendship, and thought he would enjoy the diversion. These are her words for the most part, speculation and gossip by friends who were there as to the relationship. They chatted for forty-five minutes or so, and then moved to the front door as a group to say their goodbyes."

"Masterson was with them?" McBride interjected.

"Exactly. You have the picture. This Gracie lady said they walked out the front door together, Masterson with them, and after her guests left, she turned to say good night to him; he was nowhere around. She assumed he had gone back in because of the cold, or because he thought the evening was over, as far as he was concerned."

"And that explains how he got by the front desk, I assume?" McBride finished Ornstein's thought for him.

"That's what I'm thinking. He saw an opportunity, and he just walked off. I don't think it was planned, nor do I think anybody else had anything to do with it. I don't even think it was on Masterson's mind; he didn't take any personal belongings with him. His wallet and what little it contains are still in his dresser drawer. He didn't even lock his door. I think he intended to come back to his room. There is one other thing."

"What's that?" asked McBride hopefully.

Ornstein continued, "Everybody here likes Masterson, likes him a lot, but they know what's going on, that he's challenged. He covers well for himself, but everybody knows, and they humor him when he talks about his wife as though she is still in the picture. How can I best explain it? . . . They're rooting for him. That's it. They're *rooting* for him."

"You mean enough to cover for him, right?"

"If it came to that, yes. But I don't think that's the case here. There is one guy in particular, his best friend, let me see here . . ."

McBride could hear Ornstein thumbing through a small notebook. "Here it is, Martin, Bevy Martin. He is very close to Masterson, and unlike many of the people in this place, this guy's a player. He was a fighter pilot in Vietnam, has a million stories, and proud of 'em; he's very sharp. I spoke to him briefly, and he gave me one of those *all knowing* smiles, you know, like we share a secret or something. I think he's figured out Masterson's deal here, that he is under official supervision. He seems to know that Masterson worked for the Agency, and that he was stationed in Brussels for a decade. He knows how things work, and I think he's connected the dots regarding our close monitoring and the risk Masterson's condition poses for us. He's also talked to the daughter on a couple of visits, and they seem to have some kind of understanding that Bevy's looking out for Masterson, shares a bond with him, or something; you know, like they served their country. So he sure knows things from her perspective. That's not going to work in our favor."

McBride agreed, "You're right. She does not think well of us, which she has made abundantly clear."

"What's my next step?" asked Ornstein.

"I'm thinking." McBride paused while he bit his lip contemplating whom he had to bring into his circle. "He's been gone overnight, and I suspect he didn't sleep in an alley, so somebody has probably seen him. I think we need to consider a Silver Alert to get some help from the public, although that is most effective when coupled with an automobile, which he doesn't have, right? You sold his personal car, didn't you?"

"Yes, sir."

"At the very least, I need to notify Hallanger in Washington, and he may need to bring someone else in, as well. I didn't get the feeling this operation originated with him from the way he felt about it when we discussed it. On second thought, let's not proceed with the Silver Alert; we don't really want the world to know that Masterson may be in play. That's exactly what we are trying to control. The confidentiality in our government security agencies is a sieve, at best."

Ornstein offered, "How about I just check with the local police departments, hospitals, etcetera, and see if anything has turned up. I'll keep it quiet for now."

McBride thought for a minute. "Good idea. I'll call Washington and find out how they want to handle it. Touch base with me later this afternoon, and we'll see where we are."

"Okay." Ornstein ended the call and began surveying all the local Florida law enforcement agencies.

Fulton McBride made the dreaded call to Hallanger at the Bureau's headquarters in Washington, D.C., receiving the response he expected. After a few expletives, Hallanger told him to sit tight while he conferred with the other agencies involved. He agreed that making Masterson's disappearance public might only exacerbate the problem.

Hallanger arranged a conference call on secure lines with Hollis Cavner at the NSA and Hank Brogan at Langley. By two o'clock, he had brought them all up to speed. They all agreed that until there was some more information on Masterson's whereabouts or intentions, it was best to keep their search efforts out of the public eye.

"But what are his options?" Brogan chimed in. "He has no money, no identification, no credit cards, no means of transportation, and nowhere to go. In addition, he does not have all his faculties. He has to turn up soon."

"I think you may be underestimating your guy, Hank," said Cavner. "He got away from the assisted living facility, and he has been on his own for eighteen hours."

"I agree," added Hallanger. "Remember, this guy spent his whole life working with the limited resources at his disposal in stressful situations, quite successfully, I might add. He covers for his shortcomings very well, according to McBride in Miami, and consider that, in his line of work, it is second nature to have back-up plans and exit strategies. He may very well be on a mission. I'm sure something will turn up to give us an idea what he's up to, if anything. In the meantime, he's easy prey for undesirables. I will instruct the Miami office to continue low-key inquiries. We will look around his old haunts."

After the call, Hallanger did exactly that.

McBride and Ornstein conferred once again and decided the young agent would look around Masterson's old neighborhood.

Ornstein volunteered, "Say, didn't Masterson's daughter tell us he was preoccupied with his late wife's memorial. I think I'll drop by there and ask a few questions."

"Good idea," said McBride.

ℒ◯℃℧

As Masterson made his way out of St. Augustine, the highway opened up for a while south of Jacksonville, and he started to make good time as the traffic and speed limits permitted. The skyline of downtown office buildings loomed on the horizon ahead of him, and in no time, he found himself engaging the urban traffic of the largest Florida city in land area, attributable to the fact that the county and city of Jacksonville shared the same boundaries.

The downtown passed off to his right, and the traffic signs indicating route changes for US 1 made things difficult for him. He had to reverse his direction twice to backtrack for turns he missed because he was too far into the intersection when he noticed signage. On heightened adrenaline, he increased his vigilance, so as to avoid additional missteps, but his concentration was wearing on him. Briefly his route joined I-95 for a mile or so before separating again to the urban traffic flow.

By noon he was on the north side of Jacksonville, and the highway opened up again to a limited access thoroughfare with a sixty-five-mile-per-hour speed limit. He was welcomed into Georgia, where state highway budgets were obviously limited, the road two lanes, and the surrounding countryside decidedly rural. He spoke to Helen from time to time, breaking up the monotony of the trip, describing the pastures and fencing along the roadsides.

Masterson was making good time, and he felt a sense of progress now that the Florida border was behind him. He no longer looked in the rearview mirror, feeling free of the burden of watching out for anyone who might be in pursuit. How he came to be in possession of the Mercedes was not even in his thought process; he was focused solely on his goal, getting home to Silver Spring and his daughter where he would be among those who loved him.

The miles passed steadily by, as Masterson made his way through Waycross and Alma without incident to Baxley, where he soon crossed the Altamaha River. He remembered stopping there as a boy with his parents on one of his Florida vacation trips. They had a sort of impromptu picnic along the riverbank to break up the trip, drinking Dr Peppers and eating potato chips and sandwiches they had purchased in Lyons, next door to Vidalia, a few miles to the north.

He and his brother had waded in the murky brown water along the edge of the river, careful not to get caught in the swift-moving current. It was obviously a popular stopping place, evidenced by the roughhewn picnic tables that had been set up by someone just below the steep bank off the highway, on the flat area by the water. *No time for stopping now,* he told himself as he crossed the older trestle-type bridge with its heavy ironwork overhead. Soon thereafter he passed through Lyons, adjacent to Vidalia. Images of Willard Scott from the *Today* show and his constant references to the onions that made the town a household name flashed through his mind. He had no idea where that came from.

There was little traffic on the two-lane road now, and he kept his pace up, passing an occasional car the old-fashioned way, judging the rate of closure to the vehicle ahead and timing his approach to coincide with a lane free of oncoming traffic. He slowed only for the small towns where there was little activity, putting Swainsboro, Wadley, Louisville, and Wrens in his rearview mirror. He noted pleasantly the three or four Tractor Supply Co. stores, remembering how kindly he had been treated earlier in the day by the nice young man who had invited him in to clean up after sleeping in the car. That seemed like eons ago.

He was moving along so well, he was not prepared for the frustration of another big city, as traffic and population increased at the south end of Augusta. Again he had to step up his vigilance when US 1 made unexpected turns in the old Georgia town. The great golf history of the famous home of the Masters was lost on him; he saw neither a sign nor a sign identifying the world-famous landmark, Augusta National Golf Club. Golf didn't have much of a place in Masterson's past. He only took up the game late in life, after his retirement. A career that required he live in Europe and work with unpredictable schedules was not conducive to advance scheduling of four- to five-hour blocks of his time. He did, however, enjoy the historic look of the Old South in the local architecture with its brick facades behind columned front porches.

Carefully he made his way through the town without incident by paying close attention at every intersection for signage and religiously pausing if he went more than five or six blocks without an indication he was on the right route. When that happened, he reversed his path to the previous sign and reproved his navigation, just to be sure. His greatest fear was that he would get off the track and continue unawares until he was too far misplaced to find his way back. He still knew in the back of his mind that someone was surely looking for him, and he didn't want to call attention to himself by stopping to ask for directions.

Shortly after he left Augusta behind him, he was welcomed to South Carolina and picked up his pace again, as the countryside switched from ramshackle old buildings and warehouses to fenced pastures. By midafternoon, his attention was drawn to the panel in front of him, and he noticed that the gas level on the fuel gauge indicated twenty-five percent. He turned to Helen and explained, "We are going to have to stop for gas again sometime this afternoon. It should be easier, since it's daytime; they will be more willing to make change."

Helen maintained her silence.

Although making his way to Maryland and his daughter was always on the forefront of his mind, Masterson couldn't help but notice the beauty of the countryside he was passing. Occasionally he had to slow for small towns, and he was reminded again of the trips he took on this road as a child when his family made its annual pilgrimage to Miami Beach at Christmas or spring break in the 1950s. He was just a small boy then. While one might think they would be periods of agony, two kids and their parents traveling two long days in the confines of a Buick sedan, Masterson remembered mostly good times. They entertained themselves with games like "I spy" or "twenty questions." His least favorite was "slug a bug" where the first to spot a Volkswagen Beetle punched his seat mate, and Masterson's brother was four years older and a lot bigger, so Masterson got the short end of that stick. They did enjoy a game identifying license plates, which played to his strengths, as he had the best vision in the family. He shared these memories with Helen, who had heard them all before.

As the heavy steelwork of the bridges crossing the Congaree River began to take shape in the distance before him, visible for quite a ways due to the flat terrain on the west side of the waterway, he started feeling the fatigue of a long day's drive. His back was aching from his fixed position, and his head was hurting from the lengthy periods of concentration required of him in the bigger towns he passed through. He had learned that he could ameliorate the stiffness in his legs and back by shifting his seat back little by little to freshen his posture, but that was no longer effective after such a long day. To relieve his discomfort he arched his back and twisted sideways in his seat, trying to stretch his muscles. As he settled back into his sitting position, he got a whiff of his body odor from under his polo shirt, as trapped air escaped around his neck.

"Whew!" he muttered to Helen. "That was awful! I really stink. We're going to have to stop somewhere and get me a change of clothes. I don't know how you can stand sitting next to me," he said, mixing his metaphors.

As he neared the river, he saw a huge Walmart shopping center on his side of the road, complete with a bank of gas pumps on the corner of the property. "We're in luck, dear. We can kill two birds with one stone. I'm going to get some gas and do some shopping in that Walmart. Then we're going to give it a rest for the day, as soon as we can find decent accommodations."

He pulled into the service station and slid in next to the first available pump, leaving it on the right side out of habit. The car shut off automatically. Masterson climbed slowly out of the car and tried to stretch his legs and lower back. He padded his left front pocket to make sure the wad of hundred dollar bills was still there and ambled slowly toward the cashier and mini-mart.

There were about a dozen people taking care of business inside, and a line was queuing up in front of the cashier. He used the opportunity to use the restroom facilities, hoping the line would go down while he was in there. He returned to find fewer people in front of him and waited until he was at the front of the line.

A perky young black girl smiled and asked what she could do for him. *Southerners are so warm and friendly,* Masterson thought. "I need gas for the silver Mercedes out there," he said, pointing out the elevated store window. "Can you break a hundred?"

"Fill 'er up?" she asked.

"Yes, mam."

"Certainly, sir. Give me the hundred and go pump your gas, and I'll make change when you come back. Bring your receipt." She smiled at him again.

He placed the bill on the counter, and she marked it with a counterfeit detection pen and held it up to the light. The color was good.

"Okay, sir. Fill up on pump seventeen," she acknowledged and pushed the lever for the designated gas pump.

That was easy, Masterson mused, as he turned to the door to go fill his car. The need for changing his hundred dollar bill dealt with, he selected the cheapest octane option and inserted the nozzle and began filling, all activities directed by years of habit. The Mercedes took a little over sixteen gallons. Returning to the cashier in the mini-mart, Masterson grabbed a couple of granola bars off the rack to add to his purchase and collected his change from the still smiling attendant.

Returning to the car, he was dumbfounded to see his dash lit up and the car still running. "Helen, I know you didn't do it, but for the life of me, I can't figure out why this car won't turn off," he mumbled in the direction of the urn. "Oh well, let's work on getting me a change of underwear and some fresh clothes at the Walmart and find a comfortable place to spend the evening. I could use a toothbrush, too."

He pulled out of the row of pumps and angled diagonally across the huge parking lot to the front of the store and parked. The engine shut off as he stopped against the parking bumper, and he tried to think through the challenge of finding his way around the store. Since he didn't have a car key, he contemplated the risk of leaving his priceless Helen in an unlocked car. As he sat for a moment in thought, he felt the rumble as the car started up again. Instinctively he hit the stop button on the dash and the motor shut off.

Satisfied that passersby would not have an interest in the car's contents, Masterson slid the canvas bag under the passenger seat and put his windbreaker over the urn and left the car. As he bent over and stood, he got another whiff of his body odor, which reminded him of why he was here. The cool breeze carried the scent away as he walked toward the automatic glass doors of the building, feeling somewhat self-conscious.

Just inside the front doors of the Walmart, he was greeted by a smiling older man, about his own age. Masterson surveyed the immense volume of the store, much larger than the tractor supply store he had been in that morning. The floor was lined with merchandise of all kinds imaginable, arranged in aisles that ran beyond his vision, and he was overwhelmed at the prospect of finding what he needed.

"Welcome to Walmart," the greeter said. "How can we be of service?"

The nice senior made Masterson feel comfortable, and he ventured asking for help. "Yes, you can, I suspect. I need to purchase some clothing, khakis, and some underwear and a few other things. Where would I find that?"

The greeter, dressed casually with a blue cotton jumper over his shirt bearing the Walmart logo and a name tag that said SIDNEY, pointed to the row of shopping carts next to the checkout lines, much like a grocery store, and suggested, "Why don't you grab a cart and follow me. I'll direct you to the clothing section, and you can take it from there."

The man seemed genuinely interested in being helpful, and Masterson liked that. He could not remember ever having been in a Walmart before, and he marveled at the selections of every conceivable household staple displayed on the shelves, as the two walked down the aisles, turning occasionally toward the middle of the building.

In no time, Masterson was confused about where he was, and he said so to his guide. "I'm not sure I can find my way back. This is very confusing," he said.

Sidney saw the look of concern and offered, "Not to worry; I'll stay with you and see that you find your way safely out. The men's casual clothing is just ahead on the left." He nodded forward, looking ahead where the shelving switched to wire racks of pants dangling from hangers. There were all colors and sizes to choose from.

Again, Masterson felt tension at the sheer volume of selections and froze in front of them, unsure of where to start and how to go about making a selection.

Sidney sensed the confusion of his charge and felt sympathy for him. He was no spring chicken himself, and he had seen the look in his contemporaries, since he himself had aged. He felt fortunate that he could still supplement his retirement income with an actual job where he could be useful to others, albeit financially not so rewarding, but important to his sense of being.

"What exactly are you looking for, sir? Maybe I can be of help."

Masterson was comforted. Sidney was genuinely concerned for him, and he could feel it. He made his request simple. "I really just need to get out of these clothes into something fresher. I've been driving for two days, and I don't have anything to change into. Just some fresh khakis and a shirt, and some underwear; can't forget the underwear."

Sidney led him to a rack of generic khaki pants with plain fronts. Turning to Masterson, who was standing by his shopping cart, he surveyed his size. "I'm going to guess you are about a thirty-six-inch waist, thirty-two inseam," he suggested, careful not to say anything offensive. He knew some shoppers were sensitive about their sizes.

His friend and neighbor insisted he was a thirty-four, had been since high school and proud of it, and refused to buy anything else. The result was an overhang of his huge belly above pants he wore low on his hips on an ever-shrinking butt. Sidney chuckled to himself as he remembered a stock reply to the question, "What size are you?" His answer was always, "I'm a thirty-four, but thirty-sixes feel so comfortable, I wear thirty-eights!"

Sidney watched as the shopper selected a pair. "Do you want to try them on? There's a changing room at the back of the store."

"I don't think that will be necessary; these look like they'll do," Masterson replied, holding the khakis to his waist. He did not want to complicate matters any further, feeling a little guilty about monopolizing the greeter's time.

Sidney took Masterson to a bunch of shelves containing inexpensive shirts, where they selected a blue button-down oxford, sixteen by thirty-three. They moved over a couple of aisles and added some boxers, three to a package, and a value pack of beige cotton socks to round out the wardrobe. Sidney suggested a small, cheap canvas carry bag to put it all in and asked, "Is there anything else you need?"

Masterson was feeling much more at ease with all the personal attention he was receiving, and replied, "I desperately need a toothbrush."

Sidney could sense that his customer was calming down. He felt good that he could be of so much help. "I get the idea that you are traveling light; perhaps you need more than a toothbrush. Let's head over to the pharmacy section on the other side. I think we have just what you need."

Masterson followed Sidney to the other end of the store, convinced now that he could not have handled this without all the help. He felt very grateful and noted to himself that he would always speak highly of the Walmart chain if the subject ever came up in conversation.

In the pharmacy section, Sidney showed Masterson a prepackaged Dopp kit. "This contains everything I think you will need on the road. It has two disposable razors, toothpaste, toothbrush, shampoo, and other personal hygiene stuff."

Masterson held it in his hand, a blue canvas bag with a zipper across the top, not unlike a smaller version of the bag he had found in Helen's niche. "Good idea. That's terrific!" Masterson said, feeling like he had everything under control now.

Sidney led him back to the front of the store toward the checkout lines, where he tried to engage him in conversation as they loitered casually at the end of one of the lines. "So, where are you headed today?" he asked, almost rhetorically.

"My wife and I are moving to Maryland to be with our daughter," Masterson answered automatically, not thinking about the inconsistency of his response.

This got Sidney's attention. "Your wife's traveling with you? Where is she?" he questioned, his antenna on full alert. He felt strongly that something was amiss here. *Why would this guy be moving to another state, an event that is usually planned well in advance, traveling with his wife and not have anything to show for the expected traveling requirements?* he wondered.

Masterson realized he had made a misstep. He was flustered by the question, and he knew his answer would be remembered. He began with, "Oh, she's waiting in the car. We sent everything on ahead." He thought he had recovered, but Masterson had spent his life spinning scenarios to explain the unexplainable, and reading faces at the delivery of others who were doing the same to him. He knew the greeter had not bought in, but he feared if he went any further, he would only make matters worse. He tried to smile his way out of it. "I can't thank you enough for your kindness. My name is Stewart." He stuck out his hand, and Sidney took it.

"You're most welcome. Thank you for shopping at Walmart," he replied, keeping his attention on Masterson as he made his way to the checkout cashier and emptied the contents of his shopping cart on the conveyor.

Sidney was still watching the checkout process, when an assistant store manager in his short-sleeved shirt and tie started giving him a reprimand. "Sidney, what the hell are you doing? You're a greeter, not a personal shopper. Get back to the front of the store where you belong," the manager groused angrily.

"Just trying to help one of our customers," Sidney tried to explain. "Thought that was part of the job," he added sarcastically, as he moved back to his station just inside the front doors.

The manager turned away and looked for someone and something else to exercise his authority over. Criticism of employees was something that came naturally to him.

As Sidney moved around the checkout lanes to the front of the store, he kept an eye on Masterson, somewhat surprised when the older man pulled out a thick wad of bills and peeled one off for the cashier. It looked like a hundred dollar bill; Sidney wondered if the whole wad was made up of hundreds. Masterson didn't look like he was paying specific attention to which one he selected; he just took one off the top. *That's odd!* he thought.

He continued to monitor Masterson's activities as he walked out to the parking lot in the midafternoon sun. Sidney watched him take the longest time trying to figure out which direction he should walk, as he looked repeatedly left and right, as though he had forgotten where he had parked his car, finally settling on a row close to the front doors where he threw his bag on the floor of the front passenger seat of a new, top of the line, silver Mercedes Benz. He seemed to be talking to somebody in the front seat, but Sidney couldn't make anyone out.

He shook his head and returned to the flow of customers passing the automatic front doors. "Good afternoon. Welcome to Walmart." His smile returned to his face, and he put the incident with Masterson out of his mind.

Masterson found his way out of the mall lot onto US 1 and resumed his trip north, determined to find a comfortable place to stay the night. The stress of the monotonous driving was beginning to take its toll on him. About a mile farther down the road, he saw a sign for Columbia, South Carolina, indicating it was twelve miles ahead. He could see the ironwork of the bridges over the Congaree River that was just ahead beyond the lowland river plain he was approaching.

He turned to Helen. "That's Columbia just ahead, my dear. I'm sure we will find something suitable in such a large city."

As he crossed the Congaree, the bridge gave him just enough elevation to see the taller buildings of the downtown less than two miles away, and Masterson's mood became suddenly cheery, lightened by the prospect of a nice hotel room, a hot shower, and a change of clothes. On the east side of the river, US 1 became Gervais Street, and the downtown enveloped him from all sides.

Masterson passed by several chain-type hotels, keeping his eye out for something special. He was rewarded in midtown, just a block off the state capitol, whose spire he could just make out above the low-rise office buildings on his right. Ahead on the left was a beautifully restored hotel, certainly on some kind of historic registry, about ten stories tall. The surface was clad in an off-white stone, and the windows were repeated, evenly spaced, in geometric rows, outlined in intricate wood fascia painted to match, giving the structure a magnificent, regal appearance.

"That's it, dear. That's where we're going to spend the night."

In high spirits, Masterson cut off two cars in the light one-way traffic as he made a U-turn to park at the entrance to the valet stand, where he was greeted by a uniformed attendant, eager to assist the owner of the big silver Mercedes sedan. His hand was on the driver's door handle before the car had come to a complete stop. Masterson fiddled with the window controls and finally gave up, just opening the door to free himself of the sitting position he had spent his day enduring.

"Welcome to the Orrington Hotel," greeted the valet with a smile. "How can we help you? Are you checking in, sir?"

Masterson stood straight and arched his back, trying to stretch his aching back muscles, and lifting his arms as far as he could reach over his head. "I hope so; my wife and I need a room for the night. So, do you know if there are vacancies?"

"I'm sure it won't be a problem, sir. The assembly is just out of session, so things are pretty quiet around here. If you and your wife will just head into the lobby, the reception desk will take care of you," said the valet as he automatically moved to the passenger side of the car to assist his guest's wife. He leaned over and opened the door. Peering in, he didn't see anyone else in the car. Turning to Masterson he said, "Your wife, sir?"

An instant of sadness came over Masterson, as he realized his mistake. He had become so used to talking to "Helen" on the trip north, he forgot momentarily, as he often did on the trip, that Helen was only metaphorically present. "My mistake, young man; she is here in spirit. That's her burial urn on the front seat, but she will accompany me to our room."

The valet was embarrassed that he had called attention to something so possibly painful. He felt sorry for the older man, sensing that this was probably a difficult time for him, writing stories to himself of the probable scenarios behind the situation. "Bags, sir?" he inquired, looking at the small duffle on the floor in the front.

Masterson thought for a moment, and suddenly he remembered

the zipped canvas under the driver's seat. "Oh, yes. Just the duffle; I'll take it in." He slipped back in the driver's seat and grabbed the soft bag, and reached nervously under the seat and felt the loop on the end of the "go" bag. Relieved, he slid it unnoticed into the larger canvas bag and stepped out of the car.

The valet handed him a claim stub. "Just call down five minutes before you want your car, and it will be here waiting for you when you come down. The valet number is marked on your phone in the room; all you have to do is push the button to call. Twenty-four hours," he added.

Masterson leaned over and undid the seat belt holding Helen's urn in place and gently lifted her out of the car. As an afterthought, he grabbed his windbreaker off the center armrest and covered the urn, lest it attract unwanted attention. He made his way into the reception lobby where he was pleasantly surprised to see a richly decorated space accented by oriental rugs and lavish tapestries on the walls, which were otherwise covered with beautiful stained mahogany paneling and joiner work. Filtered light beamed in ribbons from high overhead, leaded windows giving the lobby a warm cathedral-like feel. He carried his bundles somewhat awkwardly to the check-in counter and made arrangements for a night's stay in an east-facing room where he could see the capitol's dome a block away.

"It's all lit up at night," suggested the receptionist. She became concerned when Masterson said he was going to pay in cash. "But, sir. We will still need some kind of credit card to hold for possible room charges. It's standard operating procedure."

"Can't I just give you a cash deposit?" Masterson asked nervously. He had not anticipated this difficulty.

"We will also need a driver's license or other ID," she added.

Masterson was now in full panic mode, as he set his bag on the armrest of a sofa adjacent to the check-in area and started anxiously pawing through it, trying to divert her attention from the helpless look of panic he had on his face. He put the urn in the bag as well, so it would not be a distraction while he tried to figure a way out of this mess. His fingers came across the smaller canvas bag in the duffle, and he opened it, risking that someone may observe its contents. Then he spied the plastic baggie with the identification and credit cards inside. He fumbled through them and matched the Virginia driver's license with the American Express credit card that had been turned down at the gas station the previous day. He turned back to the receptionist and asked, "Will these do? But I really want to pay in cash."

She barely gave the license a glance, as she ran an impression of the credit card. "It's just our policy. . ." Looking down now at the license, she added, "Mr. Courtney. We won't put any charges on the card unless you authorize it. I'm sorry for the inconvenience; again, it's just our policy." She smiled at him.

It took a minute for Masterson to realize what the "Mr. Courtney" was about, but for the time being, things seemed to be under control.

The receptionist handed him a key card in an envelope on which she marked seven-zero-four in the room number space provided. "Can we help you with your luggage?"

"No, thank you. I can manage. It's just this duffle." He turned and picked the duffle up by the handles and headed to the elevator. Across the lobby he saw an incongruous tiny yellow neon sign over a side door that said TAP ROOM down a couple of steps from the lobby level. Over his shoulder he asked, "What time does the Tap Room open?"

"Five o'clock," the receptionist answered. "That's in about twenty-five minutes."

Masterson logged the information for future reference, focusing for now on a much-needed shower followed by a short power nap.

He took the elevator to the seventh floor and, after fumbling a moment or two, figured out that the key card did not need to be inserted anywhere, just passed over the black disk above the door handle.

When he saw the opulence of the room, he wondered if he should have been more curious about the cost. He set his bag on the bed and removed Helen's urn from the duffle and placed it on the dresser opposite.

"You can have a nice view of the capitol from here, Helen." He smiled.

It took him only seconds to strip off his smelly clothes and get in the hot shower. There was soap and shampoo on the shelf over the tub, and he made full use of both to rinse the grime of two days on the road off his body.

Finally cleansed, he returned to the room to retrieve his Dopp kit and strip the cellophane from a razor. He used soap from the wash-basin to lather up and gave himself a needed shave. Back in the room, he opened the package of white cotton boxers and put on a pair. Relaxed for the time being and cleaned up, he fell on his back on the king bed and closed his eyes for a few minutes, not minding the late-afternoon sun that barely made its way into the room through the angle of the east-facing windows.

Masterson awakened from a sound sleep to a darkened room.

∽∽∽

While Masterson was making grueling progress north on US 1 toward Maryland, Ornstein was making steady headway connecting some dots to help him paint a picture of events following the retired agent's disappearance. He shared these with McBride late Thursday afternoon.

"What news do you have for me, Lyle?" McBride asked.

"Well, at first nothing. I checked with all the local departments of law enforcement, and no one had any record of an event with a senior citizen that had not already been identified. The only thing I came up with was a conversation with a guy named McCutcheon at the Broward Sherriff's Office who volunteered an isolated event he was investigating that didn't tie to anything. So, I thought there might be some connection, crazy as it sounds."

"What's that?" McBride's intuition sparked.

"He's investigating a routine traffic stop in Deerfield where the driver of the car, who did not appear to be the owner, overpowered the police officer, and literally put him in the hospital, seriously injured. The perp is vaguely described as an older white male, about five-ten. The car was a new Mercedes S550. The details of the confrontation are unclear: McCutcheon thinks partly attributable to the embarrassment of the arresting officer who was overpowered, since he is apparently quite large and intimidating. The person who took advantage of him was apparently professionally trained, based on how things turned out."

McBride interrupted, "You think it may have been Masterson?"

"It's possible, but there's more. The Pompano Beach Police have a report of a stolen Mercedes with a description and registration matching the incident in Deerfield. McCutcheon is investigating this as well, says the owner is from Fort Lauderdale. He is somewhat unclear as to the circumstances of the theft, but it appears the car was taken from the shopping center parking lot approximately across the street from Tropic Isle."

"Bingo," said McBride.

"Wait, there's more. You remember we talked about visiting the mausoleum where Masterson's wife is interred."

"Yeah."

"I ran by there, in Boca Raton, and spoke with the manager. He showed me his visitation logs for last night, and sure enough, Masterson was signed in around eight thirty and out around nine fifteen. I talked to the guard on duty by phone, and he confirmed that he signed Masterson in, said he was a regular, but hadn't been by in weeks. I asked him if he knew how Masterson got there, and he said he didn't know for sure, but that our guy came in from the entrance that leads up from the parking lot, so most likely, by car. He didn't see the car, but the lot was most likely empty."

"Good work, Lyle," McBride complimented. "That's a lot of information. I think we can conclude that Masterson is in possession of the Mercedes, and he is on his way someplace. Do you have any ideas where he might go?"

"Without resources, I don't think he can go anywhere very far. I would imagine he will just stay in the area. I'll check with McCutcheon and see how much gas was in the car, but based on what I observed at Tropic Isle, Masterson didn't take a wallet or identification or credit cards. He can't have much cash."

"Unless he had help from his friends at the facility. Remember you told me they were *rooting* for him. Maybe you should go back and visit with his fighter pilot friend, see if he gives up anything," McBride suggested.

"Will do, but it's unlikely. We agree this was not a planned event. The Mercedes was happenstance for sure. I'll see what he has to say."

McBride thought for a minute. "Do we know how Masterson stole the car? That wouldn't be one of his talents, would it?"

"That's still a mystery. I'll find the owner through McCutcheon and see what I can find out. We should reconsider issuing a Silver Alert, get some help from the public."

"I'll think about it," McBride answered. "You learn anything, call me anytime, day or night."

"Okay." Ornstein ended the call and set about tying up the loose ends.

Karen's phone rang while she was washing the dishes from dinner with the boys, who had now settled in the corner of the simple family room to do their homework. She quickly blotted her hands dry with the kitchen towel and answered, "Hello?"

"Karen, this is Bevy Martin, from Tropic Isle. You remember me; I'm a friend of your father's. I told you I would keep an eye on him for you."

"Sure, Mr. Martin, I remember you well," Karen responded, feeling somewhat upset with herself for not following through at dinnertime to call her dad again. She hoped nothing was wrong. "I tried to reach him earlier today, but he wasn't in his apartment. I left a message. Is anything wrong?"

"I'm not sure, Karen. May I call you Karen?"

"Of course, Mr. Martin."

"Please call me Bevy, or Bev. I assume you haven't heard anything from the offices here, then." It was a statement, not a question.

"No, nothing."

"Karen, I spent last night with your dad at dinner, and later he visited with friends of one of the other residents here. He didn't come down for breakfast this morning; we have coffee almost every day, first thing. I didn't think anything of it until that FBI guy showed up this afternoon and started asking questions. No one has seen him since last night, and I think that FBI guy, I think you told me he was your dad's legal guardian, is very concerned. They don't know where he is either."

"What are you suggesting? That he has run away?" Karen asked.

"Something like that. It's not terribly uncommon for challenged residents to wander off from time to time, but they usually turn up in short order. This seems more deliberate. May I be candid?"

"Certainly, please do be."

"It's none of my business, really, but I find it highly unusual that you are not your father's guardian. I know Stewart worked for the CIA at a fairly high level. Are they concerned about him? Is he possibly in their custody for a reason?"

Karen sighed, relieved that she had a sympathetic ear. "You don't know the half of it." Feeling more emotional by the minute, Karen poured out the whole story, crying from time to time, as she explained the parts where her reputation was crushed in court. She finished with the events of the day involving her suspension from her teaching job.

Bevy listened patiently to every detail and started putting the scenario together in his mind. He felt awful for his friend's daughter and wanted to help, felt obligated to help. He was no friend of government bureaucracy, having been a victim of it during the Vietnam War, and more importantly, ignored by it after his return to America. He had seen how bureaucrats could mess things up trying to cover their asses. He was particularly bitter about his government's unwillingness to intercede in his rescue from prison in Hanoi after he successfully reached the French embassy following his escape. His heart went out to her.

"We need to come up with a plan. Something is amiss here; your dad has been unaccounted for almost twenty-four hours now, probably. I think the FBI believes he is going somewhere. That fellow Ornstein stopped by again late this afternoon and grilled me about how much money your dad might have had, even suggesting I or someone else here may have helped him. I overheard him say something about a Mercedes Benz on a call he took while he was with me. Do you know anything about that?"

"He's probably just referring to Dad's midsize he had before he moved there. They sold it a couple weeks later, so he doesn't have that available to him."

Bevy thought a minute. "You know, they also didn't seem to want to go public with this. I suggested a Silver Alert, which would be logical, but that guy didn't seem open to it just yet. Wanted to wait. Karen, do you think it's possible that the FBI is worried about someone else finding your dad? You know, it would explain a lot about what's happened. Your dad knows a lot of sensitive information about the Mideast. His dementia may be considered a threat, and he may be in danger."

"Oh, my God!" Karen gasped. "I never thought about it that way. It makes sense."

Bevy offered, "We should work together. If we can figure out what your dad is doing, maybe we can intercede. I'll think about it and speak to you tomorrow."

"Thank you, Mr. Martin . . . I mean Bev. Yes, let's touch base tomorrow. Let me give you my cell phone number in case I'm not home."

She did, and Bevy did likewise, putting her contact information in his iPhone.

Karen took a few minutes to think through what she had just learned, trying to make some sense out of it. The only place she could think that her dad could be going was home to her, but that just didn't seem possible. She was sure the guardian had sold his car a month ago, so where did a Mercedes fit in? In any event, she felt sure she would be hearing from Lyle Ornstein shortly. They would need to bring her into the loop at some point, she figured.

✶

Now fully up to speed, John Hallanger set up another secure conference call with Cavner and Brogan early that evening to find out how much publicity they were willing to endure in their effort to find Masterson. He outlined everything he had learned from Lyle Ornstein and Fulton McBride earlier in the day, and the conclusions they had reached about Masterson's whereabouts.

"What is taking you so long?" whined Brogan. "It took you nearly twenty-four hours to learn that a seventy-two-year-old senior citizen stole a car and beat up a policeman? Who knows where he could have gone in that time? Why is this taking so long?" he pressed.

Hallanger felt defensive. "Hold on here, Hank. This is your problem, remember? You are the one who has put restrictions on us. We can't go public, the obvious solution, because of your precious secret. And there are other factors. We have a car that went missing for twelve hours before it was reported stolen because some guy doesn't want his wife find out he got drunk and went to a strip club. And we have a Nazi cop who doesn't want anyone to know he got beat up by a senior citizen, so we don't really have good information to go on regarding the perpetrator. We have a runaway senior who may be getting help from someone, and we don't know where he's going, so we don't know where to look. If you have any other wiseass remarks to make about our abilities, get Hollis to authorize you to go to Florida and handle it yourself. This babysitting job isn't what the Bureau does."

Hollis Cavner from the NSA chimed in, "Let's keep it under control! I think it's time to go public. Finding him quickly is more important than the word getting out to the Russians or Iranians. I would hope the Israelis are on our side, in any event. Jack, what will that do for us?"

Hallanger responded, "A lot, I should think. A Silver Alert will go public on all the interstate highways and turnpikes. We have a description of the vehicle and of Masterson. We have portable digital license readers that we can move to service plazas, and state highway patrolman can surveil, increasing our range. Ornstein and McBride feel strongly that the only place Masterson could go would be north toward his daughter, although that is only a hunch, not based on anything concrete. If he were just hanging around South Florida, he probably would have turned up by now."

Brogan added a tidbit to the mix: "I may have helped there. Yesterday I sent an anonymous copy of the daughter's arrest record to her employer, the school where she teaches. I'm told she has been suspended, so that ought to soften her up a little."

Hallanger flew into a rage. "You did what?! What the fuck's the matter with you? Don't you realize that we may need her help before this is over. How did you think that would be of benefit to us? We've already screwed her over in every way imaginable, and now you get her fired. You're a moron, Hank. You've made a bad situation worse!"

"She was only suspended, and she doesn't know who sent it. I thought it would soften her up . . . put her on the defensive," Brogan responded, trying to pass it off as a satisfactory explanation.

Cavner concurred. "I have to agree with Jack, Hank. That was not a smart move and certainly questionable ethically."

Hallanger continued, "Are we in agreement, at least, that we go public with this? We can get all the law enforcement agencies working on this. It shouldn't take us long to find a Mercedes on I-95, if indeed Maryland is where he's headed. We should also put the daughter's home under surveillance. Hollis, can you help me get a warrant for a wiretap on her phones, house, and cell? We can find out if she knows anything, or if anyone makes contact."

Hollis said, "I'll do what I can. But first, why don't you be thinking about what crime she has committed? That's going to be the first question we're going to hear from the judge."

"That's why I'm asking you. Maybe we can play the national security card. That's your department."

Hallanger made a call to McBride to coordinate a joint operation with the Maryland office of the Bureau. "Fulton, you've done good work sorting this out, but if Masterson is truly trying to find his way north, we will need to be working on things at this end. I am going to assign Howard McCall in my office to liaise with you. You may use him for support for anything you need here in the Mid-Atlantic region. I am leaving the primary responsibility with you until such time as we know for sure that Masterson is no longer in your area. Then we will make a transfer if appropriate. Are you good with that?"

"Yes, sir. That only makes sense, although I may send Ornstein to Washington. He knows more about Masterson and his family than anybody else; no need to reinvent the wheel."

Hallanger concurred, "That's a better idea. If Ornstein gets here in time, we'll put him in charge, since he already knows all the players."

McBride continued, "I'm still not convinced, nor is Ornstein, that our guy can get very far, even with a car, without some support, money, etc. We did check with a dementia specialist here locally who is not sure Masterson could pull this off, I mean getting to Maryland, without a lot of help, unless there is something in his background that we are not aware of. He won't be able to access the car's navigation system, and he probably can't even follow a road map."

"Good points, Fultie," Hallanger acknowledged. "So you're thinking he may still be in your neck of the woods?"

"Well, for starters, Ornstein tells me the car had less than half a tank of gas when it was taken, according to the owner. So, unless Masterson has a way to purchase fuel, he should be within a hundred miles of here. Now that we can go public with a Silver Alert, if he's around here, something should turn up in short order."

Their business concluded, McBride rang off and called the Department of Elder Affairs of Florida to initiate the Silver Alert for Masterson.

The attendant at the call center recorded Masterson's description, including the clothing he was last seen wearing, as well as the make, color, and license plate number of the car he was presumed to be driving. The DOEA accepted McBride's authority as agent in charge for the Miami office of the Bureau as meeting the requirements to issue such an alert, saving a lot of time getting the word out on the street. As a result, all Florida Department of Law Enforcement agencies were placed on notice that Stewart Masterson was officially a missing person. In addition, highway recognition and notification equipment were electronically initiated on all regional interstates and service plazas.

Within minutes, ten thousand travelers per hour were presented with Masterson's situation throughout South Florida. Unfortunately, virtually all of these notifications were witnessed by people traveling the high-speed throughways and interstates in the Southeast and Mid-Atlantic.

CHAPTER FIVE

Patricia Madison, known to her friends as Pepper, sat in a corner booth of the Tap Room at the Orrington Hotel in downtown Columbia, South Carolina, nursing an Italian white wine, while she surveyed the early evening gathering of visitors, businessmen, and the like. Her observations were made discreetly from the booth where she assumed a noninviting demeanor while evaluating the potential marks filling the room. She had learned over the years that an interruption by someone she did not consider a suitable candidate could only lead to complications, and never in her experience did some man who approached her at her workplace ever result in a successfully completed transaction. Moreover, the few attempts she had made over the years to turn such an advance into a profitable venture had deteriorated into unmitigated disasters, even to the point where her personal safety was at risk.

Simply put, Pepper was a very complicated person, one of those individuals who could not be summarized in a footnote, if she could be described at all. She was very attractive and engaging, when she wanted to be, which was a help to her in her chosen professions. Her friends and associates knew her best as a well-educated, world-traveling flight attendant, which she certainly was. This accounted for her need to be on the move at unusual hours, and her frequent periods of unavailability. She had, in fact this very day, returned from Europe, part of a four-day whirlwind of travel that was typical of her monthly schedule with Delta Air Lines, where her tenure gave her sufficient seniority to bid almost any schedule she fancied. Her preference was the Atlanta-London-Paris stint followed by a Parisian layover and return through London to Atlanta, which she made three times a month, leaving her the rest of the time off to do as she pleased in pursuit of other interests and even provided enough block hours for a little overtime pay.

Her other profession was one that has been long recognized as such. In cold, unambiguous terms, Pepper was a prostitute, a carry-over from a long and complicated history that dated back to her college days, but most people, including her clients, would not characterize her that way. As she liked to think: *It's complicated.*

In high school and college, Patricia, her given name, was always that girl anyone could bring home to his or her family, and she would be unqualifiedly welcomed. She was fit and trim, about five-feet, six-inches tall, with thick, naturally blond hair that always fell just right. She could wear it short and play the tomboy role, as she did when she was a cheerleader in high school, or long on her shoulders, when she wanted to look a little sexy. When she put it up, she looked sophisticated, but no matter how she did her hair, when she smiled, her white teeth and dimples overrode any perception other than just plain wholesome and cute. She was the girl who had everything growing up, so it seemed to her, except for the part that she couldn't share with anyone, the part she thought of as the dark periods.

Pepper's parents had divorced when she was eight years old for reasons that she was not quite sure, never made clear to her. They assured her repeatedly that she was not responsible in any way, but as an adolescent, her own insecurities clouded her judgment. She always asked herself, *How could I not have something to do with it?*

Her mother had remarried when she was eleven, and although her stepfather was pleasant enough, Pepper could not help feeling a little bit displaced, on the outside of the family dynamics.

It was not long after her new family moved to Charleston where her stepfather's contracting business, which specialized in historic building preservation, relocated that she sensed something was not right about her sleep. One night she awoke from confusing dreams and thought she saw her stepfather darting out her bedroom door. Shortly thereafter, she awoke late one night and felt him touching her between her legs. Aghast and terrified, immediately awakened from adrenaline, she sat up and looked him squarely in the eyes. As she and her stepfather made eye contact in the dim glow of the night-light by her bed, she felt an empowerment over him.

Although Pepper was very confused about the entire situation, she was old enough to know that this was not something that was her fault and that it was a terrible violation of her being; she also knew that her mom's husband was fully aware that she knew what he had done and had probably done before. Her embarrassment about what had happened overrode her need to share her experience with anyone because she knew the drama of the consequences would destroy the fabric of what little security and home life she enjoyed. She did not want to endure the pain of another family dislocation like the one she had experienced just a few years before. So the subject was never brought up between her and her stepfather, but she knew she could stop him in his tracks with a look, an all-knowing look.

It changed the dynamics of the family hierarchy, but if her mother noticed, she never let on. If there was ever going to be a closure of sorts, that possibility ended when her stepfather was killed in an automobile accident on his way home from a construction superintendents meeting when she was a sophomore in high school. Over the years, Pepper came to realize that she had a closure after all; it was in the knowing looks that she occasionally exchanged with her tormentor, for they were an admission of wrongdoing. That was enough for her, but the scarring would weaken her self-esteem as she matured, leaving a trail of consequences that led her to the Tap Room on this Thursday evening.

As she sipped her wine, evaluating the people arriving and leaving the cozy bar, Pepper reflected on her life's unusual avenues. Her mother had inherited the construction business, but like most specialty construction companies, this one was grounded in the personality of its founder. Not long after her mother tried to take over the responsibilities of running the business, she realized she was in way over her head and totally dependent on the craftsmen who did the work. They, in turn, soon realized they didn't need a housewife to share in income derived from their labors and moved out on their own. After the jobs that were in process when her stepfather died were completed, the business was shut down. The construction loans that were funding the work took what little cash was left after the subcontractors burned off the bulk of contracted prices with "adjustments" and change orders, which Pepper's mom was unprepared to defend herself against successfully.

When the dust settled, the family was left with little money. Mortgage life insurance did take care of that obligation, fortunately. Pepper's mom had to get a job to take care of living expenses, and Pepper found part-time work while she finished high school. Thankfully the house was paid for, or they wouldn't have gotten by. Pepper was popular in school, having a head start because of her looks alone and supported by her accommodating personality. She dated, and lost her virginity to a popular football jock in her junior year. Her grades were good, complemented by better than average SAT scores, so in her senior year, she approached her mom about the possibility of going to college. Money was tight, but her mom agreed to put a small credit line on the house if Pepper was willing to make sacrifices in the choices of an education and promised to work summers to reduce the debt. Pepper wanted a full college experience like many of her classmates, not just an education, and she and her mother worked out a compromise that she could go to the University of South Carolina in Columbia, if she agreed to live in low-cost dormitory facilities and find some kind of scholarship assistance to lessen the financial burden.

Pepper's first two years as a Gamecock went as planned, albeit the summer job did not prove the financial success the family hoped for. The income from the scholarship she was not able to secure was replaced by a job as a dorm proctor, which gave her rent-free living, but the excitement of college life got the better of Pepper's judgment when she accepted an invitation that summer to share an apartment near campus with three other girls for her junior and senior years. The distraction and party environment caused her to lose focus on her penny-pinching culture, and before long, money issues began to surface. The purchase of a beat-up Honda Civic from a classmate did not help matters when her arrangement for financing put her further in a hole. She made it known to her friends that she was desperate for money halfway through her junior year.

The young man who sold and financed the car for her, after threatening her with repossession if she did not make the next installment, suggested an alternative source of money. He introduced her to a friend of a friend who was involved in an escort service. She agreed to meet, just an introduction to see what was involved, she was assured. The following morning she met with a gregarious young man in his midthirties named Gary for breakfast at an IHOP; neither he nor the location seemed particularly threatening.

After a few moments of chitchat, he suggested, "A girl like you shouldn't have a money worry in the world; you're sittin' on a gold mine!"

Pepper noted that he was trying to be funny. He went on to promise her that all of his customers were upper-class citizens, many in town for business at the capitol. He explained that he was not a pimp, that he just set up "dates." Everyone involved in the arrangement knew what was actually happening, but any sexual transaction would be consensual between Pepper and the client.

"Look," he said, "all my customers want is to know that I will connect them with a good-looking young lady, such as yourself. They want to know that you are classy and that you are willing to deal. You don't have to have sex with them, although let's face it, if you get too picky, you're going to stop hearing from me. I can't have unsatisfied customers. My success is dependent solely on my reputation, but if you occasionally get in a situation where you are not comfortable, you can just bug out. You have no idea how many coeds I have on my referral list. You probably know some of them, but you'll never hear who they are from me. Discretion is very important in this business."

Pepper mulled it over in her mind. This guy did not fit the profile of a drug-filled world of prostitution and filth. She was no prude, but at the same time, it was not lost on her the significance of the step she was being asked to take. Gary sensed her hesitation.

"I have an idea. Why don't I set you up on one *date?* You can see for yourself. If you don't like the way it's progressing, just bail. I'll even run some interference for you in setting it up, so the guy will be prepared, knowing you're new to the business. I can make it up to him another way if it goes sour."

"I don't know."

"Just give it a try, think about it being a blind date. Some of them don't go so well either, do they?"

He's got a point, she thought. "How would I know how to go about it? I've never done anything like this before."

Gary knew he had her hooked; he just had to close the deal. "I'm going to have one of my girls call you, and you can meet. She will go over all the technical stuff with you. There are some things you need to know, and she'll explain everything. I'm going to give you my cellular phone number. I have it with me day and night. If you have any questions, or if anything comes up, you can call me at any time." The meeting ended on that note.

Pepper got her indoctrination from a perky young girl who called her later that afternoon. She couldn't have been more than eighteen or nineteen and said she had been providing escort services for Gary for over a year, that she had had no real issues. Pepper was given a crash course in the do's and don'ts of the business. The girl would tell Pepper nothing about herself, except that she lived in the area part-time, and none of her friends were aware of what she did on the side. Pepper suspected she was a student at the university.

"What should I tell Gary?" the girl asked.

"Tell him that I'm willing to give it a try," Pepper responded cautiously.

A few days later, she got her first summons to meet a man in his early thirties outside the hotel lobby at the Sheraton Capitol Hotel. She was given his name and a description of the blue blazer and gray slacks he would be wearing. She saw him pacing nervously outside the hotel lobby as she crossed from the public garage, and she introduced herself to him by extending her hand, the way she had been counseled, very formal. She did not give her real name. As he turned and smiled at her, she thought she had been set up on a date with Tom Cruise.

"Let's get a bite to eat," he suggested as he took her arm gently and held the car door of the rented Toyota for her, handing the valet a few small bills.

Pepper smiled to herself as she remembered that evening. It took her a while to realize she had been pretty well set up that night. Only occasionally did she have such an experience, but she was hooked on the money, and she learned the ropes pretty quickly. She got periodic advice from Gary, and in fact, she was able to reject a couple of rotten apples that came across her path. Gary encouraged her to give him a report whenever things went amiss. He did caution her when she got too "picky," as he put it, but in most situations, he was reasonable.

She was making such good money that the hardest part was to keep her mom from suspecting what she was doing. A year and a half later, she graduated, settled the line of credit on the house, and took her art history degree to Delta Air Lines, where she began instruction as a flight attendant in the Atlanta training center.

Over the years, her job paid well enough. Pepper was certainly comfortable from a financial point of view; however, her social progress didn't seem to fit on a track that she had imagined. Her constant travel was not conducive to dating in the traditional sense, although the stewardess stereotype presented her with numerous opportunities for companionship. The men in her life seemed to revolve around a common theme: traveling businessmen looking for a liaison that was only temporary in nature. She had long ago put the idea of a life in escort services behind her, but that history made part-time dalliances something she was comfortable with. Then, over the years, as her seniority built up and she traveled to more interesting places in the world, she found the opportunities for short-term relationships more appealing. She did not have a core awareness of a biological clock to interfere or put pressure on her lifestyle; consequently, the years went by without milestones to mark the passage of time.

Not long after she incorporated the casual dating into her lifestyle, she was very surprised when her companion for the evening mistook her affections of the moment as a business arrangement. It was on a layover in San Francisco after a pleasant evening of dinner and a visit to the touristy piers on the bay, followed by a night in his hotel room at the Mayfair, that he asked her if she wanted to be paid in cash and what was the agreed-upon amount. Her immediate reactions were disgust, shock, and disappointment.

"I'm so sorry; I just assumed . . ." was followed by moments of embarrassment and affected outrage, while Pepper took a few minutes to get dressed and prep herself to leave the hotel. As she stormed out the lobby onto Polk Street searching for a taxi, her thought process made a one-eighty, and her indignation settled as she wound her way through town to the hotel near the airport where she had registered the evening before.

The proverbial lightbulb flashed in her brain, as the possibilities of this situation began connecting dot to dot. She didn't mind casual sex with strangers; frankly, she often enjoyed it, and it was not that different from what she had been doing in college, excepting the significant difference that she was able to be selective—or "picky"— in her choice of partners. As her thinking developed further, she began to realize that her sexual encounters on the road all had similar characteristics. She met some man in the course of performing her job, usually while in uniform. The men were all seemingly successful businessmen, clean-cut, handsome, and educated, often married and just looking for a good time while they were on the road.

It occurred to Pepper that this scenario was common and that the basics could be packaged and marketed to her advantage. Why not? She was already engaging in all the moving parts, and the experience seemed to be in high demand. So, why not profit from her endeavors, if that was in the cards? It wasn't like she had another life or person she would be betraying, other than the disrespect she was already handing out to the families of the guys she was screwing. She did not give the difficulties this might have on her own emotional well-being a second thought, so she carefully put her plan in place, supplementing her income substantially as the opportunities knocked, about twice a month on average. In her mind, she sold fantasies to traveling businessmen at very respectable prices.

So now she sat in the Tap Room lounge, not far from the Cornell Arms, her own apartment just down the street from the Orrington Hotel on Gervais, surveying the comings and goings of potential marks as they entered off the street side entrance or from the hotel lobby. She was enjoying her glass of wine for the moment, and if nothing turned up, she would go home and have a quiet evening with a good book, completely satisfied either way. That was the key to her success; she felt no pressure. Although just forty years old, she could pass for much younger. She planned to keep this up as long as she was capable of delivering the fantasy she was selling. This could be quite a while, as age was relative, and whereas she might not be able to pull off the appeal to the younger businessmen, there were always more mature ones, and in her experience, they generally had more resources to draw from.

Pepper took a sip from her glass and noticed a nice-looking, older gentleman enter from the hotel lobby and head for the bar proper, sliding onto one of the barstools facing the highly polished mahogany counter with its ornate joiner work. She gave him only a passing interest because of his advanced age, but she couldn't help but notice how well groomed he was. Although dressed casually in khakis and a blue oxford button-down shirt under a beige cotton windbreaker, she could see that he was very handsome, and he carried himself with some authority. *It's not so bad,* she thought, *if that's what I have to look forward to. I may have a longer future at this than I would have guessed.*

After a quick glance around the room to confirm there was nothing else interesting worth keeping an eye on, she returned her attention to the older gentleman, as he took a sip from the draft beer the bartender put in front of him. She watched him fumble around his pockets for something, and she went into full-alert mode as she watched him pull a thick wad of bills out of his front pants pocket, peel one off, and put it on the bar top. In her experience, men who carried their cash loosely in a front pants pocket were financially much more capable than those who carried bills in their wallets, almost as if they had a disregard for the stuff.

Clearly the white-jacketed bartender was not happy with the payment. He shrugged his shoulders and held his palms up, as if begging for a different form of compensation. Again the older gentleman rummaged around in his pockets and returned the bartender's shrug, obviously not able to comply with whatever the request was. The bartender gave a disapproving look and moved to the cash register where he took out a bunch of twenties and smaller bills and put the change on the counter.

This transaction had Pepper intrigued. She slid out of her booth, nearly empty glass in hand, and moved to the bar to order another glass of wine. She hoisted herself up on the barstool next to the man, who was taking a healthy sampling from his lager, and placed her glass on the bar and ordered a refill. She made eye contact with the older gentleman, as he toyed with his pile of twenties and change, looking as though he was deliberating on how much to tip. Then he picked it up and put it in his other front pants packet, and noticing her attention, he smiled broadly at Pepper.

It occurred to her how kindly he looked. Encouraged by the money situation, she deduced correctly that the bartender didn't like having to break a hundred for an eight-dollar beer, and was annoyed by the inconvenience. She wondered to herself if the whole wad of bills had been hundreds. Obviously so, or he would have given the bartender something smaller when prompted. On a whim, Pepper decided to engage the man with one of her comical openers.

Returning his smile with her best, dimples and all, she inquired, "Do you come here often?" She had found this to be a good icebreaker on the infrequent occasions that she initiated contact with a mark. The role reversal with such an obvious cliché conveyed mountains of information. Clearly it was a come on, so both parties knew what was going down, and the response gave Pepper a basis for gauging the man's sense of humor and interest, as well as a sense of his intelligence.

The man's reply confounded her: "No, not really. I've not been to Columbia before; I'm just passing through on my way to see my daughter in Maryland."

"I was trying to make a joke."

Masterson just looked at her blankly, the humor having gone over his head.

Now more determined to get to the bottom of this, Pepper tried the direct approach. "I mean, it's like a line out of a bad movie, you know? Like I was trying to pick you up, or something. That's why it's funny, see?"

Masterson looked at her for a moment, seemingly processing the information. Then he said, "Does that mean you're *not* trying to pick me up?"

Pepper burst out laughing, thinking she had been bested in a verbal duel until she noticed the serious look on his face.

He continued, "Because if you are, I would love to have someone to talk to. I've had a long day sitting in a car alone, well, not really alone; my wife, Helen, is with me, sort of."

This was a first! "Why don't you talk to your wife? Where is she, anyway?" Pepper looked around the area for signs of her.

Masterson thought about his response, as the bartender brought her fresh glass of wine. He caught the bartender's eye and ordered another beer, as he downed the last of the first one.

"She's in heaven, I suspect," he finally answered, as though it was a most natural response to the question.

"Okay, now I'm totally confused. I thought you said you were traveling with your wife." It was a statement, but Pepper assumed an explanation would be forthcoming. She raised her eyebrows in question, prompting him again, only to see sadness descend over his face.

"I guess that's confusing, sorry. My wife passed away, and I'm taking her ashes home to my daughter in Maryland, where we can all be together. So, I can't really talk to her, you see. Well, actually I can talk to her, and I do, but she can't answer." His face showed pain, but then his smile returned. "But I can talk to you," he continued hopefully.

"And I can answer." Pepper reached over, and in what seemed like a completely natural gesture, she put her hand on top of his. Then feeling self-conscious about it, she withdrew, but she continued smiling at him. Pepper began to realize that this kindly older man was completely open and direct, almost childlike in his demeanor. She suspected that he was still grieving heavily from his loss or that he was just starting to lose it from age. It triggered an emotion within her that she had not felt in a long, long time, a sort of deep sensitivity to another's feelings. She almost wanted to cry.

The bartender came over with Masterson's order, and asked, "Do you want to start a tab, or do you want to settle now?"

"I'll pay now," Masterson replied as he reached in his left front pocket and pulled out the thick wad of hundreds, removing one and placing it on the bar.

"That's enough, buddy! You think this is the Franklin Mint?" the bartender complained gruffly, not having any idea what the Franklin Mint actually was, but thinking it sounded appropriate from having heard it somewhere. "I've got better things to do than make change for rich bastards like you; I'm not impressed with your money, but maybe your new friend is." He nodded toward Pepper.

Pepper's face turned red with embarrassment. Masterson's face showed a level of anger that quite surprised her. Amped up by a sudden rush of adrenaline, he voiced forcefully, "I think you owe the lady an apology." He paused a moment, and hearing no response, he continued, "You know, I've dealt with punks like you all my life, and your arrogance only works to your detriment." With that, he pointed his index finger at the lip of the glass of beer and slowly tipped it over in the direction of the bartender, spilling its contents slowly across the bar top and down the front of the bartender's white cotton serving jacket.

"I don't think we're welcome here, but I'm famished. Would you like to go somewhere and get a bite to eat? There are lots of upscale restaurants all around this area," Pepper said, smiling up at him appreciatively, taking a chance before she had a sense of encouragement from her target, thinking to herself that maybe he wasn't a target at all.

"Rich bastards like me don't usually collect our change; we like to leave it to people providing us with competent service. In your case, I think we'll make an exception." With that, Masterson scooped up the hundred, rotated, and slid off his barstool, and Pepper did likewise.

"Wait a damn minute!" the barkeep shot out in anger. "You didn't pay for the beer."

"Well, I didn't drink it, did I?" Masterson smirked. Standing next to his barstool, he turned to Pepper and apologized for making her uncomfortable.

"No need," she replied, as she took his arm for support, noticing the strength of his upper torso, surprising for someone his age.

The bartender glared at them as they made their way through the door to the hotel lobby and out the front door onto Gervais Street.

As promised, Masterson eyed two casual dining pubs across the street and others lining the perpendicular cross streets heading toward the capitol. They strolled arm in arm across Gervais and toward the dome just visible a couple of blocks ahead.

"I've eaten here. The food's simple, but good," Pepper suggested, nodding at the single-story bistro on the left, which featured outside patio seating accented with Japanese lanterns weaved throughout the overhead latticework demarking the perimeter of the outside dining area.

They climbed a few steps to the hostess stand where a lovely young girl flashed her smile as she showed them to a table along the edge, where they had a view of the passersby on the sidewalk a few feet below. The night air was dry, if a little cool, and Masterson was glad he had brought along his windbreaker.

He remarked on the hostess's smile. "Everyone here is so pleasant and upbeat; not like where I've been lately," he ventured, remembering the orderlies who marshaled him at Tropic Isle as they took their seats opposite one another at a rough wood table.

"You mean like the bartender?" Pepper responded sarcastically, but with a smile.

"I hadn't considered that."

Pepper leaned forward to make sure her voice was clear above the ambient noise of the conversations that were going on around them. In the corner, a group of millennials were celebrating a hard day's work in the offices of government, their voices spiking from time to time as they gained satisfaction from contributions they were making to their conversations.

"Where exactly have you been lately?"

Masterson looked puzzled and somewhat defensive.

Pepper explained herself, "I mean you said people are pleasant, *not* like where you've been lately. Where is that?"

"Well, to tell the truth, it's sort of confusing. I'm traveling with my wife, Helen, from Florida to see our daughter in Maryland. We're thinking of moving there," he started slowly, repeating his conversation from before. His face fell in a look of sadness.

Pepper's awareness ticked up a notch. She was beginning to realize that something was not quite right with her new friend. Not wanting to put him off, she reminded him gently, leaning in even closer to show compassion. "You explained that your wife died and that you're traveling with her ashes."

"Oh, yes. I forgot."

"So, tell me what you meant by *people where you come from are not pleasant.*"

Masterson did not remember making the reference, but he

certainly knew what she was talking about. He did his best to explain the circumstances of his life at Tropic Isle, but his thoughts were random, at best, and he had a difficult time trying to put forth a coherent explanation for her.

After a few awkward attempts to talk about it, mostly just getting out his feelings, Pepper interrupted, "Why don't we start at the beginning? What is your name? I'm Patricia Madison. My friends call me Pepper." She smiled and held out her hand across the table.

Masterson took it and noticed her warm, firm handshake. She made him feel comfortable, and her smile drew him in. "I'm Stewart Masterson," he offered up.

"So, why don't you begin with telling me your story? I know you are coming from Florida, but how did you get there? What do you do? Where did you grow up? Nobody starts out in Florida."

"Do you mean from the very beginning?" Masterson asked, feeling now on very solid ground, where he was sure about his memories.

"If you like."

They were interrupted by a waiter who gave them menus bound in leather, and he informed them his name was Jerry, that he would be their server. His name tag confirmed his identity. He asked if they would like a beverage. The couple looked over the wine list on the back of the menu, and Masterson confessed he could not read the selections in the dim light. Pepper came to his rescue after determining that he preferred a red wine and ordered a Pinot for each of them.

"I'll give you a few moments to go over the selections while I get your drinks," Jerry said as he turned to place their orders at the bar inside the restaurant.

Masterson stared ahead blankly for a moment.

"You were going to tell me your story from the beginning," Pepper prompted.

"Oh, yeah." Masterson relaxed again, back in familiar territory.

For the next hour and a half, he related his life story from his youth in suburban Washington, D.C., through college at Georgetown and his time in Vietnam in the army. He explained that he received his commission as a second lieutenant after graduation through his participation in the ROTC program and his service in Saigon in the late sixties as an intelligence officer. Without the limitations of his training to inhibit him, Masterson gave full details of how he was recruited after his separation from active duty in 1968 by the Central Intelligence Agency, thanks to his work in G2, the intelligence arm of the army, not because of a keen sense that he wanted to be a spy, but because it got him out of his required army reserve obligation following active duty. He explained training at Camp Peary, known as the Farm, before beginning his career as an analyst at Langley, Virginia, in the early seventies.

"What's *the farm*?" Pepper asked. "The term sounds familiar, like I've read it in a spy novel or something."

Masterson looked like a deer in the headlights. "It really exists. It's where the Central Intelligence Agency trains its field agents. It's on about ten thousand acres in eastern Virginia; I think it was started before the war for other purposes. They had to buy out two whole towns to put it together and called it Camp Peary. When I started with them, everyone had to receive initial training there, but I think now it's just used for agents who are working in the field. Later I needed more training because I was responsible for networks of field operatives in the Mideast, so I had to have a full understanding of their methods and tactics to be effective."

Pepper's eyes lit up, and she leaned forward across the table, speaking excitedly in a hushed tone. "My God! You're a spy then."

"Was," he amended.

"Still! I'm having dinner with James Bond; I can't believe it." Pepper was fully aware that her companion was not running on all cylinders, but she sensed truth in his story and felt that there was a lot more going on with this kindly gentleman, who had not been afraid to stick his neck out in her defense when the situation warranted, for which she was deeply appreciative. She wanted to learn more. "So, when were you in the Mideast?"

"We'll come to that. First, you have to learn about Helen."

"Your wife?"

"Yes. We met in Washington when I was new to the agency, and we fell madly in love." Masterson continued with the details he felt were important. He explained that his parents moved to North Carolina in the seventies when his father retired from his printing business. They kindly offered their house in Silver Spring, Maryland, to their son and his new young wife, provided that they mortgage it with sufficient proceeds to pay for the modest North Carolina retirement home, which Stewart and Helen were happy to do.

Pepper started to connect the dots. "And that's where you're going now, to Maryland? Is it the same house you lived in?"

"Yes, when I retired, I gave it to my daughter and her two kids; that's why I'm going there, to be with them."

Masterson continued on with his story, focusing on his late wife and her tragic passing. He spoke emotionally of losing her to cancer, how difficult it was for him, and how his life seemed to collapse when she died. Pepper learned of his sense of loss and the loneliness that followed, and her heart ached for the pain she saw in his face and heard in his voice.

Again she reached out and placed her hand on his to show that she understood how important this was to him. She looked in his eyes and asked, "How long ago did she pass?"

"I'm seventy-two now. I remember my daughter and grandchildren coming down to Florida for a visit to celebrate my seventy-first birthday. Helen was already wasting by then. We drank champagne in her bedroom, so I guess it was over a year ago." Masterson's eyes looked up a little, almost as if he could see the scene in his bedroom in Boca Raton, his eyes focusing off in the distance.

"A year ago?" Pepper looked surprised. "You said you have been going to her memorial every day since she died. Where have you been living? Who has been looking after you? Why are you moving now, and how did you end up with her urn if it was at her memorial?"

Masterson's answers started to become less clear, as he tried to explain that his government superiors had taken over responsibility for him and had put him in an assisted living facility where nobody cared about him, except maybe for a few friends like Bevy. He described his life there as full of emptiness. He knew he was being watched, and he explained that he was not let out like the other residents. When Pepper asked him about his daughter's reaction to all this, all he could remember was that his government made her cry and that some young man from the government tried to keep her out of his life. He said they did get to talk by phone every so often.

Pepper sat back in her chair aghast at the story she was hearing, the dots connecting very quickly for her now. She had a chance to organize her thoughts when Jerry arrived with the salad and light pasta dishes they had ordered after their drinks arrived. Pepper asked him to refresh their wine glasses, and he left for the bar inside.

She asked Masterson to confirm what she was thinking: "So, if you think the government put you in this assisted living facility and is trying to prevent you from getting out, they must be afraid of you for some reason, don't you think?"

Masterson nodded.

"Why would they be afraid of you? What exactly did you do for the CIA?" Pepper asked.

"I was the station chief in Brussels for seventeen years before I retired," he volunteered cautiously. This woman seemed so warm and inviting. Masterson had good instincts for whom he could and could not trust, and he felt completely comfortable discussing his past with her. She seemed to take a genuine interest in him, and she made him feel relevant to her world as well as his.

"So you dealt with some pretty high-level stuff, right?" she asked.

"I suppose so. I was responsible for all of our intelligence networks in Russia, Iran, and Israel, as well as other sovereigns we surveiled in the Mideast. I was familiar with the portals for *chatter* in our communication lines."

"Chatter?" she asked.

"It's complicated and not important for you to understand. Frankly, when I think about it, I remember what the importance of all of it was, but for the life of me, I can't remember the *it* part of it— what I actually knew, exactly."

Masterson hoped that would conclude her inquiry because he was unsure if he could explain it if he wanted to, but he did remember it was sophisticated and complex. Chatter was the technique of obfuscating when intelligence was being transmitted by keeping a constant flow of meaningless information moving through lines of communication that were undoubtedly being monitored by enemy agencies, so that they would not notice spikes in transmission volume when something important was coming through. That way, everything seemed like garbage to eavesdroppers.

Pepper shared what she was thinking with her new friend. "Regardless, you know shit! And I suspect they are afraid who you might say something to." Then she added cautiously, "May I ask you a personal question?" Again, she leaned forward and placed her hand on top of his, trying to show compassion and interest.

He smiled and replied, "You can ask me anything."

"Do you know if you have Alzheimer's?"

For an instant Masterson felt hurt and shock, and then he looked into Pepper's eyes and saw that she was really trying to reach out to him with compassion and caring. He leaned back in his chair, leaving his hand in hers, and nodded slowly. He felt as though he was giving himself up to her, placing himself in her care, so strong was the trust he could place in her.

"How long have you known? How did you find out?" she asked.

"Since just before Helen died," Masterson answered thoughtfully. "She took me to see some doctors who specialize in Alzheimer's disease at our local hospital and medical school. They did some tests on me, puzzles and stuff, and determined that I suffered more than just old age memory loss."

"How did that make you feel?"

He recalled the meeting with the doctor at Florida Atlantic University. "I was frightened . . . and relieved."

"That's an odd combination, frightened and relieved. How so?" Pepper asked.

"It's hard to explain. I was relieved that there was an explanation for my behavior, but I was frightened that there was nothing much I could do about it. I am on a prescription for a drug that is supposed to help, but I'm not sure it does. I'm frightened because I know it's a progressive disease, and things will not end well for me. You know, I can best explain it as it's like losing your hearing when you get older. In restaurants you can hear everybody talking, but you can't really understand anything, unless they are focusing on you. That's how I feel right now. I know there are things going on that I am missing out on; I just don't know what they are or even when or if they occur, and I don't know when they matter. For what it's worth, they tell me I'm still in the early stages."

Pepper felt the need to express some confidence in Masterson. She continued leaning forward and placed her other hand on his and beamed her best smile. "For what it's worth, you seem pretty well put together to me, and I'm enjoying our time together immensely. I am concerned, however, that you may be in some sort of danger. Certainly the people responsible for you are desperately looking for you, and very likely the reason they are desperate is because they fear others are looking for you as well, people who are not at all concerned for your welfare. Aren't you worried that they will be able to trace your car?"

"I don't own a car."

"Then, what are you driving?"

"A Mercedes."

"A Mercedes? Where did you get it?"

"I found it," Masterson answered sheepishly.

"What do you mean, you *found* it?" Pepper asked, aghast.

"I don't remember." In truth, he really did not remember, suggesting to him that he did not come by it as a result of any significant event.

Pepper became more concerned for her friend. "Well, if it's stolen, most likely everyone is looking for it. You better hope you don't get stopped by the police. If they run the license number, your trip home will come to an abrupt end."

Just then the image of the fallen police officer he had disabled the previous day flashed across his mind. "Fortunately, I don't think I have far to go." Masterson smiled.

Pepper sensed he was getting edgy about all the negative prospects she was introducing to the discussion, so she switched the conversation to more mundane subjects while they finished their dinners. Masterson asked her about what she did, jokingly referring to the time other than when she was picking up lonely old men. She laughed, deliberately mumbling that he didn't know how close he had come to the truth of matters. She explained that she was a flight attendant for Delta Air Lines, that she traveled mostly to Europe about three times a month.

Masterson found that interesting and told her so. They compared notes on their favorite places to visit and talked their way through the rest of the meal. After a concluding cup of coffee, Masterson paid the check with a hundred dollar bill, leaving just enough change to take care of Jerry, who thanked them and wished them a good evening.

Pepper overlapped Masterson's forearm with hers, as she took his hand while they descended the few steps to the sidewalk. With a secure hold on him, more a sign of affection than an attempt to gain or give stability, she looked up at him with a smile.

"My apartment is just down the street. Would you like to join me for a nightcap? I think there are some things we could discuss about the last leg of your trip, and I think I might be of some help to you. For example, I suspect your idea to drive to Maryland came up rather suddenly, didn't it?"

"Yes, it did," he answered.

"Let me hazard a guess; your daughter doesn't know you're coming, does she?"

"No, I suspect not," he concluded.

"Maybe we can figure out a way to alert her, without giving up where you are so you can't be intercepted."

This seemed like a good idea to Masterson. He liked that he had a friend who was willing to help him get home, and he was feeling ever more comfortable that he could trust Pepper.

❧

The call to Florida Department of Elder Affairs was very effective in getting the word out about a missing senior citizen, but it also had unintended consequences. Intelligence agencies all over the world had developed sophisticated algorithms to monitor the release of information into the public domain from countless sources. The algorithm compared words, phrases, and numerical information published everywhere to its vast and extensive databases looking for matches. When matches were found, more sophisticated algorithms did further analysis to cull the coincidental hits from those that might prove to have interest to the agency involved. Many of these complicated mathematical formulae had been developed domestically in Silicon Valley, so it was not surprising that much of the information that warranted personal attention popped up on the radars of multiple countries simultaneously. So, it was not a shock that the Current Events Section of the SVR, the Russian successor to the infamous KGB, intelligence arm of the old Soviet Union, got a hit at about the same time as the analytical division of Mossad, the national intelligence agency of Israel, that the name *Stewart Masterson* had shown up in some official capacity in the United States.

In both organizations, the highlighted information was promptly moved through their agencies' respective processing systems, whereas in the case of Mossad, the Silver Alert for Masterson found its way to an analyst's desk in the Israeli embassy located on International Drive, Northwest in Washington, D.C. The analyst reviewed the notice of the alert and compared it to the database, immediately hand-carrying it to the station head office in the building.

Arye Kunin looked over the printed summary and called his counterpart in Miami, Mati Tahan. After some pleasantries, Arye explained what he had. "Mati, we have been following the trail of this guy Masterson since he left Brussels three years ago. He has been a supportive, cooperative ally of ours over the years, and we have tried to keep loose tabs on him, as is our policy, since his retirement. Everything looked normal until a couple of months ago when he just disappeared off the grid, if you know what I mean. There is no record of his death, and his disappearance is just a loose end we want to clean up because of the sensitive nature of what he knows about our operations and the networks we ran together in the Mideast. Our database just kicked out a Silver Alert on him in your neck of the woods. I don't suspect a problem, but we should check it out just to close out our files, if appropriate."

Mati Tahan reflected for a moment, but in the end acquiesced.

"I'll get right on it. Do you have a problem if I go to the source of the alert?"

"Which would be the FBI." It was a statement.

"Yes," Tahan replied. "We have a good relationship with McBride, the Special Agent in Charge here. My only concern is that if there is a problem, we may not have common interests, but usually we work together. You may be in a better position in Washington to talk to higher ups there. If they are aware of the situation, that in and of itself would be an indication that this is not just a routine matter."

Ayre thought about this for a moment. "I'm not sure I can do that, Mati; although, I think the idea has merit. From a policy standpoint, I would have to make that request through the embassy, which would raise the level of inquiry to the State Department, and that might be just what American intelligence is trying to avoid."

Mati Tahan was not buying it. "Come on, Arye! If I have a back channel to the local Miami Bureau for purposes of convenience, surely you have the equivalent to the NSA in Washington."

"Not that I want to talk to you about, Mati," Arye answered evasively. "But your point is taken. Let's talk later this evening and see where we are."

They ended the call and went about implementing their separate strategies. Tahan called McBride and got an earful of Masterson's recent history on the promised understanding that he was just providing background and that Mossad would not take any unilateral action without involving the Bureau in its decisions. McBride knew he was really sticking his neck out, but he had trust in his Israeli friend not to abuse their information-sharing relationship.

Tahan knew the position he had put McBride in, and he knew that it would come with a quid pro quo, payable at some future date. That's the way the intelligence services worked, at the middle levels, just as armies ran smoothly through the actions and wisdom of non-commissioned officers. The intelligence business was among the more decentralized operations in the modern world, where people in the field had to make decisions on the fly because they didn't have time to run alternatives up a chain of command.

For his part, Arye did contact a counterpart at the NSA where he was stonewalled with noncommittal responses. Officially, the NSA denied any knowledge of any government search or involvement with Masterson, but the lack of cooperation spoke volumes to Arye. Something was definitely going on, and it ran up the chain of command to very high levels.

～⌒⌒)

The SVR did not enjoy the cooperative substructure of the Western allied nations, so the process to act on this information took a completely different path. The responsible operations desk of the foreign operations section at the central offices in the Yasenevo District of Moscow quickly identified the significance of the Masterson reference from the information supplied by the algorithm and alerted his superior, Kirill Dernov, who put together a research and analysis team.

Dernov was a career analyst expert, who had been with the SVR since its inception in 1991 when it was created to take over foreign intelligence gathering from the KGB, which had been pretty much dismantled after the fall of the Soviet Union. He knew his way around the modern Internet-connected world, and his team made surprisingly critical use of social media and other publically provided sources for its investigations. His team was also fully capable of hacking into most firewall-protected systems, when the need arose. His manner was calm and not abusive, as it had been under some of his predecessors. This encouraged loyalty and devotion from those who worked for him.

Within ten minutes, four young intelligence analysts assembled in a computer-filled conference room in the interior of the building. Dernov outlined what he knew and gave the group the mission. He made it clear that this was a time-sensitive issue. The analysts were none too happy, having worked the graveyard shift in a department that worked around the clock. It was three o'clock in the morning in Moscow, and it didn't look like they would be off until well after their shift ended at eight. Because of the time difference, much of the critical work on American affairs was performed at inconvenient times, but on the positive side, Internet access was better globally at this hour.

"This guy Masterson is important to us because he was station chief in Brussels from the late nineties until he retired three years ago. In our business, that tenure is remarkable, and in that capacity, he had extensive knowledge of our networking with Iran, as well as the field operations he ran independently for the United States. At this point, we can only make assumptions about why he has been targeted for a Silver Alert, but as you may know, these alerts are government-sponsored identification devices for locating elderly citizens who have wandered off. They are normally issued in circumstances where the person of interest has diminished mental capacities, and therefore represents a danger to himself.

"Ordinarily the American intelligence agencies look out for their own, and none of the developed countries of the world are aggressive in co-opting retired agents, sort of a mutual détente, if you will, for obvious reasons. But in this case, this agent may be marginalized, so we have to check it out. Use all our resources. It's zero three hundred now; I will check back with you here"—Dernov looked at his watch—"at six o'clock this morning. That will give us two hours for follow-up if there is any, and you can all get out of here on time in the morning." He slid a file of background information on Masterson across the table.

The four Russian nerds turned to the computer stations set up in

DICK SCHMIDT

the conference room. These were identical to the ones located at their cubicles in the expansive floor plate of the general offices. No matter where each logged into the system, it was transparent to the process. Dernov had set it up this way, so that teams could work together in a separate space when necessary, where they could brainstorm their process and progress as a group.

While the team worked furiously on the Internet to find out as much information as they could in three hours, Dernov met with his superiors to share what he had figured out already and to begin a discussion of what kind of action the SVR might want to take, if any at all. The most senior of the three men in the room was Sergey Ivolgin, and he was strictly old school. He was dismissive of Dernov's attempts to examine all the implications of the Masterson situation.

"I don't see what is the problem, Kirill. One of America's most informed assets is in play, and he's vulnerable, you suspect. We should do everything we can to take advantage of the situation. I assure you that there is no one in the Kremlin who cares a shit about *correctness*. We have a good opportunity to get ahold of this guy and find out what he knows about our operations. Maybe we can plug a few leaks in our structure in the Mideast that we haven't been able to identify. You worry too much about nothing." He slammed his open palm on the table for effect.

Dernov turned to his section boss for support. "Danil, you see what I'm talking about, don't you?"

Danil Oriov was a contemplative man, thin and clearly a success because of his mind, not physical stature. He pushed his John Lennon–style glasses up on his forehead and rubbed his eyes, a delaying tactic he used when having to take a position on contentious matters. The energy level was low in the room in view of the lateness of the hour. Everyone just wanted to make a decision as quickly as possible and get out of there without uncovering his backside.

"Kirill has a point, Sergey," Oriov began cautiously. "We and our enemies have never gone after the family of retired officers after they have left service. I'm not so sure that everyone in the Kremlin would be very happy if you changed the course of established policy over a single opportunity such as this."

"Nonsense!" Ivolgin insisted, shifting his considerable bulk to a more aggressive position in his seat. He was used to intimidating people into support when he could not get his way by raising his voice, and he felt that was necessary now. "First of all, our retired agents are not in places where they represent a threat to us; they would be hard to pick up off the street here in Russia or whatever country is their nationality. Second, we need to make a decision and move fast, or we will lose our advantage. We will look stupid and weak if we don't move ahead. Let's find this guy and bring him in. We have the assets in place to do it. We may be criticized if we don't." He sat back, feeling confident he had made his point forcefully enough to get his way.

Oriov sat back in his chair and his face brightened, literally as though a lightbulb had gone off in his head. "I have another idea, comrades. We can have the best of both worlds. I understand your concern, Kirill. This action taken by us may change the face of how we deal with personnel who leave our service. It could have far-reaching consequences, and who in this room wants to be the one that others will turn to for an explanation? I certainly don't, but how about this as an alternative? What if Masterson is picked up and interrogated, but it's not by us?"

Dernov and Ivolgin turned to Oriov and said in unison, "What do you mean?" Their eyebrows rose, which in Sergey's case was a transformative event, very Groucho Marx–like in effect.

Oriov continued, "We aren't the only ones who are interested in what Masterson knows. The Iranians would have an even greater interest in shutting down leaks in their nuclear program and other state initiatives." He paused.

"Go on," Dernov prodded.

Oriov's contemplative nature was enhanced by his delivery method, always slow and piecemeal, causing his audiences to lean forward in their seats, as if to urge the completion of his thesis. "Don't you see? Why don't we turn this over to the IRGC and let them run with it? We can provide logistical support and guidance for the debriefing, get the information we need, and deny culpability in the act. It will also give us further protection in the event that, God forbid, something goes wrong in the pickup and Masterson is injured or killed, which would be really bad for us. What do you think?"

"Do you think the Revolutionary Guard can pull this off?" asked Dernov, referring to the IRGC, or Islamic Revolutionary Guard Core, the intelligence arm in Iran. "They probably don't have the assets or technologies in place to put all the necessary pieces together, do they? And, if we give them too much logistical support, our fingerprints will be all over it, don't you think? So, we will still have exposure."

The three of them thought about this for a minute.

Ivolgin finally acquiesced. "I have to admit, that's a good idea. I'm sure we can find a way to participate without implicating our-selves." Looking at his watch, he observed, "It's almost six o'clock. Kirill, why don't you see how your computer geeks are doing, and meet us back here at six fifteen? If we have made any progress, we'll put together a plan. In the meantime, I'll call our night desk in Tehran and have them start inquiries to test their appetite for an operation like this. If things fall into place for us, we can hit the ground running."

That concluded matters, and the three of them went their sepa-rate ways to offices in the building.

Dernov returned to the conference room to find the usual chaos when a group of computer nerds got together for a brainstorming research project. Coffee cups and notepad papers were scattered around the table. The youngest one, with all the acne, was wadding up pieces of paper and trying to loft them into the empty coffee cups, while the others were still tapping on their keyboards, squinting at the high-definition flat screens.

"What have you got for me?" he asked.

They all looked up and smiled. He took notes on all the information and rushed back to the meeting room where he had spent much of the last two hours with Ivolgin and Oriov. On a notepad, he sketched out how he would present the information. When the others arrived a few minutes later, he filled them in on his considerable progress.

"Here is what we have as of this minute. I think you will be pleased," he began.

The other two, seated across the table from him, leaned forward in their seats.

"Masterson retired almost three years ago, in June 2013. He reported directly to Langley where he got the usual career debrief. He and his wife left the Washington, D.C., area and moved to South Florida in retirement. Two years later, his wife died of cancer. We have no report on any activity until February of this year when his daughter applied to the Circuit Court in West Palm Beach for a guardianship for her father."

"What is this *guardianship?* I'm not familiar with it," Ivolgin interrupted.

"It's the smoking gun we've been suspecting was there," Oriov started to explain.

Ivolgin ignored him and turned to Dernov. "Continue," he said.

Dernov explained, "When an individual is no longer capable of making reasonable decisions, due to age or illness, a family member will usually come forward and become that person's legal representative."

"For how long?"

"For as long as is necessary, usually until the afflicted person dies."

"It makes no sense to me. We do that here. When people become old, their families take care of them until they die. Why do they need guardians?" Ivolgin continued to show his ignorance.

Dernov explained patiently, "It's the way their legal system works. Americans have more assets than typical Russians do. When someone can no longer make decisions for himself, the court appoints a representative who is authorized to sign documents, make medical decisions, etcetera. None of that is really important here. What *is* important is that Masterson needs a guardian, which means that his family determined he is not able to act on his own. So you see, he is compromised, probably has Alzheimer's disease or some type of dementia."

"I see now," Ivolgin murmured, feeling Dernov was talking to him like he was a jerk. He didn't like that. He missed the days when the people who worked for him treated him with respect. He was not so obtuse as to think he couldn't use the help of people who were more knowledgeable than he; he just didn't like his nose rubbed in it. He filed the emotion away for another time.

"But there's more," Dernov continued. "This is where it gets interesting. His daughter was not successful. The court records show her petition was denied. However, on the same day, the same judge entered a court-appointed guardianship for a guy named Lyle Ornstein."

"Who is this guy Ornstein?" Ivolgin asked.

"Funny you should ask. He works for the Federal Bureau of Investigation in the Miami office." Dernov let that sink in for a moment to give it effect. He could actually see the rate of cognition move across Ivolgin's expression.

Ivolgin realized that was significant, but he wasn't sure why. He sensed there was more coming, so he just nodded and waited for Dernov to continue, assuming additional detail would provide clarification. Dernov continued, "The U.S. Postal Service reflected a change of address for Masterson a week later, and since February eighteenth of this year his permanent address is twenty-six hundred North Federal Highway in Pompano Beach, Florida, at the Tropic Isle Senior Living Facility."

Things were falling into place for Ivolgin. "So it would appear that Masterson's condition, whatever it is, is of concern to his former employer, and they have taken steps to control access to him." It was a question.

"That's what we think," Dernov confirmed. "What we have learned next is not as solid, but it fits together pretty well." The others looked up from their scribbling with renewed interest. "The Silver Alert filed early last evening, U.S. time, is associated with an automobile, a 2016 Mercedes S550 sedan, the luxury model, silver in color."

Oriov finished the thought, "So Masterson can drive. His condition must not be too bad. My father-in-law had Alzheimer's, and he would get lost if he drove out of sight of his own house, if he could operate the car at all. Either way, it certainly expands the size of the haystack we have to find him in. Why is it that he has a car, anyway? Wouldn't they have taken it away?"

Dernov smiled. "I have two good answers for you. My nerds, as you refer to them, have researched the hell out of the disease. They have learned that it's progressive, hardly noticeable in the early stages. Most of those afflicted recognize they have symptoms early on, but denial causes them to cover up their mistakes of memory initially, probably due to the stigma attached to the disease. After a period of recognition and acceptance, if diagnosed, a person can go years living a somewhat normal life before they can no longer care for themselves. The symptoms just progress slowly until they are dealt with, so Masterson is probably in those early stages."

Ivolgin had a puzzled look on his face. "Why do you suppose the CIA would go to such lengths to get control of him? Putting him in a home is pretty extreme, don't you think? It doesn't sound too American to me."

Oriov thought for a moment and suggested, "Two reasons. First, he must really have valuable, relevant information, and the other should be obvious. We're thinking about taking him in, aren't we?"

Now Dernov was confused. "But if they had just left the guy alone to be with his family, we never would have shown any interest!"

"Point taken," Oriov noted.

Dernov continued his analysis. "In any event, regarding the size of the haystack you refer to, Danil, we don't think we need to find him; we think we know where he's going. We just have to be patient and wait for him to get there and hope the Iranians can intercept him first."

"You mean if the Americans don't pick him up in the meantime?" Oriov pointed out.

"Yes, that's a risk we have to take."

"Where do you think he's going?" Ivolgin thought ahead.

"The only place in the world he would want to go and have a chance to get there. He's trying to find his way home to his daughter. So the big question is, Kirill, can you set up some kind of surveillance operation for the Iranians so they can be the first on the scene to pick him up? Undoubtedly the Americans will also have figured this out, so we have to organize a snatch and grab, and get out of there quick."

Ivolgin thought about this for a moment. "Well, the Iranians are good at the physical stuff, and I assume nobody will be expecting them. We will have to help them with the technical stuff. I don't think they are capable of tapping phones and such on short notice."

"One last piece of information that may be helpful as background," Dernov added. "My analysts searched police records for the area around the time of Masterson's disappearance, and they came up with a Mercedes matching the description of the one he is suspected of driving being reported stolen from a parking lot across the street from his adult community."

"Is that significant? We know he got a car somewhere; do we care how?" Ivolgin asked.

"It is in conjunction with a police report later that night of the same make, model, and color vehicle involved in an altercation with a police officer a couple kilometers north of the theft. The police officer was beat up and hospitalized by what was described in the police report as a mature gentleman." Dernov just let that hang in the air for effect.

"No, shit," Ivolgin and Oriov said in unison.

"That puts a different slant on things, don't you think?" Oriov continued. "I think we should give our mark a little respect. You say, Kirill, that your computer analysts put this together off the Internet in just a few hours? I think we owe them a little respect, too."

"I'll pass that on; they will be gratified to hear it. Sergey, do you have what you need to take it from here?" Handing the operations chief a folder, he added, "You will find everything you need inside, including the daughter's address in Maryland and other particulars. I will let my guys go home with instructions that they stay in communication, in case you need any additional research or clarification."

Ivolgin took the proffered envelope and stood to begin his assignment. He sighed as he turned to the door, knowing he was going to have a long day ahead of him, as no one would be awake in the United States for another seven or eight hours. It was early Friday morning, and he didn't think he was going to have much of a weekend to look forward to, either.

CHAPTER SIX

Pepper and Masterson walked the few short blocks down Gervais from the restaurant to the Cornell Arms and took the elevator at the back of the lobby past the doorman's desk to the seventh floor. Pepper's apartment was a spacious two bedroom on the southeast corner with a great view of the capitol and its grounds a few blocks away. The capitol lighting highlighted the domed features of the official state assembly building, and its prominence drew attention to the magnificent view from the balcony that wrapped the corner of the apartment.

The apartment layout was inviting past a generous vestibule at the entrance, furnished in traditional colonial hardwoods and fabrics. The living room featured seating on large sofas in the middle, oriented in an "L" toward the captivating view of the seat of government directly in front of the apartment's view. Double-wide doorways off to the right led to the spacious master bedroom, taste-fully decorated in beige carpeting and drapes and shears, accented again with dark hardwoods. The guest bedroom was the other direction off the vestibule down a hallway that separated the island kitchen and casual dining area to the left.

Pepper took Masterson's offered jacket and hung it in the closet in the vestibule, put her sweater on the arm of the sofa, and crossed the living room to the sliding glass doors to the balcony and cracked them open a little to let in the fresh evening air tainted with the scent of magnolia.

Masterson noted that the apartment was very classy. "The airline business must be very good to you, Pepper," he observed.

"It is, and with my free time, I am able to supplement my income," she told him, not adding any explanation. "Can I get you something to drink? I have a similar Pinot Noir to the one we were drinking at dinner, if you like."

"No, thank you; I would just have a glass of ice water, if that's all right," he countered. "I have had a very long day, and I might end up spending the night in your apartment if I have any more wine."

Pepper gave him her best smile. "That would be all right, too, wouldn't it?" She saw the immediate look of confusion and concern fall over his face, as he tried to digest her invitation, deciding in the end that he just didn't get it right.

The thought of the alternative interpretation made Masterson feel uneasy, a feeling that came naturally to him just being in a strange apartment somewhere between Florida and Maryland.

Pepper prepared two ice waters and brought the remote phone over to the sofa and sat next to Masterson. She tried to make him feel more comfortable with her by reaching up and straightening his shirt collar with her fingertips. She smiled at him and held up the phone extension with her other hand and said, "Now, let's see if we can figure a way for you to get in touch with your daughter, so she knows you are coming." Not sure what she was trying to accomplish, deciding she was just trying to get her friend comfortable with her touching him, she patted his neck and withdrew her hand.

The two spent several minutes assessing the situation. Both agreed that the FBI and possibly others were actively looking for him, and that it would be best if they did not leave a trail behind that could lead the pursuers to them. Pepper had seen enough *Homeland* episodes to surmise that the government resources were formative when looking for people, particularly with today's Internet-speeded communication techniques. It didn't take much imagination for them to figure out that Karen Kenny was Masterson's only option in terms of a place to go; if they knew that, surely the government knew that.

"Stewart, I think we have to assume the government is monitoring all of your daughter's calls, both home and cell phone. So, if we just call her, I'm pretty sure they will trace the call back to me, and that's not good. I don't care if they come here; I won't tell them anything, but you need time to separate yourself from me before that happens. Is there anyone you can think of who we could call to have them relay a message to Karen?"

Masterson thought for a minute. Somehow this kind of strategic thinking was familiar to him. "The only person that comes to mind is my friend Bevy Martin from Tropic Isle. I know him the best, and I'm sure he's worried about me. We could kill two birds with one stone; he could tell my other friends that I'm all right."

"Stewart, I think that's what we're trying to avoid. We want as few people as possible to know your whereabouts or circumstances."

"Yes, of course," he said, remembering.

"We only get one chance at this; are you sure he won't tell anybody? I don't know how to be polite about this," she said aloud, fearing that this friend may have the same limitations as Stewart. "Your friend, Bevy, he's all right, isn't he?" This was awkward, and she put her hands on his upper arms and looked him squarely in the eyes, trying to show compassion, lest she be misinterpreted. "I mean, why is *he* at Tropic Isle?"

Masterson looked confused for a moment; then he caught on. He threw his head back and laughed. Placing his hands over hers and folding them together in front of him, he leaned over and kissed her fingertips in a friendly way to show he was not offended. Still laughing he said, "No, you don't have to worry. He's not like me, if that's what you were thinking. He's just there because he has no family and nowhere else to go."

Pepper joined him in a chuckle, relieved.

He continued, "Pepper, please do not worry that you will hurt my feelings if the subject of my Alzheimer's comes up. I am fully aware of it, and I am appreciative of your willingness to help me deal with my limitations. It's a disease of short-term memory loss and cognition, not stupidity."

That being said, the two set about figuring a way to contact Bevy Martin. Pepper opened her laptop on the coffee table in front of them and searched the Internet for Tropic Isle Assisted Living in Pompano Beach, Florida. Google rewarded her with an elaborate website of the facility. As Masterson looked over her shoulder, she took a moment to work through the pages on the website to get a feel for where Masterson had been living.

"Very impressive," she commented, as she perused the splendor of the loggias and apartment suites, fitness center, and multiple dining facilities. "It doesn't look like a prison to me," she added.

"It's not, until you realize that you aren't permitted past the front door. I never said I wasn't treated well. It just was not a place where I felt anyone really cared about me. I was totally alone; not free to make my own choices," Masterson answered.

Pepper let that comment slide for the moment and returned to the home page to look for a phone number, which was not easy, because the webpage was designed for interested parties to make an electronic contact with the facility, not to call and speak to an actual person. Finding none, she resorted to AT&T information and got a phone number.

Putting the laptop on the coffee table, she looked at Masterson with a serious expression on her face. "Are you ready?" she asked. He nodded. "We can't undo this after I make the call," she said as if to give him one more chance to change his mind. He nodded again, so she dialed the 954 area code and number.

"Tropic Isle," a male voice answered. "How may I direct your call?"

The staff had been trained not to ask who was calling, as management learned that some family members found this an offensive intrusion on their privacy and rights. The facility did a good job at making family members feel that this living arrangement was a normal progression in life for the residents.

"Mr. Bevin Martin, please," Pepper said.

Masterson couldn't remember his apartment number, just that it was on the second floor.

"I'll put you through" was the reply.

After three rings, Bevy picked up. "Hello," he answered, seemingly alert.

It was nearly ten o'clock, and Pepper feared it might be late for him. She held the phone at an angle to her ear, so that Masterson could lean in and hear both sides of the conversation.

Masterson became aware of Pepper's perfume, a subtle sweetness carried by the night breeze coming from the open sliders to the balcony. The scent transported him to a younger age, when he was more aware of such things, and he couldn't push the thought out of his mind that he was sitting very close to a beautiful woman in an exciting situation, a real adventure actually. Silly how this image would come to him now at his age, but he felt as nervous as a teenager. Leaning over from this angle was putting a strain on his back, and he fumbled with a place to put his hands to support himself and relieve the pressure, finding Pepper in the only places he could conveniently get support. He settled for an elbow on the back of the sofa, but it put him inside the circle of intimacy with her, as he listened to her begin her explanation to Bevy.

Sensing his closeness, Pepper smiled reassuringly at him, and shifted the phone to her other ear, so he could hear better. "Mr. Martin, I am a new friend of a gentleman you know from Tropic Isle, and I'm calling at his suggestion. Forgive me for the late hour, but he feels it is important that I reach out to you on his behalf."

"What's a new friend?" he responded curtly. "Just put Stewart on the phone. I want to talk to him. You don't have to worry; nobody's listening in on this call."

His response caught Pepper totally off guard. Not feeling like she had an alternative, she handed the phone to Stewart, who maintained his position so Pepper could hear, as well. Their closeness gave him the comfort and support he needed right now.

"Hi, Bev," he said.

"What's going on, buddy? You've got the whole world looking for you, and you're in a peck of trouble, I suspect. Tell me what's going on. Who's your new friend?" he demanded.

That was too many questions for Masterson to process, but he knew what he wanted his buddy to understand, so he kept it simple. "Bev, I'm absolutely fine. I'm just moving back to Maryland with Helen to be with our daughter and her family. I have been lucky enough to meet a lovely young lady who has agreed to help me sort out the process because we have some concerns. If you'll just listen to her, I think she can do a better job of explaining what's going on than I can. After you talk to her, you can ask me any other questions. The important thing is that I am fine. We just need your help to get word to Karen. Okay?"

As he handed the phone back to Pepper, they could hear Bevy shouting words to the effect of, "Things are not fine! You are in a lot of trouble!"

When he settled down, Pepper began calmly to explain that she had just met Stewart Masterson that evening, and in their conversation, she had learned a bit about his circumstances. She assured him she was only trying to help a kind, confused man.

"The FBI is looking for him!" Bevy snapped. "That doesn't sound *fine* to me."

"We are aware. Please, Mr. Martin, bear with me; let me tell you what I know, and you can share what you know, and from that we can put together a plan."

"Okay, you first." Bevy calmed down and listened patiently to what Pepper had to say.

Pepper recounted what she had learned from Masterson. She began by explaining how she had met him at his hotel cocktail lounge a few hours earlier, that the two of them had struck up a conversation where she had learned of his travel plans. She also explained that she knew about his Alzheimer's disease and had figured out the probability that he was being monitored by the FBI, that he had somehow procured an automobile and made his way north to where they were now.

"And just where is that, exactly?" Bevy interrupted.

Pepper paused, not wanting to answer the question.

Bevy chimed in again, "There is little likelihood that this call is being monitored, Ms. Madison. The FBI learned only this morning that Stewart is missing, and they only suspect he has a car. They didn't believe he has any resources to travel as of this afternoon, and it's only an hour ago that we learned there is a Silver Alert out for him. I think they believe he is still in South Florida. The agent who stopped by here seemed to have very little information, but he is really uptight about the fact that Stewart has gone missing. They haven't had time to get surveillance on our phones here, even if a judge would grant it. So I think we can talk freely."

Masterson nodded again to her, and Pepper told him, "Stewart is here with me in my home in Columbia, South Carolina."

Bevy was impressed; his friend had gotten himself over halfway home.

"I thought you said he was at a hotel." It was a question.

"We are nearby at my apartment trying to work out a plan for him to get in touch with his daughter, to let her know he is coming."

"I see."

"We have come to the same conclusion you have, that he is sought after by the FBI, and that they are trying to protect the government from his inadvertently divulging information he has from his years with the CIA where he was pretty highly placed."

Bevy was impressed again, this time that the woman, whoever she was, and his friend had figured all this out. He was encouraged that Stewart's abilities were not all that diminished.

"How is he paying for all of this? The FBI thinks he doesn't have any money. They suspect that he may be getting some assistance from someone here at Tropic Isle, although I can assure you no one here has any idea what's going on. He seems to have just taken advantage of an opportunity."

Pepper explained what she knew: "We haven't gone into that yet. All I can tell you is that he has a thick wad of hundred dollar bills in his pocket, and he flashes them around. I noticed it right off. It's concerning because of the attention it draws."

I'll bet you did, Bevy thought to himself cynically, the picture clearing up a little in his mind. "So, what is your plan, and how does it involve me?"

Pepper explained that they were concerned that the FBI had already figured out Masterson's destination, and they had undoubtedly put Karen under surveillance. That would mean that Masterson could not just show up on her doorstep. Karen would have to prepare for her dad's arrival if this was going to work out. "We have to assume her calls are being intercepted, so we can't call her directly."

"I see. So, you want me to call her for you; is that it?" Bevy finished for her.

"Exactly."

"And what do you want me to tell her, exactly?" Bevy requested.

Pepper asked Bevy to let Karen know of her father's plans. She suggested he ask Karen to get some legal help to see what her rights might be in Maryland if her father came to her, so that she could be prepared in advance of his arrival. She also asked Bevy to call her back and let her know how the conversation went, so she could advise Masterson on any change of plans that might be necessary. She asked him if he needed the phone number for Karen, and he advised her that he had spoken with her earlier in the day and had already been given her contact information.

For his part, Bevy Martin said he would be happy to act as an intermediary, and that he would call back and fill them in on his conversation with Karen. They also mutually agreed that if either were contacted by authorities, they would admit to the calls and decline offering any information about them. "Only a judge" can make you divulge your personal conversations, Bevy advised, but to deny they had had contact could be obstruction of justice, and that was a felony. Bevy said goodbye to his friend and ended the call to begin his assignment.

"Now, how about that glass of wine?" Pepper offered.

"It's late; maybe I should think about getting back to the hotel," Masterson countered.

"Nonsense, Stewart. You're not going anywhere," Pepper said as she moved off the sofa in the direction of the kitchen to fetch the bottle of Pinot. She returned with two glasses and a corkscrew, which she handed to Masterson with the bottle, indicating he should open it. "We have a lot of work to do to get ready for tomorrow, and don't forget, Bevy is going to call us back here to tell us about his conversation with Karen, and you don't want to miss that, do you?"

She sat next to him on the sofa and watched as he deftly opened the wine bottle and poured two glasses based on years of familiarity with the process. She was impressed. "You've done that before," she complimented. "Why don't you take your shoes off and get comfortable?"

Pepper unstrapped her sandals and folded her legs beneath her on the sofa. She had already decided to try to seduce him, if he was willing, so she was really piling on the charm and smiles.

For his part, Masterson was a mixed bag of emotions. On the one hand, the idea of a sexual encounter had not been on his radar for years, but as the air continued to waft her perfumed scent his way, and the incandescent lighting in the apartment set a certain glow to his mood, he couldn't help but notice Pepper's moments of casual touching and visual invitations. He had absolutely no idea how he would go about advancing his interest, but at the same time, he did not feel it would be unwelcome. He was so wrapped up in the moment that a thought of Helen did not even enter his mind.

They sat in silence for a while, Masterson facing forward, but looking over his right shoulder at Pepper's smiling face, Pepper sitting in a relaxed, lounging fashion with her legs tucked up under her right side, leaning a bit left toward Masterson's shoulder. A moment passed between them, as they toyed with their wine glasses. The phone rang.

"It's Bevy," Pepper guessed as she picked up the remote receiver and answered. She nodded confirmation to Masterson of her assumption when she heard his voice. Again putting the phone jointly to their ears so both could hear, they learned from him about his conversation with Karen.

"Okay, I just talked to Karen at her home, and I assured her that her dad is fine. I didn't give any specifics about where he was or divulge anything that we don't think the FBI doesn't already know. I just gave her the general picture that she should go somewhere safe in the morning and call me, so that I could give her some particulars.

We agreed on a time. So I suggest you tell Stewart to get a good night's rest to prepare for his drive to Maryland. Do you understand?"

"Yes," Pepper replied. Frankly, she was a little disappointed in the lack of substance in the information Bevy had to report, and she told him so.

Bevy was patient with her, sensing that maybe she really did have his friend's best interest at heart; she was certainly putting herself at risk getting involved at this point, knowing about Masterson's background and all. "Pepper, listen to me. We have to think through very carefully what we are doing or we are going to have some unwanted consequences."

"What do you mean?" she asked.

"First of all, I told Karen everything she really needs to know right now. And that is that her dad is fine, and he is trying to get home to her. Anything else I might elaborate can only give those who are looking for him more information to work with. Remember, our government may not be the only one trying to find him. You remember why he ended up at Tropic Isle to begin with?" It was rhetorical. "So, I didn't need or want to go into any unnecessary detail. We can deal with that tomorrow when pursuers have less time to react."

"That makes sense." This adventure was suddenly taking on a new perspective for Pepper, but the element of risk only made the emotions run higher. For the first time in a long while, she felt like she was putting another person's needs ahead of her own, and she liked the way it made her feel. "Are we in any danger?" she asked.

"I don't think danger is the right word. But consider this. Although I don't think my calls are being monitored right this minute, I have left a trail of contacts in the telephone system here at the center. By late morning tomorrow, if the FBI is on the ball at all, they will know I have talked to both you and Karen within a few minutes of each other, and I am sure they will connect the dots. I expect to hear from them, and you may as well. That's why we have to get Stewart on his way as soon as possible. He would be a sitting duck around your place. After tomorrow morning, our communications link will have to be shut down, or it will compromise Stewart's chances of getting home to his daughter. When I talk to her in the morning, I am going to suggest that she get an attorney on standby to help her navigate the legal difficulties and to keep herself out of trouble for obstruction of justice. I suggest you take Stewart out in the morning and get him a prepaid phone, you know, what they call a burner phone. Make sure it's not a smartphone, or the government can interfere with it and trace Stewart's whereabouts. He can use it to call Karen when he is getting close, so they can work out a rendezvous someplace nobody else can identify."

"That's a great idea!" Pepper proclaimed.

"That way Stewart can be in communication if he needs to be, but those older phones can't be diddled with by hackers. If he and Karen are careful, they can hook up under the radar until the cavalry arrives," Bevy said.

"Who's the cavalry?" Pepper asked.

"Well, I hope it's our legal system, ultimately," Bevy guessed. "You know, this story would have a great deal of public interest, if it got out, don't you agree? That may be Stewart's ultimate solution, but it will take time to get the story out. Let's worry about that later. For now, get Stewart to bed so he can rest. He's going to have a tough day tomorrow."

That is precisely what Pepper had in mind, although she suspected she and Bevy were not on the same page regarding his request.

"Let me say goodbye to him before you hang up," he added.

Pepper handed the phone to Masterson, who had been listening in next to her ear but not grasping fully what had been said.

"Hi, Bev," he greeted. "Sounds like you and Pepper have worked out a plan. Tell me, please, exactly what I need to know."

"We think things are under control for the moment, buddy. What you need to know is that Karen knows you are coming, and she is going to do her best to get things ready for you. Your friend is going to get you a cell phone to use tomorrow. She will explain how and when you are to use it, so listen carefully to what she has to say. She seems pretty sharp; someday I'd like to hear the story of how you two got connected, but it will have to wait for another time."

Masterson nodded his agreement. "I think you will like her. She has been a great help, and I feel very comfortable with her. I trust her," he added, looking in Pepper's direction and smiling. She smiled back.

"Let me talk to her one last time, buddy."

Masterson handed the phone back to Pepper.

Bevy said, "I have one last word of advice for you."

"What's that, Mr. Martin?" she asked.

"You and I are in this up to our necks, so I think we should be in sync with what we are going to say when the Feds pay us a visit."

"Mmmmm."

"I would suggest you answer all their questions truthfully and honestly when it comes to your meeting with Stewart or the fact that we have shared some phone calls. You haven't broken any laws that I can think of. You are just trying to help a confused senior citizen get in touch with his daughter and find his way home. I am going to take the same position. Officially, we don't know that he is a suspect in a car theft, or sought after by the FBI, or anyone else for that matter. As I see it, we don't have any requirement to disclose the content of our personal conversations until a judge tells us to, and that won't happen until long after this has all been resolved. I think the only way we can get ourselves in trouble is the broad claim of *obstruction of justice*. So, don't tell any lies. I won't either, and I think we will be good. Are you okay with that?"

"That sounds good to me, and thanks for all your help," she

agreed. Pepper hit the off button and set the handset on the coffee table. Turning to Masterson, she said, "What do you think?"

"I'm not clear what I'm supposed to use the cell phone for; you're going to have to explain that to me."

Pepper put her wine glass on the coffee table and swiveled on the sofa to face him. She said softly, "We don't have to worry about that right now. It's something we will take care of in the morning."

Pepper was overcome with emotion as she looked at this handsome older gentleman. Just a few hours ago she had considered him a possible mark but now considered him a friend who had stood up for her in an embarrassing public situation. He was old enough to be her father, but at the same time, she perceived him as rather studly. Overriding all of these feelings was her need to nurture him and keep him safe. He was simply the most genuine, kindest man she had ever met, who, in spite of his diminished capacity, had an outrageous sense of humor. *Does this mean you're not trying to pick me up?* she recalled from their earlier conversation at the bar. He cracked her up, and to Pepper, funny was the sexiest quality a man could possibly have. She melted for him.

Masterson took a sip of his wine, and as he moved the glass from his lips, Pepper leaned over to him and took the glass gently out of his hand and set it on the coffee table. Masterson sensed something was coming but felt totally unprepared. As he sat comfortably on the left third of the sofa, with his back slouched somewhat against the back cushions, Pepper raised herself up on her left knee and rotated to face him. She brought her right leg over his body, so that she sat astride him, causing his adrenaline to start flowing. Masterson was on full alert now, as Pepper squatted lightly on her haunches and leaned forward, placing her hands on either side of his face, cradling it ever so softly in her hands. Masterson could see her white linen shift rise slowly up her thighs, exposing the tops of her tan, muscular legs. As she leaned in to kiss him, he could smell the faint scent of her perfume, mixed with the fragrance of the magnolia wafting in from the balcony. She gently placed her lips over his upper lip and compressed it erotically. Her movements were slow and nonthreatening.

Masterson sat frozen in his position, totally out of his element, unsure of the appropriate response. After a few seconds, he squeezed her lower lip back, but then stiffened ever so slightly. Pepper immediately sensed she had overstepped a boundary and broke off the kiss. Leaning back, placing more weight on Masterson's legs but still cupping his face in her hands, she frowned and said, "Stewart, I'm so sorry. Please forgive me if I have made you feel uncomfortable. I should not have done that; it was very forward of me."

Uncomfortable was not exactly the emotion Masterson would have used to describe how he felt. Confused a little, maybe, or some residual guilt, thinking the only woman he had kissed erotically in almost fifty years was his beloved Helen. He really liked this woman, and he felt completely comfortable with her, but the feelings had not crossed the line to attraction. Although he recognized that Pepper was a beautiful woman, while young enough to be his daughter, she still fit into an obscure image of a woman he could have a sexual interest in, if the concept could ever even enter his mind. If he were going to fantasize about a female, she certainly wouldn't be a high school cheerleader. So while Pepper's aggressive move had been completely off his radar, it did channel his thinking down a road that had been barricaded for many, many years. Now it was open.

Pepper sensed him relax, as he looked up at her sitting on his lap, so she didn't move from her position. The two just looked at each other, digesting the nature of the change in their relationship. After a moment, it became awkward, and Pepper reached behind her for their wineglasses. Handing one to Masterson, she rotated hers by the stem, using it mainly as a prop, while she sorted out what should come next.

Masterson took a huge gulp of his and handed it back to her to replace on the coffee table, which she did reaching behind her without looking and missed the edge by a millimeter. The glass tumbled to the area rug below and spilled the small content Masterson had not consumed. Pepper jumped up. "Oh shit!" she exclaimed and bolted for the kitchen to get a wet towel before the red wine could set in. For his part, Masterson moved aside on the sofa to allow her room to kneel down between the sofa and the heavy glass top of the coffee table and wipe up the mess.

Masterson apologized for his complicity. "Here let me help you." He leaned over and grabbed a corner of the towel and made motions to assist.

Pepper smiled up at him. "Not necessary; it's completely my fault." She made fast work of the little spill and put the towel under cold running water in the sink. She returned to the sofa and sat next to Masterson, taking his hand in hers. The moment had been lost, but doors had been opened, and she just wanted to fold this man in her arms and hold him close to her. She looked earnestly at him and asked, "When was the last time you had sex?"

"I can't remember," Masterson replied, taking her question seriously.

Pepper took his answer for a metaphor, and responded, "It's been that long, huh?"

Masterson looked at her blankly and said, "No, you don't understand; I literally can't remember. I mean, I remember times I've had sex, I just can't remember when the last time was."

Pepper felt an uncontrollable explosion well up from her gut. She laughed uncontrollably to Masterson's bewilderment. She melted completely, and throwing her arms around his neck, convulsed with laughter, holding him close to her. Her laughter was infectious, and after a moment, he began to laugh too, and he put his arms around her shoulders, hugging her back.

After a moment, when their laughter quelled, they moved their lips together and kissed, ever so gently at first, and then with more ardor, as passions within Masterson that he had not felt in a long, long time began to surface. After a bit of nervous kissing and fumbling, Pepper stood, taking Masterson's hand, and led him quietly to the bedroom.

Amir Resaei parked his maroon Dodge Caravan on Tunlaw Road NW, a block down the street backing up to the Embassy of the Russian Federation in Washington, D.C. It was two o'clock in the morning when he got the call from his cell leader, who based his operations in the Georgetown Islamic Center in the heart of Southwest Washington, asking him to report to the Russian embassy to meet with a member of the embassy security staff for instructions about an upcoming covert operation. His controller, whom he knew only as Arshad, briefed him in person at the mosque. His mission was to receive some technical equipment from the embassy to be used for eavesdropping on a local resident, for the purpose of kidnapping a former high-level CIA agent and moving him to a safe house in Virginia for debriefing. There was no traffic to speak of, so Amir took precautions scouring the area for anything out of place, knowing that his presence alone was an unusual event at this time of the night.

He had met with Arshad for over an hour to receive very detailed instructions of how he was to go about his mission. Amir knew it must be important, an assignment from the highest level for his cell, which consisted of four—two Iranians who had both entered the country legally and two American converts to Islam. They would not have been put at risk of exposure for anything less. He knew that missions with high profiles often resulted in disclosure to U.S. authorities of the covert network; consequently, he would not have been called to action unless his assignment was of extreme importance to his nation's jihad.

After checking his mirrors for evidence of patrol traffic, he made his way to the back entrance of the embassy. The massive white building had prominent stacks of vertical windows, which rose to the ninth floor parapet surrounding the structure. It was surrounded by a high wrought iron fence interrupted in the rear by a small guardhouse for screening unofficial visitors. Two uniformed security guards were stationed inside. Amir's arrival brought them to their feet, suddenly invigorated by a visitor, which was unusual for this time of night, but not unheard of.

One of the guards checked his daily sheet and saw that someone was expected at this hour. Looking around nervously, Amir announced his arrival with his name, and out of habit, looking at his shoes, he requested to see Denis Pavlenko. He was expected.

The tired security guard phoned somewhere in the interior of the big building, and he was advised that a member of the embassy staff would be out shortly to escort Mr. Resaei to the building for his meeting. Once cleared for entry, the guards softened somewhat, and returned their attention to their cell phones and social media accounts while Amir waited nervously on the vacant seat in the guardhouse. While he waited, he mulled over in his mind the glory that might be attendant to his mission. He couldn't wait to see what the "high tech" surveillance equipment they were going to entrust him with might be.

After a short wait, Pavlenko himself came to collect his guest. They walked up the rear pathway to an outside stairwell that accessed the embassy's basement. Pavlenko entered a passcode on the keypad adjacent to the door, and he and Amir entered a long, dimly lit hallway toward the center of the building to a secure conference area deep under the quiet facilities above them. Amir could see offices around the perimeter of the secure area, which were generally unoccupied at this hour, and he noted this aloud to his guide. He was acknowledged with a finger to Pavlenko's lips and *ssshhh*, followed by a stern voice that said, "Don't talk until we are inside the conference room and the anti-eavesdropping system is turned on."

They entered the room, and Pavlenko closed the door behind them. He turned on the lights and activated the white noise security system mounted on the wall next to the light switch.

Amir found himself in a sparse room with concrete walls, little furniture other than a plain table and six chairs, with no wall coverings and no consideration given to warmth or decoration. On the back wall was a single framed color photo portrait of Vladimir Putin, positioned obliquely with his arms folded across his chest as though he were observing the goings on. On the table was a rectangular wooden box about a foot and a half long with slatted wooden sides and a removable wooden top, about ten inches high. Amir thought he heard cooing sounds coming from the box. Next to the box was a small suitcase lying on its side. Pavlenko turned to face Amir and gestured toward the box.

"...the fuck is that?" Amir asked in an exasperated tone, pointing at the wooden box.

"This is your monitoring device," Pavlenko answered with a most serious look on his face.

"I thought I was coming here to learn how to operate a sophisticated listening device, the latest and the greatest. You show me a wooden box with a . . . what is that, a pigeon?" Amir said, leaning over to inspect the box more closely. The pigeon chose that moment to let out a distinctive, twilling *coooo*. Amir jumped back.

Pavlenko looked at Amir intently. "Sometimes things are not what they appear."

"What are you talking about? How is a pigeon going to help us?" Amir asked indignantly.

Pavlenko turned slowly to the table and opened up the suitcase, revealing a laptop screen and some techy-looking apparatus, head-phones, and devices that looked like flashlights. A collapsed tripod was fitted into the Styrofoam molding of the case, recessed for each of the pieces of equipment, so that everything could be transported safely and quietly.

"That's more like it," said a smiling Amir. "What's the bird have to do with it?"

"That's the most important part." Pavlenko smiled. He went on to explain in great detail how the pigeon and the fancy electronic equipment worked together. The equipment could sense vibrations from inside a dwelling via a laser properly targeted to a viable portal, such as a window. The equipment needed some calibration, which was handled internally, to separate ambient noise from the spoken word and amplify it for the operator to monitor through the head-phones. The equipment had portable rechargeable batteries and had to be operated from concealment within three hundred yards of a line of sight from the portal.

"You align the laser and focus the beam on an especially designed contact from the tripod fixed for stability, allow the machine to calibrate itself after it hears some audible human voices, and listen in on the headphones. The hardware also records what it hears for up to twenty-four hours, longer if there are periods of quiet, so it can be left unattended for periods of time to avoid detection and played back later," Pavlenko explained. "I understand that you will be monitoring your target from outdoors, as opposed to from another building, so you might want to think of using some sort of camouflage cover. The equipment, if kept in its traveling container, is relatively impervious to weather, so you can leave it unattended outdoors, regardless of the conditions, just returning periodically to download what has been recorded on one of the thumb drives provided in the case. Keep one of them in the USB port at all times, or you risk losing the information."

"And how does the pigeon fit in?" asked an intrigued Amir.

Pavlenko explained that the portal, most likely to be a window in the most active area of the residence to be monitored, needs a cue for focusing the laser and adjusting its bandwidth. The cue has to have the right absorption dampening for sound waves to enhance the effectiveness of the system. "We have developed a sort of adhesive patch," he said reaching in the suitcase for an envelope containing several three-inch square pieces of hard material, which looked much like a strip of wide duct tape, and fanned them out for Amir to see, "Like these, which can be placed on the selected windowpane for this purpose." The patches had an adhesive surface, protected by a removable paper strip.

"And the pigeon?" Amir was becoming impatient.

Pavlenko sighed. He so liked drawing out the suspense in his presentation, and the thought that he was getting his guest's goat gave him great satisfaction. "The pigeon, my terrorist friend, is so that you don't get yourself observed putting the wave enhancer in place!" Pavlenko carefully removed the cooing pigeon from the wooden cage and demonstrated how to attach the leg clamp to the bird's right leg and affix the enhancer patch to the leg clamp. "When the room is unoccupied, you light up the windowpane you select with the laser and release the pigeon. He, or she, I don't know which it is, will fly to the window and slap the patch on the window targeted by the laser and return to its cage. The bird is well trained, and its work is infallible." He put the bird back in its temporary coop and, smiling at Amir, said, "I suggest you try to set the bird up a couple of times with me just to make sure you are comfortable with the process before you leave here."

Amir, not really comfortable handling what looked like a delicate bird, nervously removed the pigeon from its box and practiced attaching the leg clamp and patch. Pavlenko showed him how to hold the bird firmly around its shoulders with one hand, while he attached the patch to the metal leg clamp above the spur on the pigeon's right foot with the other. When he was satisfied that he could handle what was required of him, Pavlenko instructed Amir on the use of the electronic equipment, working with him until he was satisfied that the young Iranian was capable of pulling off the operation. "How many do you have in your team?" he asked.

"We are four, all trained together and have been waiting for our call to serve for over a year," he bragged.

"Remember, Amir, none of this equipment can be traced to Mother Russia, even the pigeon. Do not allow yourselves to be taken into custody. We will not avow any connection to you, although we expect to be invited to any interrogation that may ensue as a result of your efforts. There is nothing else I can do for you tonight. Be careful when you leave. Our representative will reclaim our equipment after you have taken your target into custody. I believe you have been briefed on where the interrogation will take place."

"Yes, Mr. Pavlenko," Amir said respectfully, sensing a heightened level of importance to his mission.

Denis Pavlenko showed Amir back out of the basement of the embassy and down the path to the guardhouse where he had entered. Amir turned his head down furtively and nodded at the guards as he left the compound, suitcase in one hand, pigeon cage in the other. Seeing no one in the vicinity, he angled down the street to his van where it was parked between streetlights somewhat concealed in the shadows. He put his newly acquired gear in the back and slid in the driver's seat, making his way back to the mosque to assemble his team for the assignment. There were only about two hours of darkness remaining to cover his activities at the Whittington Drive address he had been assigned to monitor, so Amir drove back to Georgetown as fast as he felt he could without attracting attention.

Just before sunrise, Amir and three of his colleagues drove slowly down Whittington Drive, located in an older quiet subdivision in Silver Spring. The morning sky was just beginning to lighten the high overcast of the chilly spring day. He looked at his watch, nervous about the lateness of the hour, thinking that the advantage of darkness to provide obscurity was being lost to the dawn. He mentioned his concern to Hassan sitting next to him in the front passenger seat.

"It may be to our advantage, Amir," Hassan countered. "Cars driving around a dark neighborhood in the middle of the night would raise more concern."

Amir nodded his acknowledgment, as he scanned the addresses on the mailboxes along the curb. "That's the place," he announced with excitement as he spotted 694 on the mailbox of a modest, ranch-style home set well back from the street. There were no lights on in the house, a fortunate sign. He continued driving down the street to look for an inconspicuous place to turn around and park.

There were other homes in the neighborhood, not too closely spaced, some with one or two lights glowing from the interiors, but the area did not look as though it had come to life yet this Friday morning. He continued for another block and a half, not finding a suitable site to park. The street ended at a cul-de-sac, which bordered an undeveloped woodsy area. Amir circled the turnaround and parked facing back up the street and motioned for Hassan and the other two to follow him to scout the area.

He was fortunate that the trees defined the perimeter of a deep ravine, seemingly dry but thick with underbrush, which ran back to parallel the side of the street where the Kenny house was located. He motioned quietly to the others to follow him down the ravine. Hassan returned to the car to pick up the suitcase and the pigeon box, which he passed off to the two converts in the group, and the four made their way through the dry growth under their feet, the street no longer visible from the hillside they traversed. It was hard to be very quiet because dried branches snapped under their feet as they moved along the bed of the ravine in the direction of their target.

"This is going to be perfect for us," Amir whispered to the others. "Now I see why there are no other houses behind the lady's house. On Google Earth it just looked like a dark green spot. The image wasn't too clear in close-up, but now it all makes sense. We should be able to find a good place to set up our equipment without being observed."

Hassan moved alongside Amir, both struggling in the inconsistent underbrush and footing, which was becoming difficult to manage as the soil softened in places where the ravine still carried some residual water from recent rainfall.

"Shit, fuck!" erupted from behind them.

They turned to see Karim Hashemi—whose real name was Deshawn Moseley, born and raised in the southeast section of the D.C. area—struggle to maintain his balance with the suitcase after he stepped in a soft part of the ravine, his left leg sinking in the muck up to his calf. Teetering precariously with the suitcase high over his head, he put his weight on his right leg to gain leverage to pull his left leg out. After a brief tussle, his socked foot came free, absent his left shoe, followed by a few more colorful expletives.

Just as Karim lost his balance from the effort to remove his foot from the suction of the soft mud, Hassan caught him under the arms and prevented the delicate equipment from crashing to the ground. The two did a graceful pirouette and landed sitting upright in the leaves covering the soft ground, Karim cradling the suitcase in his arms, looking up with a terrified expression at Amir, who had a disgusted look on his face.

"Get your shit together, Karim," he whispered so as not to attract attention. "You're making more noise than a herd of cows."

Karim put his arm in the muck to pull out his shoe, muttering under his breath as he put the wet, muddy sneaker back on his foot and did his best to tighten the slimy laces with his gummed-up fingers. Amir told Hassan to keep an eye on the American pig in Farsi. Karim overheard the comment but didn't know what it was about because he didn't speak the language, something he was sensitive about. "Come on, you guys. We were told to speak English. I can't help if I don't know what you are saying," he whined.

"You don't need to know. Just be quiet so we don't wake up the whole neighborhood," Amir retorted, as he began his cautious movement down the gully toward Karen Kenny's house, still a few hundred yards ahead.

Karim sulked a moment. He never felt that he was completely acceptable to his new comrades as one of them, even though he felt he was part of a just cause. In fact, his senses were right on. He had been allowed in the cell primarily for his muscle.

Mosely, as he was known in high school where he was a star running back on the varsity football team, had been adrift since those days, when he was a critical part of an organized group. Since he had finished high school, he had lived aimlessly searching for something to belong to. It had finally come in the form of Islam. One of his former teammates had turned his own athletic ability into a collegiate scholarship before hearing the call to the true faith and devoted himself to Allah. He had recognized Moseley's need for identity and invited him into his new community. Mosely felt he had found something to give him a sense of being part of something bigger, as had his football program before, and he joined willingly, even applying himself to learning the teachings of the Quran.

The mullah of the Georgetown Islamic Center where Moseley attended prayer services recognized his vulnerable tendencies and put him in touch with Arshad Gul, a member with known ties to Iran's Revolutionary Guard Corps, as a candidate for recruitment. Arshad found a willing recruit in Moseley and made use of him for occasional tasks that required some heavy lifting. For his part, Moseley did not think of himself as a jihadist, but he did identify with the superficial respect he was given in his new assignments, such as the one he was on now. He was only aware that he and the others, which included one other locally recruited character from the inner city, were to assist as instructed to locate and kidnap the father of the woman whose house they had come to monitor.

The four-man Iranian team continued their way down the ravine, appearing comical in their efforts to be as quiet as possible, which only made the snapping twigs beneath their feet seem even louder in the stillness of the morning. After another ten minutes, they spotted the Kenny residence at the top of the hill on the left, which defined the perimeter of the gully. Amir, in the lead, turned around to face the others and held his index finger to his lips, shushing quietly. He whispered, "We have to be really quiet now while we go up the hill. We will have some protection from the bushes and trees, but a group of four of us will not be missed if someone is looking. So, stay low and quiet. When I get into position, Hassan you bring me the case, and I'll set up the equipment. You other two stay below the hilltop so you cannot be seen. Hassan, stay near so you can hand me what I need, so I don't have to move around too much."

Hassan nodded his understanding.

Amir crested the hill and crouched low as he moved forward, toward the side of the house. He found a perfect place of concealment between two trees surrounding a thick planting of leafy bushes. As he took out his binoculars to survey the house, he could hear the pigeon cooing softly from its slatted box, which was now held by Hassan at the ready. Amir stepped into the bushes and focused on the side of the house. No lights were on inside yet. The sky was brightening more and more each minute, as he looked east at the house.

There was no garage, but a driveway and carport ended at what appeared to be the back door. A green Camry was parked half under the carport, unable to pull all the way in because yard equipment and a barbeque grill blocked the end of the driveway pavement. Next to the back door was a large window followed by some space and then more windows. Amir guessed correctly that this was the kitchen, naturally located immediately inside the back door, adjacent to what must be some kind of breakfast nook and family room. He decided that most of the communication inside the house would take place in the kitchen or family room, so he had selected one of these as his target for placement of the sound-enhancing strip. He decided the middle window would capture most of the communication inside the house, hoping it could pick up both kitchen and family room conversations.

He motioned for Hassan to hand him the tripod to begin his setup. They had not rehearsed this beforehand, so he had to illustrate his request with charade-like gestures to indicate what he wanted. He pointed his hand downward with three fingers extended to indicate a tripod, but unfortunately from his elevated position, it just looked to Hassan like he was being given the finger.

"Just fucking tell me what you want!" Hassan whispered loudly in frustration.

"The tripod, you idiot! Now be quiet!" Amir held up the three fingers so Hassan could see them more clearly, but it was not necessary; Hassan already had the case open and pulled out the collapsed photographic-style tripod, leaning up the hill to hand it to Amir in his outstretched arm. Then he moved closer to the top of the hill, so he would be in a better position to pass on the remaining components of the rig.

Amir grabbed it by the articulating gooseneck and extended the legs to his best estimate of a good height to focus the laser on the window. He mounted the flashlight-shaped laser on the top of the tripod and adjusted the legs again to allow for the slope of the top of the hill he was on. Satisfied he was close to a good setup, he wiggled the setup in the ground to make sure it had a stable purchase in the dirt. After hooking up one of the USB cables to the laser and the computer, still in its case, he sighted down the scope mounted to the laser until he could locate the small mark of the beam where it showed itself on the side of the house, about three feet to the right of the back door under the gutter on the roof. He estimated his distance to be nearly one hundred yards, well beyond where a casual observer in the area would be looking for any activity.

Amir thought things were going pretty well, as he adjusted the thumbscrews on the gooseneck to bring the laser dot up to the corner of the window he had selected as his target. He was about to signal Hassan to hand up the pigeon box when the lights went on in the kitchen, and his heart skipped a beat. "Shit," he muttered under his breath, "I knew this was going too good." He looked at his watch, noting that it was after six, and the sky was getting very bright in the direction of the house. He saw a woman move past the window to the other side of the room.

Amir knew the laser would give off a refracted glow from the glass window, and as dim as it was, it might be noticed by someone inside the house. He also knew that it would be undetectable after the enhancing patch was installed. He also knew he had to risk it, or he would be in a lot of trouble. He now wished he had started earlier, but that was not an option. He turned off the laser for the time being and rocked back on his haunches to think for a moment.

His best option was to turn on the laser for just long enough to orient the beam and then shut it off while he got the pigeon ready, then turn it on for just the few seconds needed to get the patch in place and recover the bird. He saw the woman leave the kitchen. *Now or never,* he thought. He motioned for Hassan to bring him the bird while he sighted the laser on the lower right side of the window and turned it off. Hassan moved next to him and knelt next to the tripod, handing the box to Amir, who undid the latch on the lid, lifting the bird softly from its cage and affixing the patch to its right leg as he had practiced earlier. Using two hands, he gently tossed the bird skyward and switched on the laser.

The pigeon took flight, enjoying its temporary freedom and made three circles from a height of about thirty feet, searching its target, finding it on the windowpane Amir had identified. It made one more circle and moved to its target as it had been trained. At that moment, Hassan repositioned himself to get a better look at what was going on and leaned on the rear strut of the tripod, moving it forward and to the left. The pigeon performed perfectly and, in the blink of an eye, slapped the patch on the right front fender of the Camry in the driveway, where it stuck as designed.

"What the fuck?!" Amir scrambled to look through the viewfinder and realized what had happened. "You dumb ass moron," he said aloud to Hassan, who had no idea what he had done.

"Isn't that what's supposed to happen?" Hassan looked up at an enraged Amir.

"I'll deal with you later, you imbecile! Thank Allah we have spares, or I'd shoot you myself right here."

Hassan was clueless, but Karim had seen the whole event unfold from below and couldn't keep himself from laughing, burying his head in his folded arms to keep any sound from escaping. He shook convulsively for a moment, which only earned him penetrating stares from Hassan and Amir. When he had collected himself, Amir returned to the task at hand. Fortunately the pigeon performed as trained and was cooing from his cage still in Amir's hands with its top open. He handed it to Hassan to be returned in a minute for the next attempt.

The woman had returned to the kitchen and seemed to be doing some chore at the window, probably dishes at the sink, Amir assumed. *Good for us,* he thought. She is focusing on something and less likely to notice the laser point. He carefully remounted the tripod on its legs, taking extra precaution to insure the legs would not move, and realigned the laser on its proper target. Satisfied everything was in order, he removed the pigeon and selected one of the several spare patches from the case and attached it to the bird's leg, as before. This time, after warning Hassan to be absolutely still, he risked one more scope of the target before releasing the pigeon. Again, the bird made three circles at thirty feet to orient itself on the laser beam, and off it flew to its target, successfully slapping the patch on the window selected.

Through the binoculars, Amir could see the faint spot of the green laser on the center of the patch, and it was then that he noticed the short window curtains on that window had been drawn, making the patch virtually undetectable from the inside, and far enough away from the carport to not be noticed on the outside. It only took moments for Amir to hook up the other USB wires to complete the network. He opened the case and booted up the computer, activating the software icon on the screen. He watched as it went through its orientation sequencing, the imagery depicted making no sense to him until the ready prompt lit up. He hit enter and put on the headphones to listen in for a sign that things were working properly. At first there was just some background noise, but as he listened more carefully, he could tell he was hearing the sound of dishes being rinsed and the clanging as they were put in the dishwasher. Through his binoculars, he could see the woman standing in front of the window, her attention directed on the task at hand. After a moment, she finished her chore and turned around, looking back into the house. He heard her call loudly, "Tim, Bart! You guys get a move on. It's Friday and you have the whole weekend to fiddle with those video games!"

"Yeah, Mom," came a resigned, muffled reply from the interior of the house.

The volumes adjusted as Amir listened, the machine automatically modulating itself for the volume of the conversation it was picking up. *I'm really impressed,* he thought. Cleanup only took a moment, as he put the large capacity thumb drive in the USB port on the side of the computer, and closed everything back up. He spread a light camouflaged canvas over the case and the base of the tripod to aid in its concealment. It was unlikely that anyone would venture casually out in this direction, anyway.

The quartet did their best to make a quiet retreat down the ravine and back to the van, still parked in the cul-de-sac where they had left it. Now all Amir had to do was set up a monitoring schedule to swap the thumb drives every few hours and review what was on them. He wouldn't need the whole crew for that, wondering even now why he brought all three along this time. Because he was told to assemble his group for the intervention, he supposed. *Better to start working together as a unit,* he thought.

CHAPTER SEVEN

Karen Kenny couldn't sleep past six o'clock, the myriad of things she had to get done in a short time rattling around in her head. After a few minutes of tossing and turning, she realized she was not going to get in any more sleep that morning, so she abandoned her bed for the bathroom to brush her teeth. It was too early to wake the boys for school, and her mind was out of control with the difficulties she had to overcome to prepare for the arrival of her dad.

Back at her bed to straighten up the covers, she noticed the book on her nightstand, *The Practice,* a self-help guide to managing stress she had purchased earlier in the week. She was reminded that the book suggested she begin her day with some time by herself to clear her head of all thoughts, so that she would be in control of her mind, not the other way around.

That certainly applies to me today, she thought, so she sat in the ladder-back chair in the corner of her room. Sitting upright, she placed her hands on her thighs palms down, closed her eyes, and concentrated on her breathing, imagining the air coming in and out of her lungs, to the exclusion of everything else. She did not fall asleep, but before she was aware of what was happening, she opened her eyes, feeling refreshed. The clock on the nightstand said six thirty, and she was not aware that the time had even passed. It occurred to her that there must be something to this, and she promised herself that she would give the concept some serious thought.

She dressed casually for the day and headed for the kitchen where she found the pile of dishes from dinner still waiting for her in the sink. She rinsed them and put them in the dishwasher. Out the window in front of her, she could barely make out the neighbor's house in the soft glow of the predawn. She thought she heard something tap the side of the house, but leaning over the sink to avoid the glare of the overhead light, she could not see any activity in the yard. Karen glanced at her watch and decided she could wake the boys now, so she headed for their rooms to welcome them to the new day. Not surprised, she found both of them engrossed in their phones, competing with each other on some sort of collaborative game.

"You guys are something else, sitting there twenty feet from each other in different rooms and still playing with each other," she said over her shoulder from the hallway and returned to her dishes to finish up with the pots and pans, her least favorite part of the activity, because they couldn't go in the dishwasher.

As she went about her task, she contrasted herself with her mother, who had been old school. Karen believed mothers could be divided into two categories, the ones who thought you had to wash the dishes before you put them in the dishwasher (her mother) and those who thought the dishwasher was for washing the dishes (herself), but that didn't mean that her mother's chastising over the years didn't make her feel a little guilty, like she was cutting corners, when she put food-chunked plates in the machine's dish racks. The dishes came out clean in any event.

Hearing no sign of activity in the back of the house, Karen called after her boys again, "Tim, Bart! You guys get a move on. It's Friday and you have all weekend to fiddle with those video games!"

"Yeah, Mom," the boys replied with resignation.

Karen made her boys a hot breakfast, feeling it truly was the most important meal of the day, and as eight o'clock drew near, she urged them along to get in the car for a quick ride to school. She dropped them in the circle at eight fifteen sharp and returned to the house to begin preparations for contact with her dad. The first order of business was to reach out to Charlie Edgerton and bring him into the loop. Karen recognized it was going to be short notice for him to drop everything, but she sensed he had taken a personal interest in her, so that might just be possible.

She called his number from her cell directory, and his secretary, paralegal, assistant, multitasking master of his office answered. Mrs. Agnew was one of those "mother hen" office workers who was capable of almost any job and worth quadruple her salary if she liked who she was working for, and to her, Charlie Edgerton was a chick who needed her mothering. She would do anything for him, including scratching the eyes out of any woman she thought was unsuitable for her charge. Fortunately, Karen did not fit in that category, so Mrs. Agnew put her right through, even though Charlie had left instructions that he was not to be disturbed.

"Hi, Karen," Charlie opened.

"Hi, Charlie. Thank you so much for taking my call. I'm sure you're busy," she began.

"Are we still on for tonight?" he asked.

"No. No wait, yes . . . I mean okay, yes, but everything has changed; that's why I'm calling. You see, I had a call last night that's very concerning about my dad, and everything has changed." Karen's emotions got the best of her, and she started to sob. "I don't know what to do."

"Take a deep breath, Karen, and tell me slowly what's going on."

Karen was scared. She was scared that Charlie would not be available to help her on such short notice, and she was frightened for her dad. It seemed to her that everything was crashing down around her ears, this new business, and her job, and everything. She thought of her father out there somewhere all alone with no one to look out for him. Her emotional release had an immediate effect on Charlie, who was a sucker for an attractive woman in distress. She continued, no longer crying, but with some heaving in her chest as she struggled to get the words out.

"That's part of the problem. I don't think I should talk to you over the phone, but I need the benefit of a privileged communication with you as a lawyer. Is there any way you could see me this morning? Like, right now, I mean?"

"That must have been some phone call," Charlie responded, suspecting that Karen was being a little paranoid, what with reference to "privileged communication" and all. "I'm reviewing some contracts right now, is all. I can put that off. Sure, come on over and we can talk. You know where the office is."

"Sure I do." Charlie's office was on Georgia Avenue, just off Colesville Road, about fifteen minutes away. "I'm dressed like a slob right now. Give me a few minutes to freshen up, and I'll be there by nine thirty."

"We're not going to be seeing anybody. Just come as you are. We'll have more time that way," he offered, trying to help.

"*You'll* be seeing me." Karen regretted the words before they even came out of her mouth, but figured, *What the hell, so he knows I think about him.* "Okay, I'll be there in twenty." Even so, she was going to take a minute to put on some lipstick and maybe swap her T-shirt for a blouse. She stayed with the shorts and sandals, not wanting to be too obvious.

At nine fifteen she pulled in the office's underground garage and parked her Camry. After a quick glance in the rearview mirror to make sure everything was in place, she headed into the building lobby and took the elevator to the fifth floor, where Charlie's office was finished in simple woods and fabrics with mahogany furniture.

The only evidence of caving in to a splurge was the crown molding around the ceiling, which really set off everything in the outer office. Mrs. Agnew looked up from her desk and motioned for Karen to go right in to Charlie's office through the double doors. Charlie's office was done in similar taste, his desk just large enough to make a statement, but not so big as to indicate an inflated ego. There were some pictures on the walls, but no vanity surfaces depicting photos of Charlie with celebrities or politicians.

"Are those your kids?" Karen asked, pointing at the photo behind Charlie's desk on the credenza.

"Yes. Michelle and David are in high school now. That was taken about five years ago when we were at Disneyworld." Charlie smiled, remembering better times.

"And Mrs. Edgerton?" Karen asked cautiously.

"History," Charlie replied, not offering up anything else. Motioning for Karen to take a seat at the small round conference table in the corner of the room, he sat next to her to make her feel the setting was more personal, rather than sitting behind his official-looking desk. "So, tell me; what's the new news about this mysterious phone call last night that has you so upset?"

Karen began by rehashing her suspicion as to why the FBI interceded in her family business to gain control over her father. Charlie remembered the events of February very well and nodded his recollection to her. Then she described her call to her dad following her suspension from the Barrie School, only to find out that he was not in his room at Tropic Isle. Charlie listened intently, waiting for her to get to the point.

"Then last night, around ten o'clock, I had a call from Bevy Martin, dad's friend at Tropic Isle. I think I may have mentioned him to you, anyway, he's really sharp, and he sort of looks after dad, keeps an eye on him, if you know what I mean, for me. He's pretty clued in on what the situation is. Anyway, he called me late in the evening to tell me that Dad had gone missing, from the evening before, and that he, my dad, had a friend call him to let him know that Dad was all right and, this is the strangest part, he has gotten ahold of a car somehow and is driving here to Maryland to see me. Bevy told me that the FBI had been out there twice already trying to figure out where my dad had gone and that they were pulling all the stops to find him."

"That's quite a story, Karen," Charlie interrupted.

"Wait, there's more, the reason I had to see you in person."

Charlie raised an eyebrow. "What do you mean?"

"Mr. Martin, Bevy, said he could not go into too much detail, but that Dad was possibly in a lot of trouble, and I should find a lawyer, so I could call him this morning and have privileged communication to get more detail. I don't really understand that part, except that this must be serious business." Karen looked at Charlie with a pleading expression. "He kept saying he didn't want to obstruct justice, or something like that."

Charlie nodded his understanding. "Your friend is right. If you deal with this through your attorney, your communications are privileged, so if Mr. Martin has something incriminating to say, you will not have to divulge it if the communication is through me. Technically, he should hire me, as well. What do you say we just call him? Do you have his number?"

"Of course; it's the same as my dad's." Karen scribbled it on a Post-it tablet lying on the table. Charlie pulled the sheet off and spun the phone around to face him, selecting speaker mode. When he heard the dial tone, he punched in the number Karen had given him.

"Tropic Isle, how may I direct your call?" a familiar voice came on the line.

Karen and Charlie were put right through to Bevy's room, where he picked up on the first ring.

"Bevy Martin," he answered.

"Hi, Bev; it's Karen. You are on speakerphone, and I am calling from my lawyer's office in Silver Spring. His name is Charles Edgerton."

"Good morning, Mr. Martin, I'm Charlie Edgerton," he introduced himself. "It is just the two of us here in the room. Karen has briefed me a little about your conversation of last night. If I might presume, I would welcome you as a client along with Mrs. Kenny, so anything you say will have the privilege. Why don't you begin by bringing me up to date with Mr. Masterson's situation?"

"I'd be happy to," Bevy replied. He paused for a moment to organize his thoughts, after which he made an orderly presentation of everything he knew, beginning with Ornstein's first visit where he learned of Stewart's disappearance, followed by his second visit where he learned that his friend may have stolen a car and possibly disabled a police officer, and the progress he had made to Columbia, South Carolina, where he was currently in the company of a woman named Pepper Madison, who was trying to help Stewart reach his destination. When he got to this part, Charlie and Karen exchanged a look of disbelief. Bevy also informed them of the Silver Alert out for Stewart and offered his thought process regarding acting as an intermediary for the exchange of information, so that Karen's dad's whereabouts could remain private.

"That's why I asked Karen to find an attorney before calling me. I am assuming that her phone is being monitored by now, or certainly soon will be. Our plan is for Miss Madison to help Stewart purchase a burner phone so he can make arrangements directly with Karen where he can meet her when he gets to the D.C. area. It won't be a smartphone, so no one will be able to access it, and if he turns it off, its location can't be traced. They'll know where he called from, but he'll be long gone by the time they get there. Karen?"

"Yes," Karen answered.

Bevy continued, "I told him to call you about an hour out. You should be thinking of a place where you can meet him without identifying it specifically, perhaps someplace he used to take you as a child. He will remember it and know how to get there. My hope is that you can meet him unobserved, so you can get him to a safe place until you can get the legal process sorted out. Mr. Edgerton, can you be of help to us in that regard?"

Charlie thought for a minute and responded, "It's a complicated issue because it mixes state and federal considerations. At the end of the day, the government's guardianship is in the hands of a specified individual, Lyle Ornstein, not the FBI. On the other hand, that is a jurisdictional matter in the state of Florida. If Mr. Masterson is physically in the state of Maryland in the custody of a direct family member, I think we may be able to get an injunction to prevent Ornstein from taking him back until the state of Maryland has had a chance to rule on the guardianship. So, my answer is: I don't know, but I can look into it."

"It's a start." Bevy sounded deflated. "Karen, do you have any ideas where you could arrange to meet your dad?"

"I'll have to give it some thought. It will have to be a place where something happened, to be sure he will have a reason to recall it, and I would suppose it should be a public space, as well."

"Good thinking. You might want to have a backup place in mind just in case."

"I'll work on it."

"So, Karen," Bevy continued, "I suspect he won't get to your area until late this evening. When he calls, be sure to remind him to turn his cell phone off after he talks to you. Mr. Edgerton, what do you think of our plan, and can you help?"

"I will start to work on an injunction right away. I've always been upset about our government bullying their way into a personal family matter. There have been disturbing repercussions for Karen as a result, which I won't go into now. As additional firepower, I might invite my sister along for the rendezvous. She works for the *Washington Post,* and they are always looking for human interest stories that embarrass government overreach. Just her presence may be of influence if something goes wrong."

The three of them continued to discuss details and logistics for a few minutes more. When they were finished, Karen felt they had a good plan in place.

"Does this mean we aren't going to go to the Olive Garden tonight?" Charlie asked with an obvious smile of sarcasm.

"I don't see why we can't, but I won't be able to eat anything. I'll be so tied up in knots," she answered.

His even joking about dinner gave her comfort that his interest was beyond the lawyer-client relationship, and she felt good about that. She said she would stay in touch with Charlie during the day. He had her cell phone number.

"Just remember, anything said between us will probably be intercepted at some point, so be careful. Best to use a payphone, if you can find one, or borrow someone else's," Charlie added.

He walked her through the reception area to the elevators and bid her goodbye. His return was met with a raised eyebrow from Mrs. Agnew.

⁓⊃◯⊂⁓

"Hi, Fultie. It's Mati in Miami. I'm following up on our conversation yesterday about Masterson. I just want to close this file and report back to Washington that the matter is straightened out." Mati Tahan always found it best when dealing with the FBI to be direct and to the point, explaining what you wanted and why.

McBride was caught a little off guard by Mati's call, early on a Friday morning, particularly when it involved a subject of some annoyance to him. "For both our sakes, I wish I could give you a simple answer. The long and the short of it is, we have not yet been able to pick him up."

"You're kidding. What's the problem?"

"I'll level with you, Mati. We've pulled out all the stops, portable readers on the interstates, POIs to all law enforcement agencies, everything we can think of. Other than a hit yesterday on I-95 in Jacksonville, we have come up with nothing."

"This is starting to sound more serious than we discussed yesterday. You told me you had the situation under control. Doesn't seem like you do. I've got to call my boss this morning and tell him what Masterson's status is. You have to give me something, or I'm afraid they are going to want to get involved," Tahan cautioned.

McBride had never been as frustrated, and the strain showed in his voice. "Honest to God, Mati, we're doing everything we can. At the very least we know this, Masterson has a car, a Mercedes in fact, and apparently has resources to move it around. He has already been stopped once, before we knew about the situation, and he put a police officer in the hospital. We have always suspected that he is heading to his daughter's house in Maryland, which I can now say is confirmed as probable, since we identified his car as far north as Jacksonville, so we have that going for us. At the very least, we will be able to pick him up when he makes contact with his daughter, so that is our fallback. I'm assuming that if we can't locate him, no one else can either, but there are no guarantees."

"Great!" Tahan said sarcastically. "Can you give it to me sugar coated?"

"That was sugar coated!"

"Well, all I can say is, for a guy you are so worried about because he doesn't have both oars in the water, he seems to be ahead of you every step of the way," Tahan said.

McBride hesitated a moment. "I can't disagree with you there."

He sighed. "What are you going to pass up the chain? My ass is on the line, having talked to you, ya know."

"I'll tell Kunin in Washington that you are all over it, and that your plan is to pick Masterson up when he surfaces in Maryland, that it's by design to minimize publicity."

"Will he go for it?" McBride asked.

"I doubt it, but it's the best I can do. Don't be surprised if we have someone in the area to observe, just to make sure you are successful."

"You mean someone with a long barrel? That's pretty extreme, don't you think?" McBride asked, meaning the Israelis would take Masterson out.

"Possibly, but there's a lot at stake" was Tahan's answer.

McBride hung up and lowered his head onto his arms folded on his desk, while Tahan called his boss, Arye Kunin at the Israeli embassy to report what he had learned.

ひつひ

While Karen was doing the early morning dishes, Stewart Masterson was working his way through the haze from deep sleep in Patricia Madison's bedroom at the Cornell Arms in Columbia, South Carolina.

It was a glorious early spring morning, and the sky was turning a light purple off the balcony behind the dome of the capitol, clearly visible over the leafy canopy between the two buildings. As he started to stretch involuntarily, he became suddenly aware that something was amiss. Oddly, the first thing to come to his mind was not that he was in unfamiliar surroundings, but the fact that his anatomy was brushing up against the bedsheets because he was nude, and this was a decidedly different feeling for him. Then the panic started to set in as he surveyed the room, not finding anything familiar to anchor him.

A gentle breeze was billowing the sheer inner drapes covering the sliders to the balcony beside the bed. He heard the clinking of dishes coming from the kitchen. He didn't know how to react, so he just pulled the covers up to his neck and waited for some kind of memory to kick in and let him know where he was.

After a moment he heard the padding of bare feet crossing the hardwood floor moving in his direction, and then he saw Pepper as she entered the room in a terrycloth robe. When he noticed her red toenail polish, things started to fall into place for him, as flashes of his late-night lovemaking danced in his head. His first thought was of Helen, and then the absurdity of that complication got through to him.

Pepper gave him a big smile. "How are we feeling this morning, Mr. Bond?" she grinned. The connection to the reference was lost on him momentarily, and it showed in his confused reaction. "I'm referring to you, my superspy. You certainly live up to his reputation," she added. She tried to help Masterson feel at ease. "Let me clear things up for you. We met last night in the Tap Room of the Orrington Hotel, just down Gervais Street from here, where you rescued me from a nasty bartender who insulted my motives. You are on your way to Silver Spring to be with your daughter and her children, having *escaped* from an assisted living facility in Florida. You are in possession of a new Mercedes Benz, I don't even want to know from where, and you are traveling with your late wife's ashes. We have made an alliance, you and I, to try to help you get to your destination without running afoul of the whole of the United States government, and possibly other governments, as well."

She sat on the edge of the bed, not so close as to encroach on Masterson's territory, but close enough that she could show him some warmth and intimacy. Her spy was now inched back against the headboard, and Pepper could see she was not comforting him. "Is any of that ringing a bell, Stewart?" She smiled.

Slowly the pieces were fitting into place, as the adrenaline started to flow, stimulating his cortex. Her summary came at him rather fast, and it took him a minute to absorb it. Then he remembered the sex, and the comfort he found in this woman's embrace. He took his hands off the sheets and reached for her hands, which braced her as she sat on the bed, trying to lean toward him.

The barrier of terror was replaced by the bond of trust he had established the night before, and he leaned forward and gave her a nibble on her lips. She leaned farther forward and lingered for a moment. Her robe opened a little in the front, and he could see her nipple contrasted against the white skin below her tan line. That view coupled with the awareness of his nudity beneath the sheets led to an erection, which embarrassed him as he remembered her fit young body compared to the loose skin hanging about his, but he couldn't help himself.

If Pepper noticed, she didn't let on. "Why don't you use the bathroom to clean up? There's probably a spare toothbrush in the medicine cabinet, while I make us some breakfast. It's a beautiful day, but we have some things to do to get you on the road again if you are going to see your daughter tonight."

Masterson hadn't had two erections in over a year, and now he'd had two in the last eight hours. He slithered sideways out of the bed, and turned away from her to shield his condition as he headed for the bathroom, looking about for a sign of his underwear or pants. He finally snagged them off the floor by the corner of the bed and took them with him to the bathroom, where he relieved himself and jumped in the shower while Pepper headed to the kitchen to prepare something to eat for the two of them.

She had noticed his interest in her but felt their intimate fling was of the right amount of intensity, so she did not pursue anything.

Masterson walked in the breakfast nook about ten minutes later, clean-shaven thanks to Pepper's razor, and redressed in his khakis and blue button-down oxford, not looking worse for the wear.

Pepper gave him another warm smile and motioned him to a chair at the kitchen table. She put a cup of coffee in front of him along with a glass of orange juice, followed up by a plate of scrambled eggs, bacon, and toast. She set the other side for herself and sat facing him.

"Well, are you up for the day? Do you remember what we talked about last night when we spoke to your friend, Bevy Martin?" she began.

Masterson was unsure of the details. "Refresh me," he requested.

So, Pepper took care to go over everything in great detail, re-creating the evening exactly as it unfolded. She explained that Bevy was going to talk to her daughter and her lawyer this morning and fill her in on the details he didn't want to tell her last night. She explained how Masterson was to use a prepaid phone to call his daughter when he got near Washington, D.C., to arrange a place to rendezvous.

"When we're done here, I suggest we walk down the street to your hotel and get your things and check you out. Then we'll stop by MetroPCS and get you a prepaid phone to take with you, so you can call Karen. I'll go over the routing with you, if you like, although you seem to have done a good job of getting along fine this far. We know the authorities are looking for you, so apparently your choice of driving up US 1 was a good one because they obviously aren't looking for you here. Their equipment is probably more suited to the interstates and such."

They followed her plan after breakfast. Masterson retrieved his sweater from the sofa, noting the matted carpet that was slightly discolored below the edge of the glass coffee table, and Pepper handed him his windbreaker out of the vestibule closet. As they started to open the front door, Pepper was overcome by sadness, as she realized that she cared for this kindly, old-school gentleman, it dawning on her that she would likely never see him again after this morning. She stood on her toes and wrapped her arms around his neck, holding him close to her. He responded with a strong embrace in return. She kissed him gently on the lips and then buried her face in the crook of his neck. He could feel the wetness of her tears, as she trembled ever so slightly.

"I'm sorry for being so emotional, Stewart. Getting ready to see you off seems so sudden and premature to me; I'm just not ready for it. You have come to mean a great deal to me in such a short time." She sniffled a little and tried to compose herself.

Masterson lifted her chin, so he could look right into her eyes. "Pepper, one of the things you deal with in the beginnings of my condition is the inability to trust, and it's such an important element to achieve happiness. I haven't fully trusted anyone since Helen's death, except for her, and she isn't even real anymore. I know that. But you have given me that support, my ability to trust, in just one evening. It's not just the wonderful sex, but that you have given me so much trust, that I could even share those moments of intimacy with you, that have fortified me with the courage I need to continue my journey." Smiling now, he added, "And who knows; you may not have seen the last of me, yet."

Pepper smiled back and took a firm grasp of his upper arm, as they walked the block and a half to the Orrington in the brisk morning sunshine. She accompanied him to his room where he made a fast change of his shirt and underwear and stowed his Walmart purchases in his duffle, along with the "go bag." Pepper pulled the bed down, so it would look like it had been slept in, and they went downstairs to the ornate lobby to check out. He carried Helen under his free arm. They walked to the checkout desk.

Suddenly Masterson stiffened as he remembered he had checked in under one of his aliases and had no idea what the name was. Pepper noticed his tense posture and looked at him to see if she could help with his difficulty. The receptionist just smiled at him, and all Masterson could do was smile back.

Pepper interrupted with, "Checking out," to get things started. She still didn't know what the problem was.

"Room number, please," the receptionist requested, unaware that the gentleman in front of him was in distress.

Masterson froze for a second. Pepper jumped in volunteering the room number. "Seven-oh-four," she said.

"One moment please." The young man punched in the number on his computer, and turned to his left as the printer started warming up. When it finished, he handed Masterson the invoice and asked, "Only the room charges, sir. Shall we just leave that on your credit card, Mr. Courtney?"

Masterson was still flustered, but he recovered. "No thank you; I prefer to pay cash." He peeled off five crisp hundreds and handed them to the clerk.

"As you wish, Mr. Courtney. Shall I have your car brought up?"

"Yes, please, I would appreciate that."

The clerk made change efficiently the old-fashioned way, by counting out the balance in cash from the invoice amount until he got to the five hundred dollar number for the bills he had been given.

As Masterson and Pepper turned their backs to leave, the clerk quickly and unobtrusively ink tested one of the bills, before putting them in the drawer.

The car was brought around in short order, bags loaded, and Pepper and Masterson were off down Gervais, but not before a gob-smacked parking attendant glanced furtively at the hundred dollar bill he had been given. *That's one tip that's not going in the pool,* he thought. He kicked himself when he remembered that he had forgotten to tell Mr. Courtney that the key had not been left with the valet, but that the car had started normally, so it must be in the car somewhere. *Oh well, he'll figure it out for himself.*

Pepper looked over the inside of the car. "Not bad," she said pursing her lips. "I will make a suggestion, though."

"What's that?"

"I wouldn't leave everyone you meet a hundred dollar tip. That's going to be noticed."

"Until now, about all the cash I have is hundreds, but it's a good point," he acknowledged.

"When we get your phone, we'll try to get some smaller bills as change."

"Good idea."

Pepper pointed ahead on the right. "About two blocks up is a cell phone store. I think we can get your phone there."

Masterson spotted it on the right and pulled in the side parking lot. Inside, he and Pepper had never seen so many phones in one place before. It was early and the place had just opened. They were the first customers in the store. The two approached one of the merchandise counters and asked a pimply-faced teenager if they carried prepaid phones.

"We don't carry them anymore. We have a few still left in stock, but you won't be interested in them, 'cause they are all old-style flip phones. And now you can get smartphones for about the same money, so nobody wants them."

Pepper's face lit up. "That's exactly what we're looking for, an old-fashioned phone that just makes calls. Can you fix us up?"

The boy looked at them as if they were nuts. "If that's what you really want." He opened a bottom drawer in the storage cabinet behind him and pulled out a carton that read MOST ECONOMICAL in bold red print across the front, underscored with T-MOBILE. "This phone is good for one hour or one month, whichever comes first. It's fifty bucks."

The clerk would have preferred to switch them to a better deal on a more sophisticated model because he would receive no commission on this sale, but clearly these two old timers weren't interested. *Well, their loss,* he thought.

"Is it charged, or do we have to charge it?" Pepper asked.

"It's not charged now, but it comes with a charger. It will take a couple of hours for it to get a full charge," the boy answered.

"Will it charge in a car cigarette lighter?" Pepper inquired further.

"No, but we have a universal adapter we can sell you for twenty dollars," the kid replied, thinking nobody was that nuts.

"We'll take it," Masterson said. "But first we want to test it. Let's hook up the charger now for a minute, and you give me your number and I'll call you. I need to know that it is going to work."

The kid's shoulders slumped and he sighed. *What a waste of time,* he thought.

He opened the box and hooked up the charger to the surge protector on the counter in front of him and plugged it into the phone. There was no change at first, and then a pinwheel started to spin in the display window. The logo on the face of the phone said DAICHI; Pepper had never heard of it before. They gave it a minute to get enough of a charge to boot the phone up, and then Masterson asked the boy for the number at his store.

The teenager complied by sliding a brochure across the counter to them, and Masterson dialed the number on the front. After a few seconds delay, the store speakers chimed, and the kid looked at the phone next to him on the counter. Its light was flashing. "You want me to answer that?" he asked.

"If you wouldn't mind," Masterson said.

He heard the phone get picked up and the kid breathing, not knowing whether he should talk or not. Finally, the boy said, "Hello," tentatively.

"That's good. Thank you, young man." And Masterson flipped the phone shut.

He paid with a hundred and got a twenty, some ones, and some change. He and Pepper walked out with the phone and the adapter.

When they got to the car, they realized they didn't need an adapter because the Mercedes had a USB port in the middle glove box. They hooked the phone up to begin a serious charge, and went around the block to get back to Pepper's apartment, Gervais being a one-way street in downtown Columbia. Masterson pulled up in the semi-circular drive under the portico of the Cornell Arms, and just sat in silence, putting off the inevitable.

Finally they turned to face one another and, in unison, started to talk.

"You first, Stewart." Pepper laughed.

"Pepper, I don't know if we will ever meet again," Masterson began, taking her hands in his and concentrating on her eyes. "But if we don't, I want you to know, I will *never* forget you!"

Pepper's eyes welled up with tears. "I so wish I could go with you, but I think that would be a mistake, just postponing our goodbye. You have given me something worthwhile to think about myself that I will treasure." She handed him an introduction card. "This is my home and cell phone number. When this mess gets settled, I would love to hear from you to know that you are all right. I will worry about you if you don't call me. And, remember, as soon as you call your daughter, turn your cell phone off, so it can't be traced." She leaned over to his side of the car and kissed him again, not passionately, but emotionally.

He held her tightly to him for a moment before he released her, rather choked up himself. "I will try to call you tomorrow after I get settled." He smiled.

Pepper's chest heaved as she got out of the car. She watched as he pulled into the early morning traffic and headed north, not taking her eyes off his car until he was out of sight. Then she headed upstairs to have a good cry and pray.

ಬಿಂಬ

John Hallanger contemplated the thumb drive he held in his right hand, turning it over and over between his first two fingers and thumb. It was the first thing to fall out of the envelope he had just signed for, delivered without a cover or instructions. He had no idea where it had come from, and it was highly unusual for him to receive communications that were not identified and logged through his office procedures system. This had just been delivered by an interagency government courier in an envelope and placed in his hand without explanation right after he came in the office this morning, around eight fifteen.

Hallanger turned his attention to the envelope and looked in, identifying a small Post-it stuck to the inside. He pulled it out and read the brief note it contained: "You don't know where this came from" was scribbled in Hollis Cavner's non–Palmer Method script.

So, that's one riddle solved, Hallanger thought.

He slid the metal protector sleeve away from the drive and put it in his desk computer, and turned his attention to his computer screen to see what would happen. After some whirring, an icon of a human ear juxtapositioned to what looked like sound waves appeared on his desktop screen. He clicked on it.

After a brief delay, an audio screen containing icons for *play, pause, fast-forward,* and *reverse* opened up on his computer. He clicked on "play" and immediately saw a digital rendering of sound waves appear on the small software screen, accompanied by a woman's voice as she answered a telephone. Hallanger listened to the conversation twice and closed the program, removing the thumb drive and putting it in his pocket. His next call was to McBride's cell phone, where he found him in his Miami office.

"Fultie, it's John Hallanger in Washington."

"What's up, Jack? I'm just sitting here with Lyle Ornstein going over what he's turned up since we last spoke. You want me to put you on the speaker, or just between the two of us?" McBride asked.

Hallanger suggested he pick up.

With the phone to his ear, McBride continued, "We have a possible hit on Masterson. A random surveillance camera has an inconclusive photo of the Mercedes he may be driving on I-95, just north of Jacksonville where US 1 and the interstate join for a couple of miles."

Hallanger offered, "What I learned may corroborate that. I can't reveal my source, but I have reason to believe that our guy's daughter has been in touch with Masterson's friend at his assisted living facility, who advised her that her father was on his way to see her in Maryland, something we have suspected. I believe the friend may have said his name was Bevy. Does that mean anything to you?"

"Bevy? Did you say Bevy?" McBride said aloud, his eyes on Ornstein.

Ornstein nodded vigorously in the affirmative. "That's Masterson's friend at Tropic Isle," he said excitedly.

McBride nodded his understanding and confirmed it with Hallanger. "Jack, yes, that's the name of Masterson's close friend at the facility. Ornstein has talked to him, and thinks that if Masterson is getting any assistance, this guy Bevy Martin is the source."

"Then I would suggest you pay him another visit and find out who else he has called. Sounds like he may have been in touch with Masterson himself," Hallanger advised.

"That's a great piece of information. How did you come by it?" McBride asked. "Did you get a warrant to tap the daughter's phones?"

"It's complicated; don't ask. The real answer to your question is that our legal department is appearing before a federal judge at ten o'clock this morning, so we should have that in place by this afternoon."

McBride could read between the lines and knew better than to inquire more deeply into the matter, also knowing he would not get a truthful response. Having conveyed his message, Hallanger rang off.

McBride turned to Ornstein, "Get your butt up to Pompano and find out what this guy knows. You can threaten him with obstruction, or something like that, to get his cooperation. He didn't make that call out of the blue; someone or something prompted him to call, and we have to presume that it was a prior communication from Masterson."

"I'm on it!" Ornstein said as he jumped up and headed for the door.

An hour later, Ornstein pulled his black Crown Victoria under the portico and, flashing his badge, asked to see Mr. Bevin Martin immediately. He tried to sound as officious as possible to create an atmosphere of intimidation and importance. It had the desired effect. In minutes, an orderly brought an agitated Bevy Martin into the lobby where he gave Lyle the "stink eye."

Thinking he may have overdone things a little, Ornstein tried to smile, motioning the aged gentleman to an area of quiet seating off the lobby. Martin sat opposite Ornstein with his arms crossed in defiance while the young agent tried to soften him up.

"Mr. Martin, I'm sure you see us as some kind of villain here, but I want you to believe me that I and the Bureau have Mr. Masterson's best interests at heart. In his frustration to be free of this place, he may have actually put himself in some kind of danger."

"What kind of danger?" Martin perked up, thinking maybe he was going to hear some truth for a change.

"You know I can't really go into any specifics, Bevy. May I call you Bevy?" he asked so as not to seem presumptuous.

"I prefer Mr. Martin, if that's all right with you." He was feeling his power, now.

"Okay, Mr. Martin it is, then." Ornstein smiled again. "Let me level with you. We have reason to believe that you were in touch with Karen Kenny last night. I'm sure you're aware that I can check the phone system here, and the records will verify—"

"Yes, I was. I called her around ten thirty last night," Martin interrupted. "We speak from time to time, more often now that you idiots have run her father off. She's worried about him, too, wouldn't you think?"

Ornstein felt behind the eight ball here. He organized himself for a moment, and then tried to hit Martin with some surprise to throw him off balance. He had already contacted the facility manager, Jerry Reinhardt, while he was driving up from Miami, and he had received a summary of Martin's phone transmissions from his apartment phone that ran through the switchboard. "Who do you know in Columbia, South Carolina, Mr. Martin?"

This had the desired effect, as Martin squirmed in his seat a little, but he recovered quickly. "I don't see how that's any of your concern, Agent Ornstein."

Lyle continued to press, "It is if you are aiding and abetting a fugitive." He let that sink in for a moment. "It is if you were in touch with Mr. Masterson in Columbia by phone, followed by a call to his daughter, followed again by another call to the same number in Columbia." Ornstein was winging it based on what he knew and what he suspected, and Martin's body language was telling him he was on the right track. "Who were you talking to in Columbia, Mr. Martin?" He was met with belligerence. "Come on, Bevy," trying the personal angle again, "work with me here. By nature I'm really a nice guy, but don't let my age fool you; I can be a prick, too! We're going to find your friend, either now or when he gets to his daughter's house. I just hope it's before someone who doesn't have his best interests at heart does. That's why we're on a time clock, seriously. Work with me here."

Martin thought for a minute. "You keep talking about some other bad guys. Near as I can tell, you're the bad guys. You broke up the family of a kind man who served his country with distinction by forcing him to live in a place where he doesn't belong and destroying his daughter; did you know she lost her job because of you?"

"Believe me, Mr. Martin, I know nothing about her losing her job; the Bureau knows nothing about—"

Martin cut him off, "And now me; you're threatening me for helping a respected senior citizen get home to his family. Do you know I'm a decorated veteran, flew over two hundred missions in Vietnam fifteen years before you were probably even born, spent eighteen months in a north Vietnamese prison camp, beaten almost daily? And you think you can threaten *me*! I would love to see how your precious bureau would handle that public relations nightmare!"

Ornstein suddenly remembered why he was sickened when he'd first learned the circumstances behind this case, something he and McBride had spoken about and shared opinions. He looked down, not able to face Bevy Martin, let alone look him directly in the eye.

Martin continued, "I have not lied to you or told you anything that is untrue. I answered your questions. Yes, I spoke with Karen last night, and yes, I advised her that her dad was fine and on his way to see her. Yes, I have been in touch with Stewart. Again, I know of nothing he has done that is against the law, so I am hardly aiding or abetting anything. You certainly have the resources to find out who I called in Columbia, and I'm sure all you will learn is that someone let him use his phone to reach out to people who care for him to let them know he is all right. There is certainly no conspiracy going on here. So why don't you piss off and leave us be?"

"Mr. Martin, thank you for your time. If you are in touch with your friend again, you may want to tell him we are not the only ones looking for him. I would suggest he look a little bit out, as my grandfather used to say."

Ornstein concluded his interview, not feeling great about his role in all of this. On his way back to Miami, he had his office check Tropic Isle's phone records to find out who the mysterious calls to South Carolina were made to. When he got back to Miramar, he went straight to McBride's office to report what he had learned. The two discussed Ornstein's conversation with Bevy Martin in detail. After some thought, McBride gave his subordinate some instructions.

"We know where Masterson is going. I suggest you get on a plane this morning and go to Washington. You know more about him than anyone else, as well as the other players, so I think you will be of more use there in place to intercept him when he arrives. Columbia is only about six or eight hours from D.C., and you need to be on site before he gets there. Report to the main office. I will phone ahead to make sure they have the necessary resources to assist you. In the meantime, I will have the SAC in Columbia pay a visit to the person with the number Martin called and have anything useful forwarded to you for when you arrive."

Ornstein excused himself to make travel arrangements with dispatch, while McBride picked up the phone to call Hallanger and advise him of the plan. After he filled his boss in, he called the agency office in South Carolina and spoke with the Special Agent in Charge. McBride gained a little comfort in knowing that, either way, this situation would most likely be resolved by the end of the day, one less headache he had to deal with.

֍

Pepper Madison was just lounging around her apartment, straightening things up from the evening before, when the doorman rang to inform her that she had some visitors from the FBI. It was just before noon, and she thought, *That didn't take long.*

She instructed the doorman to send them up. She checked her appearance in the full-length bedroom mirror and approved of her outfit, casual Bermuda shorts and matching blouse, thinking she looked relaxed and innocent enough. The doorbell to her apartment chimed, and she put on a neutral face and opened the front door. Before her stood two men in nondescript suits with rep ties.

"What can I do for you?" she asked, as the shorter of the two men reached for his identification.

"Are you Ms. Patricia Madison?" he asked, noting that he was facing an attractive middle-aged woman who seemed very confident of herself.

"Yes, I am," Pepper responded respectfully. "Would you like to come in?" She waved her arm toward the vestibule where they re-assembled and closed the door behind them. She was on her turf now, and she made no effort to invite them farther into her home.

The agents shifted from foot to foot, as the senior agent collected himself.

"Now you know who I am, who might yourselves be?" Pepper inquired. The shorter of the two reached again for his badge, and Pepper stopped him by putting a hand softly on his arm. "No, no. I know you're from the FBI; you don't have to show me your badge again. I just want to know your names."

Again the shorter man spoke, while the other stood there like a doorknob. "I am Roy Connors, Special Agent in Charge of the Columbia office of the Federal Bureau of Investigation, and this is"—he motioned to his taller associate—"Agent Brian Fasco. Ms. Madison, we are here in connection with the disappearance of a senior citizen who is the subject of a Silver Alert in the state of Florida," the agent informed her, studying her features for a response or hint of recognition.

"My goodness!" Pepper looked surprised, putting her hand to her mouth expressing astonishment. "You two certainly represent a lot of firepower, searching for a missing senior citizen. Was it a man or a woman? And why are you looking in South Carolina for someone who is missing in Florida?"

Connors shifted his weight again, looking as if he were pleading to be admitted to the spacious living room he could see just beyond the confines of the vestibule, where he felt distinctly uncomfortable, three people in the smaller space. Pepper did not offer him any relief. She just stood there waiting to see how this was going to play out.

"It is a man. Ms. Madison, let's not beat around the bush." Connors saw no easy way out, so he decided to put his cards on the table. This woman was formidable, to say the least, and for the moment she was driving the show. "You received two calls from a Mr. Bevin Martin last night, a close friend of the gentleman we are looking for. Just answer the question for us please, and this will not be difficult—"

"I certainly don't want to be difficult, Agent Connors. I assure you my utmost cooperation," Pepper interrupted almost sarcastically, frowning somewhat. "I did speak with Mr. Martin, twice, as you said," she answered matter-of-factly.

"In that case, Ms. Madison, have you been in touch with a Mr. Stewart Masterson?" he asked, expecting a denial from the woman.

"Certainly," she answered, "I know him," as though it were the most natural thing in the world. "We had dinner together last night," she added, intending to show her complete cooperation. "Is he the man you are looking for? He certainly didn't look lost to me, as I believe he told me he was on his way to Maryland to visit with his daughter. Why don't you tell me what's really going on here, Agent Connors, and perhaps I can be of more help to you? You're behaving as though I have participated in some sort of deception, and I assure you I have not."

Connors looked at Fasco, who returned his glance with a vacant stare and an almost imperceptible shrug of his shoulders. The senior agent was starting to wonder what kind of mess the Miami SAC had gotten him into, since he obviously hadn't been told the whole story behind why he was sent to interrogate this woman. He had been led to believe that she would be uncooperative, to say the least. McBride had even gone so far as to suggest that she might be on the hook for an obstruction charge. His interest in finding Masterson was high level to say the least, so Connors decided to probe further.

"Ms. Madison, can you tell us anything more about your encounter? How is it that you know Mr. Masterson well enough to have dinner with him? What did you talk about? Have you known him long? How did all this come about?"

Pepper knew she was on precarious ground now. She decided to stay with what she had scripted with Bevy, not saying anything false or misleading, but not helping them get any closer to Stewart, either. "No, I haven't known him long; I just met him last night in fact, at the Tap Room in the Orrington down the street where I stopped in to have a drink after a long day. We met at the bar and struck up a conversation, which led to dinner. He told me a little about himself, that he was on his way to Maryland to see his daughter, as I told you. There was nothing sinister about it. I liked him; he seemed interesting. He did seem a little confused at times, which I attributed to his age, and I tried to be of assistance. After dinner, he came to my apartment and asked if he could use my phone to reach out to a friend to let him know where he was and that he was all right. He spoke briefly, a few minutes I suppose. The friend called him back after a while, and that was it."

"Where did he spend the night, Ms. Madison?" Connors was taking notes now in a small spiral pad he had in his inside breast pocket.

"I believe he was checked in at the Orrington. Perhaps you can stop by there for more information. It's only a block or so down the street on the west side; you can't miss it," she answered cautiously.

Connors seemed satisfied with that answer.

"I'm familiar with it; I *will* check there," he emphasized, thinking that he had as much information as he was going to get from the lady. He motioned to Fasco and headed to the front door, and paused, turning around. "One more thing, Ms. Madison. What do you do . . . for a living, I mean?"

Pepper was caught off guard. She looked the agent in the eyes, stone-faced, and repeated the question: "What do I do for a living? Why do you ask?"

"You said you went to the Tap Room for a drink after a long day. What do you do? . . . That you had a long day, I mean."

"I'm a flight attendant. I had just come back from an international trip, and I was tired, and I wanted to relax, somewhere around people."

Connors thought this was odd, after spending six or seven hours waiting on strangers, she wanted to be around more of them. He looked again into the interior of the well-appointed apartment with its view of the capitol and gave her a parting shot to see if it would get a response. "This is a very nice place you have here, Ms. Madison. You must do very well in the airline business," he tried.

"Yes it is; I have almost twenty years of seniority with Delta Air Lines, and I can fly the most preferable routes. If you have nothing further for me, I'll show you out."

A little testy, Connors thought, as he and Fasco passed through the front door Pepper held open for them. He heard the deadbolt slide into position with an audible click, as she secured the door behind them.

After a stop at the Orrington, where he could not confirm that a Masterson had registered there, he made further inquiries and learned that a mature gentleman had checked in the previous evening under the name of Courtney. On a hunch, he got the Tap

Room's manager on the phone and was put in touch with the bartender on duty the previous night. From him, he got an earful about the old man who had picked up a suspected hooker, made a scene, and paid for his beers with hundred dollar bills. The couple had left together, and Connors got the distinct impression that there had been some kind of altercation or exchange of unpleasantries with the barkeep during the evening.

Encouraged at the implications, Connors told Fasco to check with the valet to see if he could find out what kind of car "Mr. Courtney" was driving. Connors was even more surprised when Fasco reported back that a mature gentleman checked out this morning and left in his silver Mercedes S550 with an attractive younger woman. He was well remembered because he left a one hundred dollar tip. The front desk also confirmed that Mr. Courtney checked out around nine, electing to pay cash. He could not get copies of the credit card information that was used to collateralize room incidentals because the transaction had been deleted after it was not used.

"This is getting really interesting, Brian," Connors mentioned to Fasco. "We may have some more work to do here; all is not what meets the eye. That Madison woman knows a lot more about what's going on than she let on, and there's more to her story, too."

He used his cell phone to call McBride for further instructions, after giving a summary of all he had learned.

"Do you want me to go back to the woman's apartment and lean on her? I'm sure she can give us a lot more information if we put her in the right frame of mind."

McBride thought about this for a minute before responding. His career, which began right out of the University of Florida Law School, had led him down a path of evolving positions in law enforcement. As he gained experience, mostly in dull footwork and investigation, his position on what he was here for morphed. Every fact-finding sequence led to increasing paths of possible criminal activity, and he found if he pursued each to a conclusion, he never reached the end of the branches of the tree. Often chasing alternative patterns of behavior led him to places that were far removed from the originating investigation, which contributed nothing to the understanding of the difficulty that was the genesis of his search. They just wasted his time with no reward. Over the years, he learned to stay on the main path of an investigation, cataloging extraneous diversions for future reference. Certainly there was more going on here with the Madison woman, but it wasn't going to help him with the matter at hand, so he decided to let it go for now.

"I don't think so, Roy. Not right now. Our real issue is finding this guy, and it would appear he has a three- or four-hour head start on us. We have already found out what we need, and that is where Masterson is going and what his timetable is. I suspect if she's as sharp as you say, she hasn't told us any lies. As to whatever else she might be involved in, it doesn't benefit us to make a felon out of her at this point, but it's good to know we have more leverage if we need it. You did good work today, and we have learned a lot, filled in a lot of holes. We have now absolutely confirmed the vehicle and its origin. And we know that Masterson is well heeled and documented with identification for his needs. We just don't know where he got it, but I suspect it's a stash he had from his active days with Central Intelligence. He may have even come across it by accident, somehow. I would suggest you just sit tight for a while, and I'll let you know if we need you to pursue anything further with the lady. I've got to hand it to Masterson, though. He has a lot more on the ball than we would have suspected, based on our dealings with him the past couple months. He is very resourceful. I think he covers for his Alzheimer's well, and he has a lot of survival training to fall back on."

McBride put a summary of the findings in a case memorandum and forwarded a copy to Lyle Ornstein, so he would have it when his flight landed in Washington. As he wrote his report, he wondered why the bartender at the Orrington Hotel would volunteer that he thought the Madison woman was a prostitute.

Oh, well. I guess old habits are hard to break, he reflected, realizing that he was going down a road of investigation he had decided to abandon years ago.

CHAPTER EIGHT

Masterson had been making solid progress on US 1 since hugging Pepper goodbye. Helen was strapped in the passenger's seat next to him, and as he drove, he felt the need to share his good fortune with her. He spoke to Helen softly of the woman he had met last night, volunteering how much he trusted her and how helpful she was in getting him in touch with their daughter. As he remembered his evening with Pepper, he was struck with pangs of guilt, and felt the need to share with Helen the fact of his intimacy with the beautiful woman. After he explained things, he felt better about what he had done. His head knew he had done nothing wrong, but his heart had to be released of the burden of his secret, giving him a closure of sorts.

His route up the number-one highway in the United States took him along what had been the continental coastline from the Cretaceous period, which ended over sixty-five million years ago. This part of the highway was not located near any of the surrounding interstates, which Masterson would not have been aware of, but he did enjoy the multiple lanes and divided highway medians given over to a roadway so independently important in its own right, as it speeded his progress toward his goal.

He wasn't yet hungry when he passed through northern South

Carolina into North Carolina on a beeline for Raleigh, where US 1 briefly joined with Interstate 40. He sped past the thriving city on the bypass and did not notice the portable license plate scanner on the side of the road at the Spencer Avenue Exit on the north side of Raleigh just before US 1 gained its independence from the interstate system again.

"Do you hear that, Helen? My stomach is starting to growl, and I think I am going to need a pee stop," he said aloud, as the brief respite of the controlled access highway returned to the frustrating ebb and flow of stop-and-go traffic. Masterson leaned forward to get a better view of the business signs he was passing in the hope of finding someplace suitable to stop for a bite. He was looking for something quick, and after a few false starts that turned out to be carryout restaurants, he spied a saucy-looking Mexican restaurant in the corner of the strip center he was passing.

He was led to a shiny epoxied wooden booth in the middle of an otherwise empty restaurant. *Not a good sign,* he thought as he declined a cold Dos Equis or frozen margarita, opting instead for coffee, as he perused the multiple options of Americanized Mexican dishes, all served with refried beans and rice. He selected a beef burrito from the menu, and the tiny Latina scurried off to the kitchen with his order.

After a visit to the restroom, which he found clean and orderly, he surveyed the empty restaurant on his way back to his seat. In the time it took him to look at the flip phone, which now fully charged was in his pocket, a young Latino man appeared with a steaming plate of unidentifiable mush supporting a tortilla-wrapped something or other, which he placed in front of Masterson with a smile.

"Por favor." He beamed proudly as he placed the hot dish on the table. "Careful, is hot!" he warned.

Masterson smiled back and set out with a fork and knife to dissect the tortilla to see what was inside. The steam off the plate brought sweat to his brow, as he probed the food around the edges where it was cool enough to put in his mouth. He gave the meal an honest fifteen minutes, before he signaled for the check and left a hundred dollar bill with the waitress who was now the cashier, obviously a family operation. He heard shouts of glee behind him as he left the darkened interior for the bright sunshine of the spectacular early spring day, headed to his car, still marveling at how it always seemed to start, even though he had no key.

The traffic on US 1 was heavy, and Masterson was becoming anxious as he plodded out of town on the north side of Raleigh. He had a general idea where he was in relation to Maryland, and he figured he would not get there until nightfall. He thought again of the antiquated phone in his pocket, and after some reflection, he recalled he needed to keep it off until he was close to home, and then call Karen to arrange a place to meet.

The information sign on the side of the highway as he left the urban part of the city read, RICHMOND, VA 165 MILES. Masterson put the miles behind him as fast as he dared. The highway was rural and hilly, making progress somewhat slow, but he pressed on, pointing out the occasional landmark of interest to Helen, who seemed disinterested in his imagination.

Karen Kenny reached for her phone and got it off the kitchen wall on the second ring. "Hello," she said.

"Hi, Karen, it's Charlie. I've got some good news and something to deliver to you. I'm not far away at the district courthouse on Second Avenue." He sounded excited.

"I'm at home, if you want to stop by," she said eagerly. "I don't want to leave here in case I get an important call, if you know what I mean. Can you come by the house?"

"That's the plan. I'll be there in fifteen," he replied and ended the call.

Not yet fully briefed on the setup for the rendezvous, Charlie was careful about what he said over the phone. Traffic slowed him a little, but he pulled into Karen's driveway around two fifteen, grinning from ear to ear, briefcase in hand. He started for the front door until he heard the side door slam as Karen stepped into the carport, motioning for him to use the kitchen entrance.

She smiled her biggest, showing off her deep dimples, suspecting that if Charlie had come from the courthouse with good news, it must concern her father. "What have you got for me?" she queried. Without thinking about it or waiting for a reply, she reached out and gave Charlie a big hug and kiss on the cheek.

Charlie stiffened a little, not expecting the physical contact, but in a flash, he relaxed and returned her affection. After the two of them got comfortable in the family room off the kitchen, Charlie explained what had transpired.

"I was lucky. After you left this morning, Ms. Agnew called her friend in the clerk's office and got me a ten-minute slot on the docket for a presentation. In a nutshell, I explained the circumstances to the judge, who ordinarily would not rule on a matter like this, since nothing could be shown to establish that your dad was even in his jurisdiction, which he is not at the moment. But after some explanation he agreed to take a risk and issue a preemptory injunction—"

"What does that mean?" Karen interrupted, showing concern because she didn't understand the terminology.

"Let me finish . . . granted a preemptory injunction to prevent your dad's guardian from moving him from the state of Maryland until the matter could be reviewed by the court, with all the parties of interest in attendance. He was most concerned that another jurisdiction had overridden a direct family member's right to provide guardianship for your father, particularly when there was more than one to consider, by that I mean the possibility of your brother," he explained.

"I don't see why Bob is an issue in this," she stated.

"Who's Bob?"

"My brother. He was never a consideration to act as a guardian; he lives too far away and doesn't have the time or resources."

"I know that." Charlie was a little frustrated, having just won a huge battle, feeling unappreciated. "You're missing the point. Now, when your father gets here, they can't make him go back, at least not right away!" He opened his briefcase and showed her the order he had drafted in his office, complete with the judge's signature and seal. "This is your copy to keep." He reached over the space between them and handed it to her.

Karen glanced down at the paper, not reading it, but felt overjoyed by what it represented. Without inhibition, she leaped out of her chair and jumped in Charlie's lap to give him another hug. The moment turned out to be awkward, and she retreated to her chair. "This is beyond my wildest expectations; I'm so happy." She was shaking with excitement. "Does this mean I can meet my dad here at the house tonight, if he gets here?"

"I've been thinking about that. In theory that would be fine, but logistically, I think it could pose some problems."

"What kind of problems?"

"Well, for starters, although you have the legal document, the FBI has not had a chance to process this new information, which will come as a shock to them. They may take it upon themselves, since it will undoubtedly be after normal business hours, to hold him overnight, while this gets sorted out. There will be no one to appeal to, so I suggest that we stand by our original plan to meet him somewhere else and get him to a place of safety until things sort out."

"Okay, that sounds like a plan."

"Have you given any thought to a place for the rendezvous and where he is going to spend the night?" Charlie asked.

"If we make our connection, I was going to put him up at the Courtyard on Fenton, downtown. I've given the matter of where to meet him a lot of thought. When he calls, I have to suggest a place without mentioning its name, right?" Karen raised an eyebrow in need of confirmation.

"Yep. You don't want to give away where it is in case someone is listening in on your calls, which we have to assume they are," Charlie cautioned.

"Well, I have the perfect place. When we were kids, my dad used to take my brother and me most weekends to various prominent Washington memorials, sort of as an educational visit, like a field trip. He would give us some historical background of the reason for the memorial to make it more real. The one I have in mind is the Titanic Memorial at Washington Channel. My brother and I were horsing around at the memorial when I was in third grade. He pushed me down and I chipped a front tooth on the base of the statue. It was very traumatic for all of us, and I'm sure my dad would remember it. The memorial is easy to find, and it's a very public place."

Charlie nodded his agreement. Fidgeting a little, he asked about their dinner plans, if she had any thoughts about that. They both agreed that she needed to stay at home by the phone until her dad had made contact. It would not be a good idea to miss his call after so much planning had gone into things.

"Do you know what kind of car he is driving?" Charlie asked.

"Bevy Martin told me it was a late-model silver Mercedes, the big one."

"Not bad," Charlie said with some admiration.

"I was just going to make the kids some mac and cheese. We could order in some pizza if you want to join us; I know Tim and

Bart would prefer pizza, and that way you could be here when Dad calls," Karen offered.

"That sounds great; I'd like that." He smiled. "So, if he left Columbia early this morning, I would suspect he won't get to the metro area until later this evening. I'm thinking after eight, anyway. If he calls around the time he crosses the river, we'll have to leave about the same time to get to the Washington Channel. We're about the same distance away. I sure would like to be a part of this reunion. May I feel free to join?"

Karen smiled up at him and said, "I wouldn't have it any other way."

Charlie looked at his watch. "I'm thinking I've got some time to get back to my office and get some work done."

"Be back here by six thirty, or the boys will eat your share. Sausage and mushroom sound all right?" Karen asked.

"Sure, whatever you like; that would be fine. Can I pick it up on my way over?" Charlie offered.

Karen nodded. "Sure, I'll place the order on the Internet and request that it be ready at six fifteen. You know the Domino's on Colesville? It's on the way from your office."

"I do, so I'll take care of that then."

Charlie and Karen did another awkward hug, and Charlie turned for the door. Over his shoulder he said, "We are going to have to work on that."

Karen's laughter followed him outside.

It was almost three o'clock when Charlie pulled his BMW out of the driveway. Karen left right after to pick the kids up from school.

⁓◯⁓

The newbie assigned to Ornstein stuck his head in the office. "We got another hit, Mr. McBride. Lyle told me to let you know if anything popped up while he was on his way to Washington."

"Where is this one?"

"A North Carolina authorized reader picked it up on Interstate 440 in Raleigh."

"God damn it!" McBride pounded his desk. He took his frustration out on the poor kid who had just been assigned from Quantico. "What's the matter with you guys? We know who the suspect is, what kind of car he is driving, its license number, and where he's going, and within a hundred square miles, where he is! Why the fuck can't you find him?! Let Ornstein know; he must be on the ground by now. What time did you say the hit was?"

"One thirty, approximately. Mr. McBride, we have POIs out to every law enforcement agency between here and Raleigh and beyond. State highway patrols have extra manpower covering all the interstates between here and there. I don't know how we keep missing him. I'm sure it's just a matter of time."

"We don't have any more time. The guy is just hours away from his destination. God help us and him if somebody else gets to Masterson first." McBride rested his aching head in his open palms, massaging his eyes to relieve the stress.

❧

Amir Resaei and Hassan cruised slowly past the Kenny residence, noting no cars in the carport or in front of the house. The street was quiet, no one about, as they parked the van facing out of the cul-de-sac at the end of the street, where they had entered the woods in the predawn earlier this morning.

They made their way as quietly as possible down the embankment in the trees, where they retraced their steps along the ravine. It took less time in the daylight to cover the quarter mile behind the residences that backed up to the wooded ravine where they had left their equipment. Amir found everything as he had left it. Keeping his profile as low as possible to avoid detection, he removed the camo cloth and opened the case. Everything seemed to be working properly. He lifted the computer screen and saw the same graphics flashing as he had in the morning. He removed the thumb drive and replaced it with an identical one and closed the lid. After recovering the equipment, he took one last look through the viewfinder to verify the laser was still on target.

The pair retraced their steps as quickly as they could back to the van, speed being the order of the moment to avoid detection, as opposed to quiet earlier in the day. As extra precaution, Amir drove to a strip mall parking lot before opening up his laptop and inserting the thumb drive in the USB port. When the Mac booted up, he selected the icon for the monitoring software and listened to what he had captured. The software shut the system down after several seconds of silence and reactivated it after noise was heard. There were some sounds around the kitchen, which the automatic modulation system amplified, and the loud voices of the woman urging her kids to load up for a ride to school. The last sound for a while was that of the back door closing, and then silence. Each reactivation began with a beep accompanied by a time posting in the graphics on the screen.

The first beep led to several wasted minutes of someone entering the home at the back door. This was followed by a phone call to someone named Charlie Edgerton, based on the responses to the person on the other end of the line. Amir and Hassan both listened to the woman as she pleaded with the person she called to meet with her that morning. She made reference to the fact that she thought her calls were being monitored. When Amir and Hassan heard that they looked at each other, somewhat startled, thinking she was talking about them. The call ended with her apparently making her appointment. They heard some additional muffled noises coming from the interior of the house, and then nothing. The next beep, after the woman answered her phone, revealed the woman agreeing to meet someone at her home. The final beep, around two thirty, was the arrival of her visitor and the usual greeting sounds.

They listened to the conversation, which seemed to include some legal mumbo jumbo, and then references to her father. The woman explained that she planned to meet her father when he got in that evening at the Titanic Memorial over by Fort McNair on Washington Channel. Hassan gave Amir a shoulder shrug, indicating he had no idea where the memorial was, but it took them no time to locate it on their phones.

The conversation also alerted them to the probable time of Masterson's arrival, sometime after eight thirty. The rest of the conversation did not seem to be of consequence, so after backing up and listening again to the important elements of the recording, they made their way across town to the Islamic Center, to reassemble the team and organize a plan to intercept Masterson when he arrived.

Back at the mosque parking lot, Amir, Hassan, Karim, and the fourth recruit looked over the shiny black town car. Karim looked very proud of himself as he handed the keys to Amir, beaming, "This what you were looking for?"

"Where did you get it, Mosely?" Amir used Karim's birth name, not being able to resist a subtle dig at the youth's roots—letting him know he was not really one of them, positioning himself as the real Muslim.

"You don't want to know," Karim frowned, shifting from foot to foot, sensing his cell leader's arrogance. He was patient and eager to please, to find acceptance, but there were limits.

"But I do want to know, brother," Amir said, trying now to mend things, having sensed Karim's resentment. "Are we at risk? Will this car be missed and reported stolen by somebody? What about the plates?"

"It's doubtful the car will be missed; it came from long-term parking at Dulles, and the hood was still warm when we picked it up. The plates have been changed. I believe it's what you asked for," Karim answered, standing a little taller.

"I have to admit, it looks pretty good. Good job, Karim. It's big, but doesn't stand out, big trunk, so we won't have any trouble shoving somebody in it. Good job," he repeated.

Just then Arshad Gul walked over from the side door of the mosque. He motioned to Amir, who stepped aside for a private conversation in Farsi. "Did you pick up the equipment?"

"Not yet; I was thinking of doing it tomorrow."

Amir was rewarded with a cuff to the side of his head.

"What don't you understand about the Russians not wanting to be connected with this operation? You go back tomorrow, and most likely the place will be swarming with federal agents. We can't let them see Russian equipment at the scene. It's five o'clock now, time for prayers. You've got time, go take care of it."

Amir tried to ignore his humiliation in front of his crew, but he couldn't help notice Karim smirking and shifting his eyes away, as Amir looked about.

⁓◌⁓

"Who's that?" Lyle Ornstein asked of the others who were in his Suburban, sitting at the top of the hill on Livingston at the intersection of Whittingham, watching through his field glasses as the maroon Chrysler van turned past him and disappeared down the street.

The occupants didn't seem like local residents. He handed the glasses to someone in the backseat and told them to keep an eye on them as best he could. The van seemed to have no interest in the Kenny residence as it drove quietly past.

Ornstein returned his attention to the briefing. He had previously covered the essentials of the Masterson situation when he arrived at the Bureau offices on Pennsylvania Avenue. He was actually met personally by John Hallanger, the Executive Assistant Director for the National Security Branch, who authorized whatever resources Ornstein deemed necessary for a successful recovery of his target, cautioning how sensitive this matter was becoming. He was a little overcome by the fact that he was in direct contact with a superior who was several steps above him in the chain of command, not normal for a junior agent.

Hallanger looked at the half dozen agents assembled at Lyle's request. "So, I want everyone in this room to give Agent Ornstein his, and her,"—he acknowledged the lone female agent—"full cooperation." Then turning to Lyle, he added, "Agent Ornstein, you have been the rallying point since your guardianship was granted a couple of months ago. You know more about the man than anybody else, so you are the natural choice to lead this team. Good luck. Feel free to reach out to my office if I can be of any help."

Hallanger then left matters to Ornstein, who gave those assembled a full briefing on what had been happening. There were some questions about why the Bureau was involved in domestic family matters, to which he answered, "That's above our pay grades and out of our control."

They selected two standard black Suburbans out of the motor pool and set off to surveil the Kenny residence and prepare for Masterson's expected arrival.

One of the agents observed, "These are going to stand out, aren't they?"

Ornstein explained that was not inconsistent with his plan to show a formative force on site in the event that others might want to interfere.

It was late afternoon when they stationed themselves at the top of the hill on Whittingham Drive. Ornstein was not expecting any activity before nightfall, based on the communication he got from McBride when he landed. The street was inactive until the maroon van went past, except for the white carpet cleaning utility van parked in front of the residence a few doors down from the Kenny house. The green Camry was parked in the driveway, but there was no other sign of activity. The agents, three to a vehicle, settled in for a long wait. Ornstein figured the cars could split up every couple of hours, as bathroom breaks were required.

⁂

The occupant of the carpet cleaning van watched carefully as the maroon Dodge Caravan passed by him and parked in the circle at the end of the street by the woods. He could see the driver step out of the car and head into the woods, while the passenger stayed in the front, keeping an eye on the neighborhood.

Gabe Ehrenstein watched as the driver slipped suspiciously out of sight down a hill as he entered the woods. He reached for his cell phone lying in the cup holder next to the folded sniper rifle sitting on the passenger seat. Arye Kunin answered on the first ring.

"We've got company boss," Ehrenstein began without preamble. "Two Middle Eastern types, if you will forgive the lapse in PC, just drove by my position and one of them entered the woods at the end of the street. I suspect the hill leads to a ravine of sorts running behind the Kenny residence. What do you want me to do?"

Arye thought for a moment and decided he didn't know enough to initiate any action. "Just sit tight and see what he does. If he comes back to his car, then he was just checking up on some equipment or visiting someone who is watching the house. We all know where our man is headed, just waiting it out for him to get here. Are you in a good position to take him out if things go awry?"

"Yeah, I'm just sittin' here. I'm thinking they should have sold tickets. The Bureau has two big SUVs up the street. We all know what's going down here. How could the FBI have fucked this up so badly? Our guy has been missing three days," Ehrenstein whined.

"Just sit tight. You're only there as an insurance policy, and we all hope we don't need it. My people tell me they pulled out all the stops; they were just behind the power curve. Personally, I think they waited too long to go public with this. The guy seems pretty amazing, though, wouldn't you say?" Arye rambled.

"Hold on," Ehrenstein interrupted. "The Arab is just coming out of the woods. He has a suitcase of some kind, loading it in the van."

"Must be surveillance equipment or a weapon. Just let him go; he's not our primary concern, but it does tell us there are others looking for Masterson. We may need your services yet."

"God, I hope not," Ehrenstein prayed. "Maybe you should pass it along. Those idiots should know what they're up against."

"Good idea."

⁓⁓

Amir placed the case carefully in the back of the van and started up the hill to leave the subdivision. He couldn't help but notice the brace of black SUVs as he turned away from them on Livingston and out of the subdivision. He kept an eye on the rearview mirror until he was out of sight of the SUVs. Finally satisfied that he was not being followed, he turned his attention to the route back to Georgetown.

He reassembled his team and returned the equipment, but not until after he had listened to the last of the conversations from the house. There was nothing he heard that would amend his plans for the next several hours; the earlier conversation with the lawyer had confirmed Masterson would not be in the area until later that evening, since they were planning on dining on take-out at six thirty, leave an hour for dinner, and they would not make a rendezvous until after dark.

Amir debated placing one of the Americans back at the house to monitor when the daughter left to meet her father but decided against it, thinking the manpower was more important right now. He decided to use the next couple of hours to scout out the memorial to determine where the best spot would be to intercept his target.

∾∽∾∾

Stewart Masterson could smell the barn. Much of the road was four lanes now, which made for speedier travel. Miles of open countryside came and went, small town after small town, many of which tried their best to throw him a curve ball by moving the big highway through the central business districts, requiring him to keep out a sharp eye for turns.

At first he was annoyed by the needless detours, but after he thought about it, he realized that the local residents were just trying to keep potential business in town for as long as possible. Understanding their point of view took the edge off, a psychology Masterson had developed during his lifetime as an aid in dealing with others in confrontational situations.

On a roll now, he had passed Wake Forest University, where Arnold Palmer had studied and played golf until his best friend, Buddy Worsham, died in a car crash. Next was the town of Henderson, and Masterson was starting to recall the areas he was driving through the farther north he got. A half hour later he crossed the Roanoke River on into South Hill, where US 1 turned northeast to Petersburg, and then north again into Richmond, where he hit the beginning of weekend rush-hour traffic at around four o'clock. As he drew closer to his goal, he increased his chatter with Helen in the next seat, describing places locally they had visited together over the years.

Exiting Richmond, his bladder began signaling him it was time for a stop, so he pulled into an Exxon and filled up, again with a hundred dollar bill, but this time, he was given his full change. He thanked the cashier, used the facilities, and got back on the road. He figured he had less than two hours to go to get to Karen's.

Masterson had another fifty-five miles of country driving until he hit the outskirts of Alexandria, where the road widened to six lanes, and the lines of cars queued lane by lane, as the stoplights regulated crossing traffic. The slow movement was frustrating, and although he was pretty comfortable with where he was and considered slipping over to the interstate, which was often visible off to his left, his gut told him that good old US 1 had worked out pretty well for him, so he decided to stay with it.

As he neared the edge of Alexandria, the traffic was almost at a standstill. He glanced at his watch, *after six o'clock,* and for the first time in a while he felt really fatigued. He considered stopping for a rest but disregarded the idea when he thought about being so close to the end of his journey. *Maybe some refreshment,* he thought. "What do you think, Helen? Should we get a snack?"

She was up for it apparently, as he spied a Sheetz, a full-service gas and convenience center, ahead on the right. He didn't even have to cross the street. He parked away from the pumps, dozens of rows of them facing every which way, up against the center building and went inside.

The interior was mammoth, reminding him of his first impression of the inside of the Walmart, where he had bought some clothes in what seemed so long ago. Clearly it was not as big, but for a convenience store . . .

Feeling somewhat lost, he roamed the aisles looking at the shelves, hoping he would spy something that appealed to him. He had worked his way around the entire perimeter of the store when he came upon a frozen milk-shake display. He read the directions carefully, selecting a chocolate shake from the freezer, noting that it was frozen rock hard, undrinkable. The instructions in bold print over the machine had him place it in a boxlike device and press the "prepare" button. The machine buzzed and hummed for a minute, and when Masterson pulled it out and removed the cellophane, he could feel the pliability of the cold cardboard half-quart container. He grabbed a straw from the rack, bit off the end of the protective cover, and stuck it in the opening of the lid. Sampling the contents, he decided it was the best milk shake he had ever tasted. This time he had some smaller bills to pay for his merchandise.

Back in the car, he sat next to Helen and reclined his seat a little to give his back some relief from the strain of hours on the road. He held the ice-cold container to his throbbing forehead and felt the tension and stress melt away from his body. The moisture accumulating on the outside of the milk shake reached the limits of adhesion as they comingled and slid to the bottom of the container, forming large droplets. When the weight of these exceeded their cohesive limit, they dropped onto his pants. Masterson brushed them away with the back of his hand and noticed the lump in his right front pants pocket. He reached inside and pulled out his new cell phone, triggering memories of his morning with Pepper and her instructions to call Karen when he was close to Maryland. He didn't know why he couldn't just go to the house and surprise her, but Pepper and Bevy had been very clear that he must not go directly to the house. Then he remembered the government agents were looking for him, and he knew enough not to trust them.

This seemed like a good time to call his daughter. He wasn't driving, so the call would not be a distraction. He opened the flip top and pushed some of the buttons until the screen came to life. He waited a moment, assuming it had to warm up, and punched in the number he had known since he was a little boy.

Karen was sitting at the kitchen table staring at the phone and biting her fingernails. Charlie had called her a few minutes earlier to let her know he was on his way with the pizza. The boys were watching television in the family room. She had jumped at Charlie's first ring, hoping that it would be her dad. She was so worried about him, but she assumed that if he had been intercepted, she would have been notified, and she had heard nothing.

Karen had seen enough episodes of *The Blacklist* on Thursday nights to be aware of the significance of the black Chevy Suburbans that were cruising down her street, reversing at the cul-de-sac every hour or so, so she knew the house was being watched.

Charlie pulled in the drive and knocked on the kitchen door with his elbow, both hands holding the hot Domino's boxes by the edges. Just as she let him in, the house phone rang, and Karen faced a dilemma, which to attend to first. She compromised and opened the door and held it with her foot while she reached over the kitchen table for the wall phone.

"Hello," she said breathlessly.

"Hi, Karen, it's Dad" came the reply.

Karen was overcome with emotion. As Charlie worked his way past her in the confined space, he put the pizza cartons on the table and reached out to Karen to steady her. Karen could no longer support herself and slumped into the chair adjacent the door; unable to contain her emotion, she released her burden through heaving sobs. Charlie held her shoulders affectionately.

"Daddy," she blubbered. "I've been soooo worried about you. Are you close? No, no wait, don't tell me; somebody might be listening. Please tell me you're all right."

"I'm fine, dear. No need to cry. Everything is under control. It's so good to hear your voice. I have so much to tell you."

"I'll bet you do!" Karen laughed a little through her tears. She began collecting herself to prepare for the ordeal ahead. "So, Dad, I need you to pay close attention."

"Okay, I'm listening."

"We shouldn't stay on the phone too long or your location may be traced. We need to meet somewhere. It's not safe for you to come to the house right now. There are government cars all over the place just waiting for you to show up."

"Got it. Where do you want to meet, and where do we go from there?" Masterson asked.

"Daddy, do you remember when Bobby and I were kids, you used to take us to see memorials in the city? You gave us history lessons."

Masterson did not have to think about it; he vividly recalled his form of homeschooling when the children were in grammar school. "Yes, of course I do."

"Do you remember the one when Bob pushed me down and I chipped my front tooth?"

Masterson thought for a minute, as he visualized the twenty-foot statue along the water's edge at Fort McNair with its arms spread wide, so as to embrace the souls of those who perished in the north Atlantic in 1912. He remembered Bobby and Karen chasing each other around the stone steps in front of the pedestal, his son catching her as she tried to evade him behind the base of the statue. He felt again the sudden panic as he grabbed her and Karen lost her balance, falling and landing face-first against the unforgiving stone. He heard her shrill squeal as she put her hands to her suddenly bleeding mouth, and seeing the panic on his son's face when he realized the consequences of his actions, hands stretched in front of him, palms up, pleading to him, "I barely touched her."

"Like yesterday," he replied simply.

"Can you meet me there? Do you remember how to get there?"

"Sure, honey. It'll take me about an hour, depending on traffic."

Masterson estimated he was only a half hour away from central D.C., but he was allowing for heavy Friday night traffic.

"Best if you take your time to give me some leeway to get out of here without being followed," she suggested. "Let's arrange to meet in an hour and a half, okay? I'm so excited to see you; I can't wait."

"All right, Karen. I'll be there on schedule. Be careful. Love you."

"Love you, too, Daddy. Bye."

Karen was so excited she had goose bumps. She turned to Charlie, looking up at him. "Wow! This is *really* going to happen. We're so close. But we still have to figure a way to get out of here without being followed. Have you noticed the surveillance cars out front?" Karen looked out the front window, not seeing any. "They cruise past every so often."

"I passed two of them parked at the top of the hill on Livingston, black Suburbans," Charlie replied.

"Those are they," Karen confirmed, her English grammar parsing skills taking over.

"I have an idea. Let's take my car, with you sitting down out of sight, and drive back to my office. The parking is underground. I'll have Ms. Agnew come back to the office and park next to us. We can leave the office and take her car. Nobody will be looking for it," Charlie said, proud of himself.

"That could work. She can drive your car home and we can swap back tomorrow," Karen said.

"We can take one of the pizzas with us, and leave the other for your boys," Charlie added.

"They will never get by on one pizza. Just take a couple slices for yourself. I couldn't possibly eat right now," Karen countered.

"Works for me."

Karen took two slices of the sausage and mushroom pizza out of the top box and wrapped them in a paper towel and slid them into an oversized baggie. Then she called the boys into the kitchen. "Right now!" she emphasized, adrenaline surging through her body. "Sorry," she apologized, realizing her abruptness, but it had its effect. Bart and Tim were standing at attention in front of her, sensing the stress in her voice. "Mr. Edgerton and I have to go out for a little bit, and when we come home, I may have a surprise for you, but it'll have to wait, for now." She explained that she wanted no nonsense from them while she was gone and that they were to be in bed by the time the news came on.

"Does that mean *FOX News* or *NBC News?*" Bart asked.

"Don't be cute, young man." Karen knew they recognized that *FOX News* aired an hour earlier than the other network channels.

Tim smiled at the chiding his brother got from their mom.

"We're leaving you the pizza, minus a couple of slices, so share the way you were taught."

The boys seemed content to have a free evening; they gave no heed to the "surprise" their mom referred to, for the moment anyway.

Karen grabbed a sweater to ward off the chill of the approaching evening, and she headed out the back door, noting that no other vehicles were visible on the street except for the carpet cleaning van at her neighbor's house that had been there all afternoon. She bent over and made her way silently to the car. Charlie was to leave by the front door by prior arrangement, a hopeful subterfuge. The interior light gave her away, if anybody was watching, but she slid low in the front seat, anyway.

Charlie took a moment to call Ms. Agnew and make arrangements with her. She was only too willing to participate in some sort of clandestine affair, and she left her apartment on the spot, driving to the office in her Buick LaCrosse, which fortunately was white, so it could not be confused with her boss's black Beamer.

Two minutes after Karen got to the car, Charlie opened the front door, making as much fuss as he could about getting in, trying to make it look like he was just at the house for a visit, now leaving by himself. His hope was that whoever was watching the house would notice that Karen's Camry was still in the drive, and that the residence was occupied with the lights on, TV flickering from the rear.

He backed out and drove up the hill with Karen crouching as low as possible in the passenger seat to avoid detection. Charlie turned right on Livingston, noting the parked Suburbans on the other side of the intersection. As he accelerated away out of the subdivision, he saw the headlights of both SUVs light up. The car in back followed the BMW, while the other turned right down the hill on Whittingham. Charlie knew better than to try to lose his tail, so he continued to his office, parking in the garage as near to the elevator as he could. Ms. Agnew's car was already in her spot across the aisle. On the fifth floor in his office, Charlie swapped keys with Ms. Agnew. They hugged in the excitement of the moment, as she wished him good luck in his mission.

Karen stepped to the window and watched as the black Suburban pulled under the building and then returned to position itself on the street where it could observe comings and goings from the garage onto Georgia Avenue. She pointed it out to Charlie, who took note.

"Not to worry, the garage also exits on to Cameron Street on the back side of the building. This will work out even better."

Charlie took a minute to explain what was going on to Ms. Agnew, so she could feel more a part of it. In fact, she had already figured things out, having typed the writ for the injunction earlier in the day before Charlie went to district court. They said their goodbyes, and Charlie and Karen headed for the elevator first, lest the bad guys spot Ms. Agnew in the BMW and know something was amiss.

At seven fifteen, Karen and Charlie eased quietly out of the parking garage onto Cameron Avenue, turned right on Spring Street, and right again on to Colesville Road at the light. Charlie could see no headlights of interest in his rearview mirror.

"Charlie, I can't thank you enough for all of your help. This is above and beyond, and I could not possibly have put all this together by myself."

"Karen, you don't have to thank me. This is the most exciting thing I have done since losing my virginity," he said, turning and smiling and prompting a laugh from Karen. "So, where are we going, exactly?"

"Take a right on Fenton. If you go south a ways, you can cut over to Georgia Avenue, and we will be out of sight of your office. Take Georgia Avenue all the way south, cut over to seventh, and take it to the end, then just follow the river as far as you can. We can't get too close because the road ends, but you can't miss it once you get near. It's a big statue facing away from the water, with arms spread out wide, you know, like that scene with Leonardo DiCaprio and Kate Winslet at the front of the *Titanic* in the movie where he said, 'I'm king of the world!'— probably where they got the idea for that scene in the movie."

∽◇∾

The early site visit to the Titanic Memorial proved to be well worthwhile. Amir drove the Lincoln Town Car while Hassan navigated with the aid of Google Maps. The route suggested took them out of Georgetown via Virginia Avenue to Seventeenth, where they went south to Independence, finally joining Maine Avenue SW. From there, they followed the river to Sixth, and again south to the memorial.

As they got closer, the entire area seemed to be consumed by new construction, making things very confusing. At the water's edge, the street ended at the ferry docks and the Anacostia Riverwalk Trail.

The paths to the actual memorial were blocked by the massive construction projects, and the circle that marked the beginning of the path to their destination was hardly recognizable. There were few cars in the area, and Amir proceeded as far has he could with the car until finally he could go no farther. The four men continued on foot down the double-wide sidewalk along the river front for almost two hundred yards before they could even see the statue in the distance.

"This is not good," Amir said aloud. "There is too much that can go wrong here. If Masterson gets to the monument, we will have to strong-arm him all this way to get back to the car, and that might attract too much attention. We have to find a way to intercept him *before* he gets here."

Hassan nodded his agreement, still looking at his cell phone for some clarity.

The others were just along for the ride, at this point, and simply watched as Amir and Hassan tried to figure something out.

Hassan suddenly came to life. "No, wait! It's worse than that." Studying his phone, he said, "There are *two* entrances." He emphasized two. "The map shows you can get to the statue from the side at the end of Fourth Street," he said, pointing ahead.

"Let's check out the other entrance," Amir said, as he motioned for the others to return with him to the car. After further reflection, he changed his mind. "Karim, you and Armin follow the path, and we'll meet you at the statue from the other direction. Then we can compare notes."

The American converts started south on the wide sidewalk along the water, while Amir and Hassan ran back to the car. They retraced their steps up Sixth to M Street, and cut over two blocks to Fourth, back south again to the end of the street. At the very end was another double-wide sidewalk heading toward the water perpendicular to the one they had just come down, which they could see just a few hundred feet ahead.

"There's nobody around; let's see if we can drive to the memorial from here," Hassan suggested.

"Good idea," Amir agreed, and he turned down the path. As they approached the river, they could see the statue rise above them to the left, a man standing atop a six-foot pedestal above five or six steps, his arms stretched out to the side in a reverent manner. An inscription on the pedestal dedicated the monument to the men and sailors who gave their lives to save the women and children aboard the ill-fated luxury liner. Karim and Armin were standing in front waiting for them. Amir and Hassan discussed the different scenarios that could play out, as darkness fell on their little group.

"We have to assume the daughter will wait for her father at the statue, since that's where they decided to meet," Amir began. "We have no control over which entrance Masterson will decide to use, and we obviously can't wait for them here in the open."

Hassan nodded in agreement.

"The other entrance is too far away and impassable for a car, so I suggest we wait at the top of Fourth for the Mercedes to pass by. If he parks up there, we will grab him then; if he drives down the short access we just came down, we will follow him and grab him as soon as he gets out of the car. We can have him in the trunk in a matter of seconds. There's room enough here in front of the statue to turn around and get out. I think we just have to shoot up Sixth or Seventh to get to the interstate, and then we are just about home free."

Again, Hassan agreed. "Sounds like a plan. What if the daughter puts up a struggle or tries to follow us?"

Amir shrugged. "What can she possibly do? There are four of us. Where is she going to park? We'll be long gone by the time she gets to her car."

Hassan wasn't so sure about that. "She could call for help."

"If she was willing to call for help, she wouldn't be meeting her father here," Amir reasoned.

"You've got a point," Hassan responded, still not as confident as he would have liked.

They retraced their path to the corner of Fourth and P Streets where they parked discreetly among the other cars and began their vigil.

CHAPTER NINE

Ornstein's phone vibrated just as the black BMW turned in front of him onto Whittingham and pulled into the Kenny driveway. The light was fading, but he thought he recognized the person who got out of the car, carrying two pizza cartons. The agent sitting next to him ran the plates and verified that the car belonged to Charles Edgerton, who Ornstein remembered was the lawyer Karen Kenny brought to the guardianship hearing in Florida months ago. It seemed reasonable that he would be involved, so Ornstein didn't pay any attention to it.

His phone vibrated again, returning his attention to it. He looked at the screen and saw a text message from the AD's office. It read: "Just advised by another intelligence agency that Middle Eastern operatives have been observed in your vicinity."

"That's just great!" Ornstein said out loud, sarcastically. "It's no secret which is the other agency. Only the Israelis would notify us, so obviously they are here, too," he said to no one in particular. He passed it on to the others in the second SUV. Another half hour passed without activity, when the front door of the Kenny house opened and the lawyer walked to his car, started it up, and backed out of the driveway.

"Anybody see a second person get in the car?" Ornstein barked.

"I thought I saw the interior light come on a few seconds before he got in, but I'm not sure" came from the backseat.

As the car passed, they could see no one in the passenger side. Ornstein had to make a snap decision. He directed the car behind him to follow the BMW. He couldn't risk sitting here on his ass while the Kenny woman arranged to meet her father somewhere else, but he couldn't risk being somewhere else if Masterson showed up. *Thank God we have two cars,* he said to himself.

Ten minutes later, the second Suburban radioed in that Edgerton had returned to his office. His car was in the parking garage underneath the building.

"Stay with him," Ornstein instructed, tension building by the moment.

"The fifth floor lights just came on, and we can see activity in the office" cackled over the speaker.

"Let me know the minute he leaves and follow him until you know where he goes."

"Okay."

Another fifteen minutes went by. "Anything?" Ornstein asked.

"Yes, we see lights coming out of the garage . . . It's the Beamer."

"Stay on him."

"We're about a block and a half behind" came the reply. "He's coming up Georgia, no wait, he's going south on Colesville."

"Move in closer. I don't give a shit if he knows he's being followed. The better for us!"

Another two minutes.

"We're right behind. Shit! Shit, shit, shit!"

"What's wrong now?" Ornstein was getting really frustrated, not feeling any control over the situation.

"It's a woman driving, definitely not the lawyer. What do you want us to do?"

"Pull her over; ask her what's she's doing in his car."

Ornstein could hear the abbreviated siren pulse over the radio as the agent released the mike button, doors slamming, and then silence.

Another two or three minutes.

"She says her boss asked her to drive his car home, that he had another ride."

"Bullshit! Find out what kind of car she drives and plates if you can get them. If not run it through DMV. They must be in her car."

Overcome with frustration that nothing was going his way, Ornstein let out a series of expletives and smashed his fists on the dash in front of him. He felt a jab of pain and heard a pop from the outside bone in his right hand. He looked at his hand and tried to make a fist, but the little finger kept curling up and turning inward. He was familiar with that injury from a brief stint as an intramural boxer while he was in college. He had broken his outside or fifth metacarpal, now showing the same symptom. Angry at himself, he nursed his hand, knowing that there was nothing that could be done about it for now. He would have to endure the inconvenience of the pain for a while, until he could have it looked at.

"Tell her we will be in touch, and come back here. I'll try to figure something out in the meantime."

Ornstein had never felt so stupid. While he was waiting for the other Suburban to arrive, he drove the few hundred yards to the Kenny residence and rang the doorbell. After a moment he was greeted by the older of her two kids who confirmed what he suspected, that their mother had stepped out for a while, to be home soon. With much trepidation, Ornstein made a decision. He knew it was a gamble, but he had to call in the cavalry, or he was in risk of this whole thing blowing up in his face. He searched the contact list on his phone and found the cell number of the AD in Washington and, with great reluctance, autodialed his number.

"Hallanger" was the simple response.

"Sir, this is Agent Ornstein from Miami; we met this afternoon when you helped me assemble the surveillance team to pick up Masterson."

"Yes, I remember," he replied. "What's up?"

Ornstein was direct and to the point. "Sir, I may have made an error in judgment here, and I'm afraid I have really messed things up. I need help."

Hallanger actually found this a little refreshing, thinking that, while what he was about to hear was not going to be good, it was going to be reliable and truthful. "Okay, Ornstein, let's have it from the beginning."

"Well, sir, the beginning is the end. We have lost contact with Masterson's daughter. Not intended as a defense, sir, but it was a deliberate act on her part, something that had been planned well in advance," Ornstein began.

"Go on, agent. I'll save my reaction until after you have finished." As Hallanger spoke, he heard the alert on his cell phone that another call was coming through. He held the phone far enough away that he could identify the caller on the screen; it was Cavner. *Oh, that's not good,* he thought. "Give it to me fast, Ornstein. I think I may already be hearing about it from somebody else."

"Sir, it's pretty obvious to me that Miss Kenny has been in contact with her father and arranged to meet him somewhere else, other than here. I know—forgive me—I suspect that you may have an alternative source of information available to you, from the lead we got this morning regarding calls between Masterson and his friends at the facility, and possibly some other individual in South Carolina. If that source is still available to you, I'm thinking that about the only way we are going to catch up to Masterson and his daughter is if your source can track her cell phone. Am I out of line, here, sir?"

"Ordinarily I would say yes, but I don't want to split hairs with you while things are going up in smoke, so I'll overlook it for now. You realize we may be opening up a can of worms, so let's not discuss it any further. I understand what you need, and I will do my best to find out what information is available to us. We don't have time to set up anything in real time, so any information I obtain will be stale by the time you get it, but it's better than nothing. I'll call you back when I have something. Until then, just sit tight. If you're still watching the Kenny house, they may come back."

"Doubtful in my estimation, Mr. Hallanger." Ornstein frowned, but he had no choice. The AD as much as admitted he had a source, and it didn't take much imagination to figure out what it was.

By the time he was off the phone, the other Suburban had pulled in behind him in the Kenny driveway. All six agents got out of their cars, discretion no longer a requisite for them, and discussed their options in a huddle between the two SUVs.

ᘒᗡᘓ

Hallanger selected Cavner's name on the list of "missed calls" and listened to it ring until he picked up.

"Cavner."

"Hi, Hollis, it's Jack. I saw a missed call. What can I do for you?"

"I haven't got time for pleasantries, and neither do you. There's bad news and worse news. I'll dispense with discretion, in view of the short fuse we have. Karen Kenny spoke a few minutes ago with Masterson and set up a meet. I assume you are watching the house, but I wanted to get to you before you got fooled. All I have about the place is that it is a monument somewhere in the city where Masterson's family gathered on weekends," Cavner outlined.

"That doesn't narrow it down much, say what, to about two or three hundred? I assume that's the bad news; what's the worse news?" Hallanger sighed.

"The Israelis have someone in the area of the Kenny residence, and he has identified some Iranians or other Middle Eastern clowns there as well. So it looks like Brogan's fears were grounded. This situation is serious. Make sure your guys don't let the Kenny woman out of their sight. Have you got enough resources on it?" Cavner asked.

"That ship has sailed, Hollis; they already lost them. I was going to call you, anyway. As you predicted, the Bureau was unable to get authorization to tap Kenny's phones. So Obi-Wan, you're our only hope. Can you keep the trace of her phone going?" Hallanger pleaded.

"Jesus Christ!" Cavner blurted out. "Do you appreciate what you're asking? First, this information comes to me alone, for obvious reasons. I can't put my people in touch with your people because they can't know what we're doing. All I can do is pass this stuff along to you, and I'm not going to stick my neck out to talk to your agents. So, in a nutshell, I'll do this for you, but it's between the two of us. If somebody later on wants to know how you got so smart all of a sudden, you are going to have to figure something out to cover both of us. She better have her cell phone on. I don't know if we have the time to hack it. I think the best we will be able to do is tower track it, anyway. GPS would be better, but if she's moving, you are going to be behind the eight ball, anyway. It's after seven thirty now; I probably won't know anything for half an hour."

Hallanger called Ornstein and explained the plan. "I'm sure I don't need to spell it out for you how many violations this little plan is going to rack up. So you had better make good use of the information. I wouldn't be doing this at all if we didn't have confirmation the Israelis and probably the Iranians are looking for Masterson, too. I'm thinking that if we just had left this situation alone, we would all have been better off."

Ornstein agreed with him, thinking this whole operation was distasteful from the beginning. *Mossad*, he noted to himself. *That must be the carpet cleaning van down the street; we ought to run down there and tell the poor guy he can go home. Nothing is going to happen here tonight.*

∽つつ∾

Charlie Edgerton maneuvered Ms. Agnew's Buick slowly down Georgia Avenue, careful not to attract attention by speeding. As he approached southwest Washington, Georgia Avenue became Seventh Avenue. At Karen's direction, he took it to the end where it emptied out onto Maine. There was construction everywhere, and it was getting dark. He could see no sign of a memorial of any kind.

Karen pointed ahead. "Turn right here."

Charlie did as he was told and angled around construction debris. The road was completely gone now, and he was driving on a dirt path. "Karen, are you sure this is right?" He was starting to get nervous.

Karen was nervous, too. "I don't really recognize anything except for the warehouse-looking building on the water ahead. It's been a long time. This area was all open when I was a kid. There are cars parked ahead, keep going and look for a circle. That's where we parked when I came here with Dad."

Charlie continued cautiously, not particularly liking what he was seeing in the headlights: trash, discarded soda cans, and construction debris. He inched forward when Karen pointed excitedly ahead.

"There! Doesn't that look like part of a circle, where those cars are parked?"

Indeed, Charlie did see some old pavement amounting to half a circle, the other half having been removed by the apartment building site preparation.

"This is it; I'm sure. See that big sidewalk that runs along the river? That takes us to the monument. Park here on the circle, and

241

we'll walk the rest of the way. It's just ahead; you'll see it when we get closer."

Charlie parked the car, looking around at the deserted area, and locked it. He and Karen stepped into the chilly night air and began walking up the sidewalk that paralleled the river. About halfway down the walkway, Charlie could make out the head and extended arms of the statue. Karen saw it, too, and grabbed Charlie's hand and tugged, urging him to speed up his pace. Charlie picked it up a little, glancing at this watch.

"It's not quite eight yet; we're early. We don't have to be in a rush. Your dad won't be here for another twenty minutes."

Karen led him by the hand up a few stairs to the base of the statue, and Charlie read the words chiseled on the front. She pointed to the corner next to the last step. "That's where Bobby tipped me over and I chipped my front tooth." She lifted her upper lip, and showed him. "See, the left front is a cap. I've had it since I was ten. Not the same one of course."

Charlie pretended to examine her mouth. He never would have noticed. He thought her teeth looked fine. "Excited?" he asked.

"Very. I think we just might pull this off," she answered.

The statue faced north. Behind it was the river, so water was on two sides, right facing and behind. Charlie walked to the railing behind the statue and looked into the water. Small eddies had cornered some trash where the two seawalls met, and some leaves and an oversized Styrofoam coffee cup spun in circles, trapped in the current. He wondered how long it would stay there. Karen sat on the steps to wait for her dad.

೨೨೧

Stewart Masterson needn't have worried about being early. The Friday night Alexandria traffic held US 1 almost to a standstill. Each light seemed to take two or three cycles to get through, and it was almost an hour to get over the Fourteenth Street Bridge on I-395, which he joined off old faithful US 1 to cross the river, after he got into familiar territory.

He crossed to the Washington side and exited at L'Enfant Plaza Circle to pick up Maine Avenue, which he followed to where he remembered visiting the Titanic Memorial so many years ago. He continued along the river until he was where he thought he should be, but all he could see were massive construction projects. The whole of the area seemed to be in the midst of a redevelopment.

He drove down Sixth Street, but it dead-ended a block from the water at another construction site. They all appeared to be apartment buildings going up, and he could see the dinner cruise barges tied up along the water, but he didn't see how he could get to them. In his frustration, he turned around to see if he could find another way in. He felt sure he knew exactly where the monument was, and then he remembered that it was approachable from two sides. He thought of calling Karen, but Bevy and Pepper had drilled it into him that he was not to turn on his phone after he contacted Karen, and he assumed they had their reasons. They were very insistent. He looked over at Helen sitting beside him.

"Got any suggestions?" he asked.

Hearing none, he turned the car around and worked his way around the block to the next street south, Fourth Street by the entrance to Fort McNair, which ran along the water to the west. He took it to the end by the entrance to Fort McNair, which paralleled the channel behind the monument, and right away recognized the double-wide sidewalk that led to the memorial. It was late and dark, and he remembered it was a little bit of walk, so he decided to drive down the sidewalk, which was as wide as an alley, anyway. He paid no attention to the black Lincoln Town Car parked at the corner.

∽ↄᴄ∾

It was just a few minutes after eight when Cavner reached out for Hallanger. "We've got a location on the Kenny woman. She's been stationary for about fifteen minutes, located in southwest Washington along the water. Google Maps tells us that's the location of the Titanic Memorial, for what that's worth. Good luck!"

Hallanger relayed the information to a very relieved Ornstein, reenergized that he was back in the game. The agents lit up the roadway with sirens and flashing lights from their grills. The two Suburbans were quite a sight to see rushing down Georgia Avenue at high speed. Fortunately for them, most of the local traffic had left the D.C. area for the weekend. The procession did not look that organized as six federal agents punched buttons on their cell phones trying to google directions for the Titanic Memorial in cars that were jumping around all over the place. With the location identified on their phones, they proceeded in earnest to the entrance to the memorial near Washington Channel off Sixth Street SW.

∽ↄᴄ∾

Masterson proceeded slowly down the sidewalk, which was almost as wide as the walkways around the National Mall. The path was lined with oak trees on both sides, which blocked his line of sight to the statue at the memorial itself, and the path was dimly lit with globe-like street lamps on both sides of the path. The excitement of nearing his destination had his heart rate well above normal, and adrenaline was coursing through his system. Finally, he could see the steps leading up to the statue, just as he remembered, and, as he approached, his heart almost jumped out of his chest when he saw his daughter rising to her feet on the step near the base of the statue.

He accelerated the last few yards and pressed firmly on the

brakes in the spacious area in front of the statue. He was overcome with emotion at the release of all the tension from his three-day ordeal, drained of energy, as he watched Karen run down the steps toward the car. Out of the corner of his eye he could see a young man step from behind the pedestal and join her as they made their way the last few paces to his car door.

Masterson turned to the passenger seat and said quietly to Helen, "We're here."

Feeling exhausted after the tension of his three-day quest to see his daughter, Masterson's chest heaved with the beginnings of a sob, as he gathered himself to greet her. He slid the urn out of the seat restraints and placed it in the duffle he had bought at Walmart. Lifting the bundle in his arms, he affixed the strap firmly over his shoulder, opened the car door with his left hand, and placed his feet on the ground to lever himself out of the car.

As he stepped around the open door, clutching his duffle, Karen and the young man, who seemed vaguely familiar to Masterson, were just coming down the steps to greet him. Karen's arms were already spread in anticipation of the bear hug she was going to give her father, now just steps away, when they all heard the squeal of tires losing grip on the pavement. Turning in the direction of the sound, they watched in horror as a black sedan, headlights off, screeched to a halt between the Mercedes and the steps to the monument, barely missing Masterson, boxing him between his open car door and the sedan and separating him from his daughter and her friend.

As the Town Car stopped, the trunk flew open, activated from the inside, and the rear doors sprang open. Two large men, one black and one with a full crop of facial hair, jumped out and roughly grabbed Masterson around his shoulders and legs, lifting him as he kicked and elbowed the best defense he could muster while still clinging to the duffle, and dumped him unceremoniously in the trunk of the big sedan.

Masterson did his best to free himself, but he was no match for almost five hundred pounds of a defensive lineman and a running back. Before he could sort things out in his mind, he was enveloped in darkness, curled in a fetal position, clutching his duffle in his arms, with a nasty bump on his head where it had hit the edge of the trunk when he was thrown in. In a flash, the assailants were back in their seats, and the Town Car was turning around the front of the Mercedes, speeding up the wide sidewalk from which it had come.

Karen screamed as she helplessly watched her father being overpowered by the kidnappers and did her best to run the last few steps to intervene.

Adrenaline surged through Charlie as well, and he rushed behind Karen, his heart pounding, but at the last second, he reached out and grabbed her by the neck of her shirt, having the presence of mind to know that she could only endanger herself by interfering, although he was rewarded with a smack on the side of his face as she tried to break free.

"Hold on, Karen. You'll only get yourself killed," he warned.

"But we have to do something! What can we do?" she pleaded.

"We can follow them, and maybe call for help when we find out where they are going," he offered.

"But we'll never get to our car in time; they'll be long gone," she said as she watched the taillights of the black sedan move up the sidewalk.

Charlie eyed the Mercedes. "We'll take your dad's car; it's right here," he suggested.

"But we don't have a key!"

"Don't need one. Look, it's still running," Charlie observed. "Come on, we don't have any time to waste. We have to get moving, or we will have no options," he said, pushing her toward the car.

Charlie jumped in the driver's seat as Karen ran around to the other side and got in. They made a U-turn in the generous space, still in time to see the sedan turn left onto Fourth Street. Once it reached the street, they saw the taillights come on. It didn't seem to be moving very fast.

⁊⊃◌⊰

It took twenty minutes for the pair of SUVs to reach the mess of the construction at the end of Sixth Street where the cell phones had led them. The six agents were maxed out in frustration, only compounded by the pressure they were under.

Ornstein, in the lead car, motioned for his driver to continue on the tamped down dirt of the construction site toward the water, that being his only option to bring his blue GPS locater on his cell phone closer to the red pin that identified the memorial. It looked to him like getting to the monument was going to be problematic. They wound their way to the seawall by the boathouses that lined the river where he saw the remnants of the paved circle that led to the memorial entrance.

"There! Stop!" he radioed the car behind them. "Didn't you guys say the lawyer's secretary drove a white Buick LaCrosse?"

They confirmed it and gave him the license number.

Ornstein jumped from the vehicle and looked at the plate on the back of the car. He motioned to the others to follow, saying, "That's it. That's the car the daughter and her lawyer came in."

Feeling like he was finally making some progress, Ornstein told the drivers to pull the SUVs up to block the egress from the walkway and wait with the cars, as he and the three remaining agents formed a tactical line to advance the few hundred yards to the memorial clearly identified by signage on the walkway and his GPS locater pin on his phone.

They proceeded slowly, making sure they didn't walk into a bad situation, which they could only make worse. A few minutes later, they arrived at a deserted statue, arms spread wide, face uplifted to the heavens. Ornstein's shoulders slumped, as he looked skyward, thinking that he, too, would need help from the heavens. As he scanned the walkway to his left, he saw the taillights of a car turning left off a side entrance to the memorial he had been unaware of until this very minute. In the distance, he thought he heard the squeal of tires trying to negotiate the pavement.

"We missed them!" he shouted to the others. "Quick, on the double, back to the cars!"

The four agents ran the three hundred yards at full speed, trying to holster their weapons on the fly, back to the Suburbans. It was another three minutes before they were loaded up and ready to go.

"Where to?" the driver asked.

"I have absolutely no idea," Ornstein replied, slumping in his seat.

Amir's heart was pounding as he started to speed up the sidewalk, after Masterson was secure in the trunk of his car.

"Not so fast, Amir," Hassan cautioned. "We don't want to attract attention to ourselves. Masterson isn't going anywhere, and nobody's following us."

"You're right." Amir slowed to a residential speed limit, and turned left onto Fourth. "Have you got the route dialed up?"

"Everything is right here. You drive, and I'll navigate." Hassan had already anticipated the need for GPS, since they hadn't really done a full rehearsal of the trip to the safe house that had been provided by the Russians. He just knew in general it was south toward Mount Vernon on the George Washington Parkway. "Take a left on M Street, and cut over to Seventh and take a right up to Independence." At M he said, "Turn left here."

Amir turned left on M as instructed, but things suddenly didn't look right to him.

"Hey! This isn't M; the sign says Maine," he said excitedly.

"Same thing. Just relax. I've got this; you're doing fine." Hassan could tell his coconspirator was very tense and nervous. *Hell, I would be, too,* he thought.

As they crossed Sixth, Amir could see flashing blue lights off in the distance to his left, reflecting off the darkened buildings under construction in the direction of the memorial.

"You see that Hassan?" he asked. "Do you think that has anything to do with us?"

"Maybe. They aren't a factor, though. There's Seventh; turn right."

"Okay." They proceeded north up Seventh for a few blocks.

Hassan tried to relieve some of the stress. "Up ahead you are going to turn left on Independence; it's a big street."

Amir followed the direction and turned on Independence.

"Now left again on Ninth, just ahead. You don't want the street, just the ramp that goes down to the expressway, and then join I-395 west out of town. There, turn opposite the Smithsonian Castle, you see the red building on the right?"

"Yeah. I know where I am now. I've got this from here. Just help me when we get to the parkway." Amir felt more confident now. They could hear some muffled shouts and thumps from the rear of the car, as Masterson let his feelings be known to his captors.

From his vantage point, Masterson knew he was in trouble. He was jostled about from time to time as the car made its way over rough road surfaces, making sudden turns. His adrenaline level was high, causing synapses to begin firing constantly, as he tried to sort out his situation and come up with some kind of plan. He could feel the hard form of the urn against his chest, as he held on tightly to his duffle.

After a few minutes, the road surface smoothed out considerably, and the motion of the car did the same. He began an assessment of his resources, when his attention was diverted to the bag he clutched, and he decided to inventory what was available to him. He felt the space around him for something he could use as a weapon. Finding none, he refocused on the contents of the duffle.

Charlie and Karen sped up the walkway to the intersection of P and Fourth, where Charlie turned left to go north. He could see the tail-lights of the Town Car a block ahead. It was not going very fast, so he felt he could keep it in sight without too much effort. The trick would be not letting a traffic light get in the way. He made a mental decision that he would run any bad luck with stoplights; the worst alternative would be that he would have reinforcements if the police tried to pull him over.

"Should I call 911?" Karen asked.

"Let's hold off a minute, see if maybe we can figure out where they're going," Charlie suggested.

Karen acquiesced, not feeling too sure that was the best idea, but she trusted his judgment. She kept second-guessing herself, remembering all the caution she had been given by the agents from the Bureau and from Bevy Martin that her father might be in some kind of danger. Apparently they were right, and she had not heeded their warnings. She began beating herself up about that. "Charlie, I think we should have listened more carefully to what people have been telling us. I keep thinking of all the surveillance around my house today. That should have told us something. And how do you think those guys knew where we were going to meet, and who are they, anyway?"

"Certainly not from our team, or it would have been the FBI that picked your dad up," he said thoughtfully. "They must have followed us here, or they have your house bugged."

"Wouldn't the FBI just do that?" It didn't make sense to her.

Charlie made the turn onto Independence a few hundred yards behind the sedan. Fortunately there was enough traffic that he might not be noticed by the people in the car in front of him. He thought about her question. "The FBI has to follow rules, and foreign governments do not," was the best he could come up with. "Our government would have a tough time getting approval to eavesdrop on your home without you having committed some kind of offense."

Karen saw the Lincoln turn at the Smithsonian. "Look they're turning onto the ramp to the interstate."

Charlie ran the changing light at the intersection and followed his quarry onto the expressway. "They must be heading out of town." Without the risk of getting separated by traffic lights, Charlie backed off a dozen car lengths or so, occasionally letting other cars get between him and the black sedan, but always making sure he had a good view of the car he was pursuing.

"He's got his turn signal on!" Karen shouted, her attention focused on the car in front.

"Looks like they're taking the exit to Mount Vernon," Charlie guessed. He followed his prey around the exit ramp on to the George Washington Parkway as they proceeded south toward Mount Vernon at a reasonable speed. They passed Reagan National Airport on the left and the countryside opened up to them. The beauty of the drive was lost on them due to nightfall and the fact that they were so stressed about the situation. The otherwise scenic drive took them along the Potomac for a few miles until they came to Old Town in Alexandria, where city traffic lights became an issue again.

"Still think we shouldn't call for help?" Karen asked nervously.

"Not yet. We don't know what jurisdiction we will be in, so they don't know who to send for help. Let's wait a little longer; see if they stop," Charlie reasoned.

Panicked at the turn of events, Ornstein dialed Hallanger's number again.

"Just going to call you. Kenny's cell phone is traveling down the George Washington Parkway, just passing Reagan National. Where are you?" Hallanger asked.

"We got to the memorial too late. We identified the car Kenny was traveling in, so we know they were here, but there's no sign of anyone now. Should we alert someone else, perhaps closer to them, or do you think we can still catch them? I have to assume they have been intercepted, since the car Kenny was using is still here. They had enough people to move all the cars, if they wanted to. So I assume she and the lawyer were snatched as well, or they are also chasing whoever," Ornstein said.

Whomever, you illiterate moron, Hallanger said to himself. "This goatfuck is already out of control. Too many people know about it, and our necks are out there a mile. You've got lights and sirens; use them. They're only about ten minutes ahead of you, and you can make that up if you hurry, and they may still have a ways to go. Let's try to keep this in house, if you know what I mean,"

Ornstein was already motioning for the driver to get moving, holding the phone away from his mouth saying, "Head toward Mount Vernon, fast as you can!"

Tires spun and sand and gravel flew as the high-performance SUVs powered up and blew through the construction terrain back to the city streets. The agents driving knew their way, and in a moment, the cars were speeding west on I-395 across the Potomac, sirens blaring and blue and white strobes flashing out the front grills.

Ornstein felt grateful that Hallanger was not screaming at him. "Thank you, sir, for staying with us. I appreciate your understanding of our situation."

"Don't mistake my demeanor for approval, young man," Hallanger rebuked. "You and I are going to have a serious talk about your future with the Bureau when this is all over, if either of us still have jobs by that time, that is!" He knew that elevated emotions were not going to foster a good outcome at this point, and he trusted the judgment of the recruiters in the selection of future agents. He really hoped they had done their jobs well when they screened Lyle Ornstein.

Hallanger knew he was literally going to have two phones to his ears as the chase got close, so he could relay their positions relative to each other more in real time. He called Cavner on a landline, for an update, just for this purpose.

"Still no change. They're still moving steadily down the parkway nearing Old Town" was Cavner's immediate response.

Hallanger's antenna was up. "Hollis, you got a phone in your other ear?"

"Of course I do. How do you expect me to be up to date? You better, too."

Hallanger couldn't help but smile at the irony. "Don't you think this is ridiculous? We are supposed to be the most sophisticated government agencies in the world, and we're relaying the results of Buck Rogers technology by multiple handheld telephones. What's become of us?"

"We're criminals, for one thing," said an exasperated Cavner. "None of this would be happening if it weren't for Brogan. Where's he right now? Probably boinking his secretary. Jack, please accept my apology for getting the Bureau involved in this. I have had a bad feeling in my gut since that day we met in our conference room."

"We're the ones who screwed it up," Hallanger offered, trying to be understanding, although he agreed with Cavner.

Cavner continued to beat up on himself. "I wish I'd had the balls to stand up to the west wing bureaucrats when they put pressure on me to coordinate this mess. Oh, well, standing by for now. Get your other ear in the loop, so I can pass anything along as soon as I hear."

"Will do," Hallanger responded, and he put the connection on speaker to make sure he didn't miss anything. Then he called Ornstein on his cell.

After the young agent answered, Hallanger announced, "They're just coming up on Old Town. Let's keep this line open, so I can bring you up to date as information comes in."

"Good idea; I appreciate it," Ornstein thanked him.

CHAPTER TEN

"**H**ow much further?" Amir asked Hassan.

"About six miles after you get through Alexandria. Look for the Morningside Exit on your right. You take that to the light, and then go right again, on Fort Hunt Road for half a block. We'll see a gravel driveway up a hill just past the first intersection."

The traffic was moderate for a Friday night, and Amir kept checking his rearview mirror for any evidence that he was being followed, but he saw none. The hollering and pounding from the back of the car had ceased for the last ten minutes, and he mentioned the quiet to Hassan with some concern.

"You don't think he could be up to something back there, do you?"

"He's an old man. What could he do? Just keep your mind on the driving; I'll keep looking around for anything wrong."

Hassan seemed very confident. *Maybe overconfident,* Amir thought. The goons in the back kept looking over their shoulders for the most part. At least they were silent. *Thank Allah for small blessings.*

Masterson could never have known, as the car slowed for city traffic, that he was only a mile or so from where he had called his daughter just a little over two hours ago. The parkway paralleled US 1 along the river as it came up from Richmond and neared the D.C. Metroplex. He was more concerned right now with sorting through his duffle, looking for something that would help him out of his predicament. He had given up trying to kick out the taillights from inside the trunk, where he could get no leverage in the confined space to swing his foot with any force.

With Helen's urn out of the way, he began digging through his dirty laundry and new clothes. Near the bottom he came across his Dopp kit, but he couldn't think of anything in there that would be of any use. In the corner of the duffle, he felt the loop of the canvas bag he had been carrying around with him, and he tugged it out.

The trunk was almost pitch black, except for a tiny glow coming from the taillights, which cast an eerie rose color around the confined space, so his fingers became his eyes. He felt the banded bills at the bottom of the bag, and the baggie that contained the credit cards and ID, and finally he reached the hard surface of the barrel of the nine millimeter Smith and Wesson. As his fingers closed around the familiar grip, his spirits lightened considerably.

He pushed the button on the side of the weapon with his thumb and felt the magazine eject into his palm. Carefully he set the pistol aside and tested the tension on the spring of the magazine beneath the bullets. There was quite a lot of push back, which told him the magazine was probably full, seven or eight shots at least. Another search of the bag revealed two more magazines, also seemingly fully loaded.

Masterson felt quite comfortable in his new circumstances; now he just needed a plan, and plans under stress were something he had always been good at. He put one of the magazines in the grip of the semiautomatic and rammed it home. It seated in the trigger housing with a rewarding click. Masterson pulled back the slide, felt in the open chamber for the bullet that was about to be seated, and released the slide, chambering the round. His years of training and practice had taken over now, as he prepared for action. Check, check, and triple check. Nothing was more disheartening than the dull click of a hammer blow landing on an empty chamber. He was as prepared as he would ever be, and now he just had to wait to find out what for.

❳❴❳❴❳

Ornstein had one of his earbuds in, so he could keep his hands free and monitor conversations in the car and over the radio, not that his right hand was going to be of much use to him. He kept testing his injury by making a fist, hoping that the pinkie finger would stop curling inward as he did so, but he always got the same result. The outside of his hand was beginning to throb a little. There was no doubt in his mind that the bone was broken, but the pain was not severe, more like a dull ache. He still had some basic use of his hand to hold his phone and whatnot. He certainly couldn't risk using a weapon with it, if things came to that.

"Ornstein, you there?" Hallanger asked in his right ear.

"Yes, sir," he answered.

"Where are you now?"

"Just coming up to the first light in Old Town on the north side of Alexandria. We were doing ninety earlier. Now we're just negotiating traffic, running red lights when we have to."

"Good," Hallanger acknowledged. "We've alerted the local park police and city police that we have agents in pursuit of a suspect, so they won't bother you, although they might follow, since you're in their jurisdiction. We figure it's the best way for them to stay uninvolved, at this point. Your target is just leaving town on the other end, still heading south. I'll let you know if you get close if you keep me up to date, so you don't overrun them. Stay alert!"

"Will do."

Ornstein kept the connection open, so they wouldn't have to initiate new calls if something came up.

ᘒᗒᗒᘖ

"Your exit to Morningside Drive is coming up in about a mile," Hassan anticipated. "Stay in the right-hand lane."

"Got it. What's after that?" Amir asked, eyes locked on the road in full concentration. The traffic had been light since they left Alexandria, and he could see the reflection of an almost full moon shimmering on the still water of the Potomac.

"About a mile or so at the light take a right on Fort Hunt Road, and you're almost there."

Amir saw the exit ahead on the right, so he slowed and put on his turn signal. Off the parkway he traveled on a winding road through a residential area.

"I thought this place was in the country," he said aloud, concerned about all the houses he was passing. They were on generous-sized lots, but none seemed to have much privacy from neighbors.

"I'm sure the Russians know what they're doing. Just keep going," Hassan tried to calm Amir.

Sure enough, the road led to a traffic light, and the area was much less developed, even forested to some degree. Amir turned right, moving ahead slowly, as the foliage prevented the ambient light from the moon from brightening up the terrain, as it had along the Potomac.

"The GPS says it's just a block."

The two of them peered ahead, almost missing the tiny road that came in from the right. Just past the road was an elevated, wooded area, accented with a gravel driveway that negotiated the steep hill through the trees, out of sight from the road. A counterbalanced gate blocked the drive on which was a sign that indicated it was the caretaker's entrance.

"This is more like it." Amir smiled. He extended his knuckles to Hassan, who gave him the obligatory fist bump. He pulled up to the gate.

"Armin, jump out and raise the gate, and then follow us up the drive to the house on foot. Be sure to put the gate back down after we are through. Pavlenko from the Russian embassy is supposed to have the garage open, waiting for us. Meet us in the garage."

Armin got out of the backseat and approached the gate, not looking forward to the climb up the hill. He found the gate easy to lift thanks to the heavy piece of cinder block wired to the short end of the fulcrum. Amir and the others started up the hill, tires spinning a little, as the sedan tried to gain purchase on the gravel. Armin cursed as he jumped out of the way of the flying pebbles, still getting stung by a few, and after he had some separation from the vehicle, he lowered the gate to its original position and started his trek up the hill.

Amir drove carefully up the narrow driveway of sorts; every time he tried to give it the gas, the tires just spun uselessly. The driveway turned left near the top, and he entered a spacious area in front of an elegant brick antebellum house, not quite large enough to be considered a mansion, but impressive nonetheless. It was nestled in the woods without another structure or sign of lights visible in any direction. As he turned, his headlights lit up the unattached garage, which was also brick. It had three generous wooden panel doors across the front. The top row of panels had glass windows.

As his lights highlighted the garage, the middle door began opening electrically. Pavlenko's cynical features were recognizable in the cars lamps, as Amir maneuvered the Town Car into the center stall, and killed the engine. Pavlenko lowered the door, and the interior of the garage became dim, lit only by a weak floodlight at the front of the space. He joined the others as they got out of the car and assembled at the rear to release their captive.

As an added precaution, Amir and Hassan pulled their nine-millimeter Glocks out of their waistbands and held them at the ready. There was no sound coming from the trunk of the car, and the Iranian crew worried that something might have happened to their charge during the short trip from the city.

Amir leaned forward and reached for the trunk latch; feeling the rubber grip with his fingertips, he pulled and heard the audible snap as the trunk lid released and started to open on its pneumatic actuator. Then he stepped back.

✌⤳✑✌

Charlie and Karen had no trouble keeping the black sedan in sight, as it continued down the parkway on the south side of Alexandria. Their quarry was not traveling particularly fast, probably trying not to draw attention to themselves, Charlie thought, so he was able to continue his pursuit from a safe distance. The few minutes he had before he saw the big car exit the parkway he used to try to formulate some kind of plan, while speculating on the possible outcomes of this situation. He was unable to come up with one, and the scenarios that were running through his head did not have good outcomes.

Karen's idea to call 911 was beginning to sound like the best among lousy alternatives, but he still felt they should wait until they reached their destination, wherever that might be, before calling the cavalry. He was confident that the kidnappers, whoever they were, would not harm Karen's dad until they had a chance to interrogate him, and that would take some time, and the local authorities would need some kind of description of the location to be of any help.

Suddenly Karen spoke up. "Look, they're getting off!" She pointed ahead.

Charlie could hear the tension in her voice. A quarter mile in front of him, the right turn signal made clear that the car was going to exit onto Morningside Lane. He followed as close as he dared, fearing that he might lose them if they got too far ahead, but at the same time not wanting to call attention to himself, lest Masterson's kidnappers abandon their plans. Who knows what would happen then? He knew it was unlikely that he could follow a car that was intentionally trying to evade him.

As the black sedan wound around the curves of the residential neighborhood, he decided to turn off his headlights, but that proved to be a mistake, as Mercedes had designed their cars to drive with lights on. At least they weren't the powerful lamps used for night driving, just the dimmer silhouette lighting designed to attract attention.

Staying back as far as he dared, he just saw the Town Car make a right at the next traffic light. He made a mental note of the sign, Fort Hunt Road. Charlie allowed the sedan to get a little ahead, and then he turned to follow, when suddenly Karen shouted out, "Look out! He's stopping. What do we do? We can't stop, too."

Charlie had no choice but to continue past the sedan as it waited on the gravel driveway for the man exiting from the rear to open the gate blocking the access to the front of the drive. He drove round the next bend on Fort Hunt Road until he felt he was safely out of visual range of the Town Car. After he gave them several minutes to get up the drive, he made a U-turn and cautiously approached the driveway. Seeing no sign of anyone, he pulled into the short piece of gravel drive in front of the gate.

"We can't risk driving up this hill, Karen, or they might see us coming, and we don't know what's up there. Let's go on foot from here. This isn't anything more than a driveway, so I think we've probably gotten to their destination. Whatever is going to happen is going to happen here. You agree?"

"Yes. But Charlie, I'm really scared for my dad, and for us. I think we should call for help now." Karen's voice quivered a little as she spoke.

"Okay, but first let's put our eyes on the situation, so we can give the call center a better idea of what the emergency is. We'll leave the car here."

Charlie killed the engine, and they got out of the car and walked around the gate. Karen noticed the sign on the gate that read: CARETAKER'S RESIDENCE, and beneath that in hardware store stickers, 7707.

They began their climb on the gravel, taking care to be as quiet as possible, walking along the dirt edges where possible. Winded a little as they neared the top, they could see a quarter acre open space and the beautiful vine-covered old brick house and the unattached garage. They stood at the edge of the trees and took everything in. Karen took out her cell phone and called 911. In a hushed voice, she outlined the emergency, stressing a kidnapping was involved and gave her location: 7707 Fort Hunt Road. The call specialist on the other end of the line tried to get her to stay on, but developing circumstances made that impossible.

The night was deathly quiet, the air still, which only made what happened next all the more dramatic. The dimly lit windows in the top row of the garage panels flashed brightly multiple times, accompanied by muffled, but still loud cracks of pistol shots.

Bang, Bang . . . Bang, Bang . . . Bang . . . Bang!

Each report coincided with a bright flash from the overhead windows.

ᔕᘓᔐ

"Ornstein, you there?" sounded in the agent's right earbud.

"Yes, sir."

"Listen up. Kenny just exited the parkway on Morningside Lane and took a right at the end of the street onto Fort Hunt Road. The GPS target stopped for a bit then returned to the corner immediately following Morningside. Then it continued slowly east; we suspect they are on foot now."

"Got it. We're at the one-mile warning for the turn, can't be more than two or three minutes in trail. Stay with us, please," Ornstein answered, and then relayed the information to the other car. "Off here," he told the driver. "Follow the road to the end and take a right on Fort Hunt Road, and we're about there."

He started the sirens again, having turned them off after they left the outskirts of Alexandria. *This was going to be one neighborhood that wasn't going to sleep early tonight,* Lyle thought wryly, as they roared their way through the tranquil residential community. He noticed out of the corner of his eye the flashing blue and white lights of patrol cars coming from both directions on the parkway as they made their exit.

"Mr. Hallanger, I don't think we are alone anymore," he groaned into his earbud mike.

"Great! That's just great! Fuck me!" was Hallanger's uncharacteristic reply. He relayed the bad news to Cavner, who was still bucket brigading the high-tech eavesdropping information from his nerds in the basement.

Ornstein's caravan barely used two wheels as they made the corner at Fort Hunt Road, where they slowed, so as not miss their mark. A block ahead on the right, Ornstein yelled and pointed, "There! That's the place!"

It only took a moment to recognize the silver Mercedes S550 he had been searching for parked at the edge of the driveway. "Well, I'll be damned!" he said aloud.

The agents assembled, and after a caution from Ornstein that the kidnappers may be armed, they split into two tactical groups and started up the driveway. When they got to the top of the hill, they were totally unprepared for the scene that lay before them.

❧

Masterson felt as ready for a fight as he had ever been. After days of stress and detours of all sorts, he had finally had his goal in his grasp when these motherfuckers had grabbed him and put him in the trunk of a car.

The car had sped up after leaving some stop-and-go traffic and continued at what seemed like highway speeds for about ten minutes, before slowing and turning off the highway.

Masterson could hear the occasional muffled voice coming from the interior of the car, but he couldn't make any sense of it with the ambient road noise coming from the wheel wells. He just bided his time until the car stopped. He felt he was parked on an incline when he heard someone give instructions to have a gate opened. He wondered about the significance of that, but seconds later, the car moved forward again. He could tell he was on a gravel driveway. The car leveled out and continued moving, creeping forward. Then it stopped.

He heard the rumbling and whirring of an electric garage door. It quit with a thud as it reached the end of its travel. Car doors slammed, and footfalls moved around to the rear of the vehicle. Masterson could hear hushed voices followed by a pause, and then *thump* as the trunk latch released. In the dark of the truck, his eyes had become adjusted for night vision, so he was a little disoriented when the interior trunk light came on over his head. With his Smith and Wesson at the ready, he waited for what the slowly rising trunk lid would reveal.

The first thing he saw was a black semiautomatic in the hand of the person nearest him. *Priority number one,* he told himself, as his training kicked in, riding a wave of adrenaline. The trunk was only half open, and he could see four other men assembled behind the car, but only one of them seemed to have a weapon in sight. *Priority number two.* Just like solving a puzzle, only Masterson didn't have a lot of time to react. He had killed before, so that wasn't really an issue; plus, he was really pissed off. His training had taught him to make the mental commitment beforehand, and then execute. He had. He brought his Smith and Wesson closer to his body to lessen the chance he could be stripped of his weapon. *Funny,* he chuckled inwardly, *how the shooters in the movies always extend their arms to the fullest in close quarters, making themselves vulnerable to being disarmed.*

As the truck lid inched upward, Masterson aimed for the bulk of the nearest body, squeezed the trigger, and as soon as his mark was clear, he gave the closest armed individual a double tap—two rounds in the middle of his chest—sending him flying backward. The others froze in position as they absorbed the unfolding situation, and a second later, he lined up with target number two, dispatching him the same way. As the second flew backward, the bearded one finally had the presence of mind to take action, and he did the simplest thing he could to slow down the carnage; he tried to close the trunk.

As the lid came down, Masterson fired in the direction he had last seen the man through the thin alloy of the trunk lid. The jacketed bullet didn't even notice the lid was there as it penetrated first the trunk, and then Armin's liver. He went down. The black man reached for one of the loose handguns on the cement floor and grabbed it, moving to the side in an attempt to hide from Masterson's field of vision. He pointed in the direction of the rear of the car and pulled the trigger. Nothing happened. Then he realized no round had been chambered.

He moved to a better position, not really wanting to shoot anybody, and just waited to see what the old man was going to do. After a moment, the trunk lid opened again, and Masterson started to emerge, clutching Helen's urn to his chest with his left arm, while he raised the lid with the barrel of the handgun.

Karim grew nervous again, as he watched the Russian run for the side door of the garage and make a hasty exit.

As Masterson kneeled carefully, clutching the urn and extending his legs over the back of the trunk in order to exit the car, he scanned the space. The three men he had put down were motionless on the floor of the garage, but he didn't notice the young black man crouching behind the mullion of the adjacent garage doorframe. As Masterson began to slide his bulk over the lip of the car trunk, Karim aimed as best he could and let loose a round, targeting Masterson's midsection.

His aim was right on target, only Helen got in the way. The bullet struck just above the memorial lettering on the urn: *You Will Be Missed.*

Three hundred eighty foot-pounds of torque hit the urn with the force of a speeding car, and the total of the energy was released inside the pewter amphora-shaped urn. The force sheared the finely threaded cap from the base of the urn and blew it and the contents skyward with great force. The impact pushed Masterson backward into the trunk compartment, where he sat, dazed, with one leg over the lip of the trunk, hearing now gone for the next little while.

Karim had had enough of jihad for the time being and made his retreat out the side door as well.

Karen and Charlie ignored all reason after the shots ceased for a minute, and they rushed to the side of the garage where they had seen two men, one Caucasian and one Black, flee the building at full speed, one to his car that was parked by the side door of the house, the other into the woods as fast as his feet would carry him, which was pretty fast since he was an all-state running back in high school.

Charlie fumbled for and found the center garage door opener switch against the back wall and opened the door. The automatic door opener light turned on above the car, illuminating the garage. As he walked to the back of the car, he was relieved to see the bodies of three strangers lying motionless on the floor, none of which were Karen's dad. He then followed Karen around the back of the car to look for Masterson.

As Ornstein approached the garage with one of the other agents, weapons drawn, he was totally unprepared for the killing field he saw. Before him was the person for whom he had legal responsibility, sitting half in and half out of the back of a Lincoln Town car, covered in what looked like soot and chunks of calcium, smartly dressed in khakis and a blue oxford shirt under a beige cotton windbreaker, surrounded by dirty laundry. He was holding the bottom half of a metal urn to his breast, weeping softly as his daughter and the young lawyer he had met in Florida months earlier moved in to comfort him. On the floor of the garage were three collapsed bodies, and as he got closer, the acrid smell of cordite filled his nostrils.

As he took the sight in, he could hear sirens getting louder as the Fairfax County Police arrived at the bottom of the hill. In short order, uniformed officers joined the party, stopped in their tracks as they tried to make sense of the carnage in front of them. First things first, after confirming that the fallen were dead, they verified the FBI agents' badges, called for EMTs, and secured all the weapons they could find.

Ornstein tried to assume control over the situation but was sharply rebuffed by the senior policeman. "You are out of your jurisdiction, buddy. This is a county matter now. You will get your chance after we have sorted things out and the prosecutor has had a chance to look things over."

Karen and Charlie overheard the discussion and tried to intervene. Karen tried to explain that her father had been kidnapped by the now-dead individuals, and he had prevailed in his defense . . . *"Self-defense!"* she emphasized.

"That may be all well and good, but this is way over my pay grade. We have people who know how to handle this on their way to assume responsibility. Nobody's going anywhere for a while yet, so don't get antsy." He thought a minute, nodding to the Lincoln, "That's your father all covered in ash, you say? He must be somethin'."

"Actually my father and mother," Karen answered flippantly, but with a proud smile.

She was feeling the letdown following the rush of adrenaline. Relieved that her dad was safe, she returned to him to help him get out of the trunk and clean up a little.

Father and daughter smiled and hugged each other, happy in their reunion, tears mixing with the ash on their faces.

Charlie looked on with warm feelings in his heart, watching happily as Karen and her dad were reunited.

EPILOGUE

The mid-July heat was soaring, but the humidity was tolerable, as Karen Kenny and Charlie Edgerton sat on the grass just off the walkway in front of the Vietnam Memorial on the National Mall. She looked on with joy, as her father knelt next to the beautifully engraved granite wall. Sitting in a semicircle before him were his grandchildren and Charlie's son and daughter, patiently listening to him give the history of the war that so deeply divided this nation in the 1960s.

The youngsters could hear the emotion in his voice as he described those turbulent times and the role he played with his work in army intelligence in Saigon. They listened with interest as Stewart Masterson continued his memorial tradition for the next generation.

Karen looked down at the personal handwritten note she had received from Pepper Madison. As she slid it out of the envelope to share its contents with Charlie, she reflected on the whirlwind of events that had consumed her life after that extraordinary night in March, which ended in the deaths of three foreign agents following a harrowing car chase along the Potomac.

Charlie read over Karen's shoulder the kind words of affection Pepper expressed for Stewart. She wanted Karen to know that meeting her father had a profound effect on her, that her life had taken a new, better direction as a result. She asked Karen to tell her father that her memories of him would be cherished.

Karen could only use her imagination as to what, exactly, those memories were. When she brought the subject up with her father, he only smiled and looked off in the distance.

Karen remembered the detention until the wee hours of the morning by the Fairfax County Police, when following an intense interrogation of those present, they were released, Stewart to go home with his daughter, Ornstein and the other agents to leave empty-handed. Their story was corroborated by the young black American who fled the scene only to be captured as he exited the woods at the base of the driveway by additional arriving Fairfax County Police. He identified himself as Deshawn Mosely from Washington. He was held over, pending further investigation.

It was revealed to her about a month after the event that her father's kidnappers were acting on behalf of two governments who wanted to obtain information from him about U.S. intelligence operations in the Mideast. This did not come as a shock to anybody.

Some weeks later, following an internal review at the National Security Agency, Karen received a letter of apology from some bureaucrat as well as a personal one from Lyle Ornstein, who was still working at the Miami office of the FBI, for the difficulties caused her. At the end of the day, the government's embarrassment encouraged the Attorney General to convince all local authorities to drop any criminal proceedings for actions taken by Stewart during his excursion. No charges were ever filed for his appropriation of the Mercedes, as Mr. Smith felt it would be in his domestic best interest to keep the circumstances of the weeklong loss of his car quiet. Stewart, on the other hand, was no longer allowed to drive.

The Montgomery County Circuit Court approved Karen's petition to be her father's guardian, which was uncontested by Lyle

Ornstein and the Bureau, and he now resided in his childhood home on Whittingham Drive with his daughter and grandchildren.

Karen was reinstated in her position as a fifth-grade teacher at the Barrie School. What remained of Helen's ashes were scattered at the place on the Mall where Stewart had proposed to her forty-five years earlier.

The dramatic destruction of her urn that night in Virginia had given Stewart Masterson a closure of sorts. He was now able to cherish Helen's memory, rather than be a slave to it, freeing him to enjoy the family with whom he was so blessed. He enjoyed watching his daughter find happiness in her budding romance with her lawyer friend and his family.

Stewart relished his days with his family, managing the best he could, understanding the challenges that faced him and determined to meet them with grace and dignity. He never felt as relevant as he did at times like these, when he shared himself with his grandchildren.

ACKNOWLEDGMENTS

If you have read my previous work you may be aware that I sometimes use names of people who have been known to me as I develop characters in the story line. In *Memory Road,* I have continued this practice, if for no other reason than it helps me keep the thread of the story consistent, and it is fun. If I were to change them at this point, the names would still belong to someone in the reading public, so I figure, what's the difference? If you are known to me and your name appears in this book, rest assured that the connection ends with the name; the character bears no resemblance to you, so please do not be offended by how the character is portrayed. If you are known to me and your name does not appear, likewise do not take offense; I just ran out of story. Perhaps you will find your namesake in a future tome.

There are so many who have been of help to me in this project, as I try my best to create a meaningful story based on achievable circumstances. Thank you first to my good friend Doris Kearns Goodwin, who gave me the encouragement to write so late in life. Also, thank you to Dr. James Galvin at Florida Atlantic University, who gave me a brief education on just how much Alzheimer's patients were capable of, so necessary in this work. Kudos to Jim Nantz, whose efforts to bring awareness to this terrible affliction spurred me to present the disease in a form that reflects well, I think, on the needs of families touched by Alzheimer's disease, and the necessity of the rest of us to relate compassionately when the opportunity arises.

There are many acquaintances, like Mike Kerry and Brendan Cunningham and a few others who asked not to be mentioned, who have backgrounds in our country's clandestine services, who shared nonclassified information about the inner workings of the spy world, which enabled me to add some juicy details to the obstacles Stewart Masterson faced on his journey. Bruce Lyons, friend and attorney from Fort Lauderdale was of great help to keep me from running afoul of legal missteps; thank you, Bruce, for your patience with my stupid questions about guardianship. Thank you also Gayl Hackett for your suggestion on how to title this work so it fits in a modern world of social media. Particularly I want to give credit to my good friend and former congressman, Dan Mica, who spent hours with me in Washington putting eyes on actual places described in the book. Sometimes I think he got a bigger kick out of Masterson's dilemmas than I did writing them. Thanks again to Carol and Gary Rosenberg for your copyedit recommendations and beautiful cover designs. You rock!

Thank you also to my family, Barbara and Michelle, who had the patience to hear me out as I sampled twists and turns of story development, and especial thanks to my son, David, who actually endured the three-day trip up US 1 from Boca Raton to Maryland, so that I could experience Masterson's journey firsthand. We had a blast. Thank you to a world of friends who sampled my efforts as they evolved and gave me candid opinions on what works and what doesn't, especially you, Karen Krumholtz, for keeping my office life organized so efficiently that I can set aside time to write.

THE BOY
AND THE
DOLPHIN

Dick Schmidt

PROLOGUE

The sun is high and the incoming tide has cleaned out the refuse-filled waters of Nassau's harbor, revealing a deep blue in the natural channel formed between the island of New Providence and Hog Island, which defines the outer perimeter of the harbor. The edges of the channel lighten to a pristine turquoise near the sandy beaches of the island, contrasted with the garbage and wreck-littered wharf along Potter's Cay on the south side. The tide change means more than pretty water to the ecosystem in the area. The incoming tide also washes through the reef around Rose Island to the east, which pushes the small fish and mullet away from the reef's protection. This makes good hunting for the large pod of bottlenose dolphin that frequents the area.

The cow forages the down-current side of the reef with her close traveling companion. She is a young female, about six years old and very pregnant with her first calf. Her companion stays close, so she will be able to help with the birth when the time comes, something she is familiar with, as she has had several calves of her own. They hunt well together, often batting small baitfish

with their flukes to stun them, making the catch all that much easier. Both are healthy animals with traditional markings, dark
bluish gray tops and light gray bottoms. The companion has a
notch missing from her dorsal, the result of an overzealous lover
some years ago. The pregnant cow is unmarked, unusual for a six-
year-old. Younger, she is a little smaller than her companion,
weighing in around 500 pounds, yet she eats twice as much, a
result of her condition.

The feeding is easy today, as the current brings the easy pick-
ings over and through the reef where the cow patiently waits for
an opportunity to grab small fish in her sharp conical teeth. The reef
is shallow, and at the turn of the low tide, she can hear the water
foaming around the coral where it breaks the surface. The sun is
high, the water is clear, and she can see the coral tips jutting above
the surface when she comes up for air. The current is pushing her
away from the coral as the tide starts its flood.

It is a perfect day, complicated only by the agility the cow has
lost because of the calf she is carrying. Although uncomfortable
and yearning for the release of her burden, she is prepared for the
event, having scouted a suitable location to give birth in the lagoon
of the L-shaped island next door. The lagoon is protected from
predators and weather, yet filled with mullet and shrimp for her to
eat while she prepares to introduce a newborn to her aquatic
world of adventure.

With the help of her companion, she will be able to tend to her
calf as well as her own needs, which will be considerable. The
shallow end of the lagoon will give her a fixed place where she can
put the calf, so it will be able to reach the surface for air as it strug-
gles to learn the art of breathing. The newborn will need air every
few minutes at first, until it learns how to maximize intake in its
tiny lungs. She and her companion will nuzzle the calf into position, so it will not slide off the sand shelf into deeper water, which

at nine feet will be too much for it to negotiate while it learns to use its flukes to swim in its first few hours of life. That process will advance quickly, and after a few days, the calf will be comfortable staying at the surface as it learns to breathe more deeply.

The cow and her companion will be in full attendance until the calf is comfortable with the basics. Nursing will also be easier in the shallow water; by rolling on her side, the cow can offer her mammary slits to the calf so they will be more accessible than if they were birthing in deep water. A nudge from the companion will position the calf so it can insert its tongue in the slit to access the thick, sweet milk. This will happen as often as four times an hour while the calf is an immature and cannot feed on solid food by mouth. This will take at least six months, and even then, although the calf will have new teeth and can feed on solid food, it will continue to nurse for another year.

The cow is uncomfortably full from the foraging when she feels the first cramp deep in her belly. Instinct tells her that the time is nigh for her to head for the lagoon. A signal to her companion starts them on the three-mile journey to the island. The tidal current is with them, which helps. The cow stops from time to time as she is overcome by an occasional birthing cramp.

Crossing over the sandbar and moving into the lagoon, the two find a perfect slope of beach to perch for the birth. The beach has a deep hole on one side that is filled with discarded hemp nets and metal debris left there by humans. This is all the better, as they can see countless shrimp and crawfish on the bottom, shielding themselves from the high sun overhead. They won't have to go far to feed themselves in the coming weeks, just an added bonus.

The pains increase in frequency until her last push against the cramp eases the pain somewhat, as it moves lower in her belly. Tiny pliable tail flukes push out from her vagina, and her companion helps with gentle nibbling tugs on the calf's tail. More and *more appears with each push, as the lower part of the calf becomes exposed. Being born tail first makes the survival probability better, as the newborn can exit the womb gracefully, without having to worry about breathing until it detaches from the placenta.*

During this process the calf is very aware an event is taking place. First at its tail, it feels the cold, chilling water, which is eighteen or so degrees colder than what it has been used to for the last several months. As she comes further and further into this world, it gets colder and colder, and finally the cold wetness around her finds her eyes. The shock opens her eyelids, and she is overcome by brightness, something she has never experienced before. She clamps her jaw and feels the bone around her mouth, but she has no teeth, which won't start to come in for another five or six weeks. She feels her body literally unfold, as her dorsal becomes free of the confines of her mother's womb, and at last, her head pops clear of her mother.

There is some blood, but not much. Quickly the cow's companion pushes the newborn up the sand to fresh air, and the calf takes her first breath. On instinct, she blows out the goop clogging her blowhole with a robust cough-like exhale. Air comes easily to her now, and she lies exhausted in the shallow water on the sand shelf, surrounded by her mother and the companion. They roll the calf side to side, deeper in the water and out, and begin the long and tedious process of introducing this new little girl to the world.

CHAPTER ONE

PIPER CAY, BAHAMAS ·•· SPRING 1969

The quiet of sunset at Piper Cay is profound, the sun setting over the small spit of land that forms the southwest side of the natural lagoon. The evening no-see-ums will be arriving soon to make the pleasant solace of the modest pink on the horizon a place to avoid for a couple of hours. Toby Matthias measures his time alone, as he contemplates returning to the main cottage where his wife and daughter are waiting for him, giving him the space they think he needs. Friends of the family are here for his grandfather's memorial service.

Toby has a lot to think about and many decisions to make in the next several days. His decisions will mark a turning point in his life. It is a sad time for him. He was raised here on this island by his grandparents, who took him in after his parents were killed in the freak air crash of KLM 633 shortly after its departure from Shannon, Ireland, in 1954. They were en route to New York on their way home from a European vacation. Although half of the passengers survived the crash, Toby's parents were not among the fortunate ones. He was only eleven years old, and, young as his parents were, naturally no plans had yet been made for this even-tuality. At the time, Toby's grandparents were still reasonably young and recently retired, living out their later years in the Bahamas and running an inn for tourists who wanted an Out Island experience that wasn't too far from civilization and an airport.

Piper Cay is the perfect setting, located outside Nassau harbor, across from what the locals knew as Hog Island. The island forms a natural barrier for the harbor in Nassau, situated west of the chain of small islands that form a protective reef on the north side of New Providence. While Toby was away at college, new owners began development and renamed it Paradise Island to make it more attractive to vacationers. The Commonwealth provides a stable government, banking, and currency, and communications and transportation to South Florida are somewhat reliable.

Toby's grandmother, Irene, passed away while Toby was in high school. He has recently finished a lengthy tour as a Navy fighter pilot aboard the USS *Constellation* in Southeast Asia, where he flew cover operations over Laos and bombing missions in the designated route packs in Vietnam. Now, just as Toby is preparing to decide whether to make the Navy a career choice or to leave the service, his grandfather, Vernon, has passed away.

Although married with a six-year-old daughter to consider, Toby faces a dilemma. The Navy is offering him a career position if he would like it, or he can separate from active duty. His grand-parents have left him virtually everything from his childhood, their investments, and the Out Island Inn, run down as it is, but with a good reputation of sun and sand for the following of repeat cus-tomers that keeps the place going.

A piece of him remembers the years growing up in an uncon-ventional world of the Bahamas, the private day schools, years at prep school in Florida, and the University of Florida. The memories rekindle his love of the islands and the sea. On the other hand, he lives a dream life as a fighter pilot, but absent that he must spend much of his time thousands of miles away from his wife and his precious little girl, he doesn't know if he wants to give up the adrenaline rush of a cat launch, shacking a rejoin with his flight lead, or the terror of a night trap aboard a carrier.

His only fear is of doing something stupid like inviting a SAM up his tailpipe, but that would go away with his appointment opportunity in the Navy. A new fighter weapons school is being initiated in Miramar, California, to teach Navy fighter pilots the lessons learned from Vietnam, where the U.S.'s initial air combat record is less than stellar. If Toby accepts the new appointment, he will be reassigned to the new "Top Gun" school as an instructor, where the only enemy will be other experienced Navy pilots. He will be able to live in a home, not a bunk, and his family will be able to join him, to normalize him. The best of both worlds, he thinks.

Alternatively, he can leave active duty and return to the islands to manage the cottages, living what many would also consider a dream life. The main house and cottages have become a little neglected over the years since his grandmother died. His grandfather didn't have the motivation to keep the place as manicured as he had when Irene was still alive.

Toby reflects on how common it seems that aging couples often follow each other closely to that last stop on the train. His grandfather was more like a father to Toby in his willingness to share learning experiences with him. He made Toby work hard for his place in the family with chores on the property. Keeping a cheerful attitude for the guests was a constant obligation, so Toby acquired a keen ability to work well with adults at the expense of social development with peers.

This explains why he gets on so well with superiors. He has

always been that "nice young man" someone brings home when visiting others' families. He was a devilishly handsome kid growing up, with fierce blue eyes, constantly browned skin, and long, wavy blond hair. This carries through as a young man of twenty-six. His hair, now military short, is still light, and his vision is excellent through his deep blue eyes. He isn't tall or short, about five-ten, very fit, yet he moves with a languid gait one would associate with a taller person.

He sits on the end of the dock, barefoot in slacks and a dress shirt, watching "red ball" drop toward the horizon. The dock extends a hundred feet into the cove on the south end of the island, built on sturdy iron beams hammered into the marl bottom. At the end, the last beam extends eight feet above the planking, wired for a small white light used for finding the dock during approaches at night. Unlit day markers define the narrow channel over the sandbar in front of the cove, but the light can be used with a good compass bearing of 340 degrees to navigate the channel safely on non-moonlit nights. On the other side of the dock, the iron beam is not so high and supports an eight-inch brass ship's bell. Once active, the clapper is now corroded to the point that it can no longer swing freely enough to ring the bell. Toby's thoughts turn to the bell, and he is flooded with memories as he recalls his years as a young teen in this cove with his best friend and companion. He hears the screen porch door slam shut, as his daughter, Jenny, runs out the dock to greet him.

"Daddy, Daddy, Mommy says it's time to come in for dinner and talk to the people who have come to see you." She is a mini Toby, with blond hair and blue eyes, barefoot in a simple sundress. It isn't lost on him how natural she looks in this setting. "Aren't the bugs going to bite you pretty soon?"

She sits next to him and puts her head in his lap, kicking her legs out in front of her and spreading her toes in the disjointed way she makes them look like stubby fingers. She surveys the surroundings and notices the bell, pointing it out with her toes. "Daddy, that bell is dirty! Does it ring? What do you use it for? Are you going to clean it up?" she machine-guns her musings.

"Jenny, that's a very special bell," Toby replies. "You remember the story I told you about when I was a little boy, a little older than you, and I had a very special friend named Phinney."

"You mean the dolphin you saved?"

"Yep. That's the one, but I didn't save her. She was just a little baby at the time; it was her mother I saved."

"I like that story; tell me again, Daddy, please. Please!"

"I can start it a little bit, because we do have to go in. Some of our guests have traveled a long way to pay their respects, and I need to attend to them."

Excited at the prospect of hearing the story again, Jenny sits up and looks at her father with anticipation. . . .

CPSIA information can be obtained
at www.ICGtesting.com
Printed in the USA
LVOW10s2345210318
570756LV00007B/125/P